The Glimmer in the Leaves

Milo Hays

Dedication

This fun, romantic tale is dedicated to my parents, who both passed away during the writing of this story. You carry on through me and my children. Thank you forever for your unconditional love and support.

Chapter 1

"Hey! ... Clark Kent!" yelled the pretty, fifty-year-old woman who was standing behind the rustic country bar. "In or out! ... You're blocking the door!"

Startled, and embarrassed that he had drawn attention to himself, Rowan Delaney gave her a long look to see if the earthy woman in plaid was talking to him. The live music playing in the corner of the small, enclosed space muffled some of what she had said. And the faces that started to stare at him confirmed his initial fear. He was a fish out of water put into the spotlight and uncertain about what to do next. He only had two options. One was to venture in further. The other was to turn tail and walk out. His inclination to walk further in was hindered by concern about venturing too deep into the crowd. But it was born out of necessity. He desperately had to pee.

From the narrow country road that disappeared into the darkness of trees, and where the winery resided, the property appeared shabby and distressed. But Rowan also knew he was holding it to a higher standard than he would expect if the winery were nearer to his home in the suburbs. The inside did not change his first impression from the outside. However it had an attractive air about it. Although full of patrons who seemed happy and satisfied, the interior looked dingy and tired with an eclectic collection of tables, chairs, and other furniture placed about, and intriguing paintings both hung and muralled on the walls.

The winery's parking lot was full. It was lit by a series of loosely strung white lights throughout the trees near the entrance. A noticeable hum of conversation and music radiated out through the walls of the wood building that would have sat nicely in a rustic Colorado town. Although his subconscious told him to drive on, the sight and sounds of the place had stirred his interest to go inside. It was also the only public bathroom that his quick Google search on his iPhone with only one bar of service identified within fifteen miles.

Rowan's decision to take a day trip north was impulsive when he woke early on that cold October Saturday. He had no plan for where to go, or for how long he was going to drive. He just knew he needed to shed some of the accumulated stress of sixty-hour commercial banking work weeks and his failed marriage, which was sitting in separation limbo. Twenty-five years of burning his candle on both ends to make everyone but himself happy, he realized that, at age fifty, his life was nearing two-thirds over with only the expectation of physical decline coming in his future.

The Pennsylvania tourism ad he saw during the eleven o'clock news the night before stuck in his head and seemed God sent. He bought into its message to visit the beauty of the extraordinary country that surrounded his Western Pennsylvania home. His mistake was to not check the leaf schedules the TV ad mentioned that were easy to find on the internet. Although the leaves were starting to turn, he quickly saw that he was a few weeks early for his tour.

Rowan's eight-hour drive was peppered with periodic stops at places he had heard about since childhood but never visited. Unusually blue skies and sunshine followed him as he traveled northeast up to Williamsport to see Pennsylvania's Grand Canyon, a site that proved to be more impressive than he thought it could be, even though still mostly green.

Checking a map on his phone, Rowan had considered driving farther north into New York State toward Ithaca and Ellicottville. But he had made a commitment to attend the four o'clock Steelers game on Sunday with a client. It was a meeting he neither could nor wanted to miss. His travels, therefore, had to track back toward Pittsburgh to ensure he was either home or close enough to the city to be rested to go to the game and survive its pre- and post-game revelry, food, and drink.

The easiest and most scenic path back from Williamsport traveled across the state's northern tier on Interstate 80. Rowan knew he had time to visit Cook Forest State Park to see if it was worth returning to on a later trip. With a few hours of daylight remaining, he traveled with the big rigs at over eighty miles per hour to get there before the sun set.

The sun was starting to hang low in the sky when he decided to drive roads off into the country to see where they led. Rowan relied on his iPhone's GPS to find his way to and back from the dead ends. When service disappeared, his car's GPS was his second option to find civilization. But in most cases, when the phone lost signal, the car's GPS also did not work.

Rowan's anxiety started when his car slid as it turned on to the gravel of the parking lot. His immediate concern was that the low profile of his all-wheel-drive Audi S8 sedan was going to bottom-out on the undulating roll of the poorly maintained parking area. The other vehicles scattered about were better suited for the terrain. Most were pickups of every make and size. Scattered among them were a few Jeeps. Off on a separate grassy knoll were a handful of quads and a few Polaris Razors. The Razors reminded him of dessert dune buggies, with two or four seats surrounded by a roll cage, fiberglass, and not much more.

The common thread through all the vehicles was ground clearance. The dirt on their tires and sides made it clear that the parking lot ahead of him was the easiest of terrains they had traveled. Sensing that the rowdy crowd he could hear from inside the winery may not be his type of people, Rowan considered leaving to find a better place to stop. His bladder, however, had a different plan that created an urgency to park and go inside. He briefly considered disappearing into the nearby woods to avoid entering the roadhouse. But he was concerned about being caught, embarrassed, or worse.

As he stepped out of his car, he took another look at the other vehicles, then adjusted his black fleece Patagonia pullover. The air had a crisp fall chill. There was a smell of firewood burning that was familiar from his own fire pit at home. The music remained muffled as the sound of conversation behind the building became louder. There had to be a back deck or patio.

Although notably nervous, Rowan was more intrigued and desperate to pee. He took a deep breath to straighten his lean six-foot-two-inch body dressed in high-end touring attire. He knew he was going into foreign territory and wanted to look confident. His last action before grabbing the door handle was to straighten his tortoiseshell horn-rimmed glasses.

"Excuse me buddy," said a deep voice, as he felt the pressure of a notably large hand on his shoulder.

Startled by the unexpected ask for passage, along with its firm guide to help him step aside, Rowan rebounded back to the moment. The tall mountain-man that passed by him fit the rest of the crowd of work-hard-and-play-hard individuals.

As he finished surveying the crowd, Rowan noticed that despite a band playing some marginally good Black Crowes, the groups peppered around the small, oddly shaped room were more engaged in conversation and laughter than the music. The number of empty, blue wine bottles on each table likely had something to do with it. A closer look at the bottles and labels showed that the wine was a house brand labeled with unusual names and images that made its legality questionable.

"Bathroom?" Rowan asked a young waitress as she walked by.

"In the trees, or over there," she answered, without stopping.

As she walked away Rowan thought he should have gone with his initial idea when he turned into the parking lot. However, had he chosen the trees, he knew he would have lost the courage to enter the building that was now appearing to be the top of a fascinating rabbit hole.

"Hey!" the bartender yelled again. "In or out."

Rowan's initial reaction was to raise his hand to acknowledge her call and to give an impish smile. Without thinking, he started toward the bathroom that was located on the far wall of the room. As he took each step, he felt the bartender's eyes follow him through the crowd. When he touched the brass knob that opened the flimsy wood door to the men's room, a mental image appeared of what was on the other side. When his hand slipped off the tiny brass doorknob, he knew it was locked and only a single stall. His bladder showed its displeasure by adding pressure he had to work hard to hold back.

Afraid to look back toward the bar, Rowan turned his attention to the porch area that was beyond the enclosed bar area. It had a roof that covered half the wood decking, leaving the far end open to the night air. The crowd outside was bigger than what was in the bar. It was also the obvious source of the clamor he heard when walking in from the parking lot. Running a quick mental count of people, Rowan's banker's head multiplied that count by the open bottles he saw and pricing to think that the little winery he found was *killing* it.

When he finally glanced back toward the bar, he hoped to see the bartender focusing her wrath on some other soul. Instead, he found her eyes still locked on him. An amused smile came to her face as she slowly shook her head. Her face was framed by shoulder length gray hair pulled back into a ponytail. As their eyes aligned again, the door to the men's room opened. As expected, it was the *get in/get out, don't touching anything* place he expected.

# # # #

From the muffled quiet of the bathroom, he emerged to noise and laughter in the bar that grew louder as the door opened. The waitress's suggestion of the trees began to make more sense as a first option, given the size and smell of the second one. Rowan wondered if he should buy a glass of wine to use as hand sanitizer.

As he started his return walk to the front door, he took a second look around the bar. He began to feel guilty for having used their facilities without buying anything. It was a feeling he always had when traveling. His solution was to buy a Diet Pepsi or other small item as fair compensation for the use of their restrooms.

As he made his way across the bar, Rowan could feel a happiness radiate around him. There was a looseness to the conversations he could hear. It was all casual and fun. The laughter was contagious as he felt his face moving toward a smile despite only hearing tidbits of what sounded like infantile conversation.

"OOOH NO!" yelled a thick, mid-forties lumberjack in plaid as the front door swung open. "Don't bring that shit in here!"

The crowd went quiet as a scruffy, middle-aged man peered around the corner of the door to the bar. He was dressed in a long white coat and a brown canvas-covered hat that looked like a thimble. His face was weathered. He had curly brown hair that cupped out from under his hat. The look in his bloodshot eyes, which were wide open with a sinister glare, seemed to be seeking permission to enter.

Rowan connected the line-of-sight of the oddly dressed man to the bar to see whose attention he was hoping to get. Sneering back at him with her arms crossed, laughing, was the bartender who had chastised Rowan for standing in the door when he first arrived. A quick wave of her arm granted the man permission to enter as she redirected her attention back to the work she had in front of her. A smile appeared on thimble man's face as he swooped in past his rejector, who was now standing with his arms crossed and shaking his head.

"You're lucky she didn't leave it up to me," he said to the oddly dressed man as he walked by.

A smile appeared on the face under the hat as he continued to the bar. His white jacket was a light fabric and had baggy arms and loose flaps that all flowed behind his movement, which did not stop until he was at the bar in front of the apparent boss of the place.

Intrigued, Rowan decided to hang around to people watch. A barstool sat empty near wall, giving him the perfect position to sit unnoticed and out of the way. He quickly made his way to secure the seat before anyone else noticed it.

As he settled into his new vantage point, Rowan watched the thimble-hatted man take a blue bottle of wine and glass from the bar then head off into the crowd. Rowan's gaze followed the man across the floor, watching him greet most of the patrons he saw. Thimble man's occasional twirl, followed by applause and a smile, was an image that Rowan was not going to forget. It would definitely be a topic of conversation for the Steelers game the next day.

"So, Clark …" the familiar female voice asked in a lower volume that sounded near him.

Rowan turned to look to where the words came from. After watching the whirling dervish work his way across the room, he was interested to see who Clark was.

"What will ya have?" the bartender asked with a warm smile.

Rowan's first focus was on her eyes. They were a warm gray-blue that complemented her silky, soft, gray hair. Her hands were busy working a towel over a thick, stemless glass that she quickly placed in front of him.

"Drink?" she asked again, bringing his thinking to the present.

Rowan quickly looked to the chalkboard on the wall that listed the wines they offered. Although the names were separated into reds and whites, none were familiar to him. He then began searching for a paper list that would better explain the wines they made.

"What kinda wine do you drink at home?" she asked, winking to a provocatively dressed cougar seated on a nearby stool.

The woman on the stool fit Rowan's expectations for the place more than the bartender. She was a little chunky. Her top was a flowy cotton hip-length blouse loaded with embroidery around the open collar that showed too much cleavage. Her black yoga pants resembled a sausage casing that was about to explode. Rowan waited for the bartender's eyes to return to him.

"Cabernet…" he answered. "Shiraz if you have it."

A sympathetic smile lit her face as she glanced again to her friend.

"Hey Clark, I don't know if you've noticed, but you're not in Napa," she said with a twinge of sarcasm.

"Red, then," he clarified, anxious to get their attention off him.

The bartender turned and grabbed a blue bottle from the rack behind the bar. She pulled the cork with an electric cork remover which, in his mind, was contrary to the entire presentation of everything else around him. She put the bottle on the bar in front of him.

"Do you want to start a tab, Clark?"

Rowan looked at the dark blue bottle with a strange label that hosted the familiar image of the thimble-hat man who was standing across the room.

"I just want a glass," he replied. "I'm not staying long."

"It's the same price," she answered in a matter-of-fact tone.

Rowan smiled as he handed the bartender his platinum American Express. The thickness and weight of the aluminum card attracted the attention of the bartender and her friend nearby. Their nods of approval were followed by sarcastic smiles.

Rowan used the bartender's departure and his empty glass to look away from the eyes he was feeling from the bartender's friend.

"You lost?" the woman asked.

Her confused expression surprised him as he looked to find her staring at him. He smiled as he thought about the many different cavalier replies he could use. She looked like she was a fairly simple person who may have had a few too many wines. Then he thought that messing with anyone from this crowd was probably a bad idea. He did not know who she was connected to.

"No," he replied. "I had to pee. So I stopped."

"You were just driving by? ... Here?" she asked with a grin.

Rowan smiled as he looked to check on the bartender still processing his tab.

"No. My GPS brought me here," he answered.

The woman smiled as she watched Rowan rethink his response.

"You asked your GPS for a good place to pee? Did you not see all the trees everywhere?"

Rowan smile as he nodded to confirm the stupidity of his reply. The seemingly simple, intoxicated country cougar had more wits about her than he expected.

"I'm Janis," she said, extending her hand to him. "As in Joplin... but that's not my last name."

Rowan instinctively lifted his hand to shake hers then stopped. He thought about its path through the nasty bathroom to get there, wondering if he should decline her shake. Before he came to a decision, Janis closed the gap to take hold of his hand, rolling it over to show his college signet ring. Her firm grip had no sign of letting go.

"Row..." he started, then stopped, as he noticed her complete attention was on his hand.

"That's a dainty ring," she remarked, studying its small size. "Most of the high school rings around here are twice that size with a big red stone in the center. GO WARRIORS!"

Janis released Rowan's hand as she threw hers into the air to finish her high school chant. A satisfied smile appeared on her face as she redirected her attention back to her glass of wine then to him.

"Here ya go, Clark," the bartender said as she returned Rowan's Platinum card to the bar in front of him.

Puzzled, Rowan picked up his card to look at it.

"Why do you call me Clark?" he asked. "I've never been here before, and my name is on this card."

A smile came to her face as she looked to Janis. She then lifted both of her hands to her eyes to fake a repositioning of an imaginary pair of the horned-rimmed glasses on her face. She then ran the palm of her right hand back along her hair to make fun of his perfectly set, salt-n-pepper flow. The smug look on her face showed she was enjoying his discomfort with each gesture she made. An image of the 1960s preppy, gelled Superman he used to watch on TV appeared in his head as a smirk appeared on his face.

"Superman," he mumbled, while shaking his head.

Rowan looked toward Janis, who was readjusting on her chair. The look on her face showed she was anxious to know more about the fish-out-of-water sitting at the end of the bar.

"Rowan," he said, as he started to extend his hand toward the bartender.

Janis reacted immediately to intercept his hand again.

"Janis," she declared, "again."

Rowan smiled to acknowledge her second introduction then loosened his hold to get her to let go of his hand. As her hand released, he reached across the bar to the bartender who made him feel so welcome.

"Clark Kent," he said, smugly. "Also known as Superman. But please don't tell anyone. I'm here to keep an eye on the dervish over there."

The three looked to the far corner of the room as the man in the canvas-covered thimble hat was working a table of middle-aged women.

"Oh, he's harmless," the bartender answered. "That's just Cousin Dave."

Cousin Dave looked toward them as if feeling the weight of their eyes on him. The two women waved before returning their attention to Rowan.

"What's your name?" Rowan inquired, now intrigued with the gray-blue-eyed woman with the soft, gray ponytail in front of him.

The bartender took his hand as she thought. Rowan noted hers was surprisingly warm and soft.

"Oddly," she answered. "It's Lois."

A cackled laugh erupted from Janis as she spun away. Startled by her surprised response, a puzzled look hung on Rowan's face as he watched her shift in her chair while he continued to hold Lois' hand.

"Really?" he asked. "As in Lois Lane?"

Janis looked back at the two still holding hands then erupted again in a belly laugh that took her to her feet.

"Yes," she replied adamantly, as if accepting her name for the first time. "But not Lane. It's just Lois."

Rowan released Lois' hand thinking the coincidence of her name really was not that funny. Her eyes were still watching her friend work off her hysterics. A third, softer round of laughter finished Janis' amusement before she was able to sit back on her stool and regain her composure.

"Nice to meet you, Low… is… But not Lois Lane."

Rowan smiled before he took a large pull of red wine. The two women who were teasing him exchanged glances and smiles as if waiting for something to happen.

The sweet taste of the wine made his jaw clench, causing an involuntary gag reflex. His body jerked back before he was able to settle and look into his glass. It took all his strength to keep from coughing. His response pulled the attention of the two women back to him.

"This is good…. Low-is," he said, with small gasps for air before taking a second taste of wine.

The second pull lacked the overwhelming sweet surprise of the first. It mellowed in his mouth as his taste buds recalibrated their expectations from the dry wines he usually drank. Its *Rowan Rating* was changing from *total shit* to *not bad*.

Lois nodded in agreement before looking to Janis and heading back to work. He watched her walk away, noticing her slim build that filled her flowing cotton shirt and blue jeans nicely. He took another large pull of wine before turning back to Janis, whose eyes he could feel running up and down his body.

"You never answered my question, Clark," she said, smiling that he was not happy with his new nerdy nickname.

# # # #

The first pain he felt was a throbbing in his temple that would not quit. His hand worked its way from under the blanket as it lifted to rub and soothe his forehead. It was obvious that he had had too much to drink and was paying for it. A foggy recollection of the Red Sombrero Winery and the two women at the bar came into focus as he began to recall his evening.

"Shit," he grunted quietly as his eyes popped open to see what was around him.

As the room came into focus, he could see that it was the size of a walk-in closet. It had a window with plastic blinds and a metal casement that slid sideways. The blinds were leaking sunlight, showing that the day had started long before his brain did to wake him up.

Rowan ran his fingers through his hair to think. He could feel that he still had his shirt and jeans on, which was a good sign that nothing regrettable had happened. A quick check placed his phone and his wallet in his front pockets. His shoes were missing. But his socks were still where they were supposed to be.

The room had a strange, musty odor he equated to cabins either at the beach or deep in the woods. He turned on his side to get comfortable, causing the bed to squeak.

As he released a slight exhale, he closed his eyes to relieve some of the pressure from his hangover. He gently rubbed his temples to get some comfort as fought to not drift back off into a light haze.

A light thump on the door sounded as it creaked open. Rowan was hesitant to look as he opened his eyes, having no idea who would be looking back at him. The jingle of metal was a familiar sound, like the family dogs he had during his marriage. The smell of the dog's wicked breath made him immediately sit up, fearful that he was about to vomit.

Looking back at him and breathing in a slow pant was an old coon dog. His face was curious. His yellowed eyes showed that he was well into his later stage of life. The dog was definitely there to find some love rather than protect the home he was in.

As Rowan sat on the edge of the bed, the coon dog climbed onto his bed and settled next to him. He placed his head on the pillow Rowan had just used. The dog's unneutered butt-end pressed against Rowan's hip. Rowan patted the old dog, knowing that he had taken his bed for the evening. Although thankful at first, he began to wonder when the sheets were last washed and if any ticks or fleas were left from nights before. The flea-and-tick collar around the dog's neck appeared to be new and in good shape. Rowan's initial impulse to conduct a full-body tick search became less of a priority. However, his inner leg did begin to itch when he thought about fleas.

"Travis," whispered a voice softly from the other side of the door. "Come here, boy."

The door creaked open a bit more to provide enough room to lure the dog back out into the hallway.

"Travis!" a stronger whisper called.

Rowan finished fixing his hair the best he could feel before answering the voice's call for the dog.

"He's in here," Rowan said, in a raspy voice.

The door creaked open farther to first show a woman's hand followed by a face he remembered from the night before.

"I'll get breakfast started," she said with a smile. "There's Tylenol in the bathroom. I'll be in the kitchen when you're ready."

"Thank you," was all Rowan could reply before she disappeared back into the hallway. Breakfast must have been a word she used with Travis to define his morning meal because the dog that was eager to settle into his bed quickly stood and left the room to follow his owner.

Rowan reached to rub his temple again. His urge to throw up after the dog breathed on him was gone. He could feel a wobbliness in his body that gave him concern that standing would be a challenge. With a single thrust forward, he decided to go for it and pushed upward onto his feet to stand upright. He took hold of the dresser that was on the wall opposite the bed to stabilize his stance. After taking a few seconds to find his balance, Rowan took his first steps to find the bathroom before heading out for breakfast.

# # # #

Stepping out into the hallway to walk to the bathroom confirmed his fear that he had spent the night in some sort of trailer. The hallway, which ran the front side of the trailer, had windows that he could look through out to the woods surrounding the trailer. Still unstable, with his head pounding, his pain kept him from thinking about any type of *Deliverance* scenario that could be playing out. If that had come to mind, he likely would have told them to just kill him to eliminate the almost unbearable throbbing in his head.

Rowan drank several handfuls of water from the spigot to rehydrate himself. He found, then took twice his usual dose of Tylenol to accelerate the pain relief it promised to provide. His face reflecting in the mirror appeared saggy and tired. His eyes were bloodshot. There was nothing positive in the image he saw.

"You look like shit," he said to himself before splashing more cold water on his face.

Rowan could smell bacon frying as it drifted down the hallway and into each room. On any other day, the smell of bacon was the start of a good day. But today it hit him like a gut punch. He stayed in the bathroom a little bit longer to regain his equilibrium with the smells that were continuing to grow stronger.

"Are you okay in there?" he heard bellow down the hall.

The sound of her voice brought back the reality of where he was and the stranger he had to face. He felt embarrassed that things had gotten out of hand the night before. As someone who had been married for over twenty-five years without incident, he began to wonder how to thank the person waiting with breakfast for her kindness in order to gracefully leave without offending her.

"Yes," he answered as he opened the door to proceed back past his bedroom to the trailer's main living quarters.

"I was beginning to worry about you," the woman said as she tended the stove. "First I didn't think you were going to wake up, then you took so long in the bathroom."

Rowan walked to the kitchen table that sat next to a window overlooking more trees. He remembered the woman in front of him from the night before but was having problems remembering her name. All he could remember was that it was from his childhood.

"I'm so embarrassed," he finally mumbled. "I have no recollection of anything from last night."

"Well, you had a very good time with some very fun women," she replied while stirring eggs in a skillet. "We all did rock-paper-scissors to see who was going to take care of you."

She placed two plates loaded with scrambled eggs, bacon, and a piece of cornbread on the table. A mug of steaming coffee with a container of milk and sweeteners was also added. Two small glasses of orange juice finished the breakfast as she sat in the chair across from him.

"So you lost?" Rowan asked while dressing his coffee with creamer.

"No," she answered with a smile. "I won."

Rowan's first pull of coffee brought back a vivid memory of his first taste of wine the night before. The coffee had an initial bite to it that was unfamiliar to his tastes, which were used to Starbucks Morning Joe. A second taste began to move his tastebuds to thinking that the coffee he was drinking just may be an improvement to the coffee he bought.

"Well, I don't know how taking responsibility for some drunk stranger is considered *winning*. But I appreciate your help and am really embarrassed I got to that point..."

Rowan wanted to say her name. But it just was not coming to him. He looked around the room for help, to find something that would give him a clue. On the far wall was the classic poster of Jimi Hendrix in concert. The image of that era fired some synapses in his head to connect the dots back to the night before.

"Janis," he finished, happy he knew he got Janis Joplin, minus the Joplin, right.

Janis adjusted in her chair with a smile as she took a bite of bacon impressed that Clark Kent remembered her name, which was a concern of hers, and a test to see if she even had a shot with him.

"It's nothing," she replied. "I live the closest. I just buckled you into my Razor and brought you here. You were pretty mobile for as drunk as you was."

Were he immediately thought, to correct her grammar. *What the hell am I doing here?* was next as he looked for the nearest exit.

"It's not nothing," he replied. "I would like to make it up to you some time."

How Janis heard those words was not how Rowan intended. Her face lit up as her back straightened, pushing her chest toward him. He seemed to be a keeper rather than the throw-backs she was used to.

"I'd like that," she answered with an unintended flip of her hand through her hair. "You'll have to come back."

Rowan immediately felt panic set in as she said those words. He looked for a clock in the room to see what time it was. There was a strange wall clock above the sink that was built into the body of a black cat whose tail wisped back and forth as its eyes moved left and right.

"Is it really twelve fifteen?" Rowan asked, thinking he was to meet his client at Heinz Field in Pittsburgh by three o'clock for a tailgate before the Steelers game.

"I think so," Janis replied. "Do you have to be somewhere?"

Rowan got to his feet, immediately feeling so dizzy he had to sit back down.

"The Steeler game," he mumbled. "I'm supposed to meet clients at the Steeler game in two hours…. *fuck.*"

Rowan took another big gulp of coffee to calm his nerves and to get rid of his headache. His pharmacist told him that the caffeine in coffee accelerates the pain reliever in Tylenol. *Or was it Advil?* He began to stress over not being able to remember that fact too.

"You're going to be late," Janis observed. "You also look like shit."

Janis threw in a pregnant pause to enable her comment to sink in. She enjoyed messing with him the night before, and there did not seem to be a good reason to not continue it today. Rowan chomped on another slice of bacon to fill the void as he pondered his options.

"I've got to call him and tell him I can't make it," he said. "That'll give him time to find someone to use the ticket."

Rowan's stomach churned at the thought of losing the pregame and postgame with the client he has known since childhood and spent years cultivating. They were just reaching the point of a good lending rhythm for land development projects that were all over the country. He had no other option but to try to get there. To show late was inexcusable. He had to think of a believable lie to avoid explaining why he was two-and-a-half hours away, hung-over, and that he had woken up in a trailer owned by Janis. He smiled when the thought that the actual truth was more unbelievable than anything else he could concoct.

Rowan pulled his phone from his pocket hoping to find a message from his client canceling his game obligation. He knew it was a desperate thought that was not going to come true. The battery icon on his iPhone read fifty percent as the words *no service* sat beside it.

"There's no cell service here," Janis offered as she watched his eyes shut.

He wondered what his client would think if Janis' caller ID showed up on his cell phone. The simple explanation could be that he was broken down in a *Mayberry* town up north with no cell service. Janis could be the shop-owner's wife, who allowed him to use her phone. That explanation made complete sense until he laughed about the thought of even having to make it up.

"May I use your phone to call Pittsburgh?" Rowan asked, knowing that it would likely be okay.

Janis' face went blank when she heard his request.

"I only have a cell phone," she answered. "I can't afford both."

Rowan looked at Janis' apologetic expression, wondering why she would have a cell phone when she had no cell service.

"I have cell service at work and when I'm out," she answered. "You can call from the Sombrero. They have a landline I use all the time. Sometimes they have one bar of service. But my calls always get cut off there. It's just through the woods."

"Great," Rowan replied, now seeing a trek to the Sombrero as his opportunity to exit. "I'd say I have to pull my things together; but I don't have any!"

His joke introduced a new lightness to their awkward situation and conversation. Janis smiled as she worked to finish a slice of bacon. She excused herself to change so that she could show him the way back to the Sombrero, his car, and his exit.

Chapter 2

The Polaris Razor sat next to Janis' red Chevrolet Cruze sedan. The exterior of the trailer offered no better vibe than the inside. It was old and tired with an attached wooden deck that was covered with a corrugated plastic roof held up by wood beams. The driveway and parking area were a combination of loose stone and dirt. There were lots of things that Rowan observed that he could have spent hours talking about. But he knew his questions would be insulting. So he kept them to himself.

"What do you do when the snow comes?" he asked as they climbed into the plastic seats of the two-seater Razor.

"It doesn't snow as much as it used to," Janis answered. "We just deal with it. My ex plows me out. So I'm good to get to work as long as I can get to the main road."

Rowan tried to recall his drive to the Red Sombrero from the highway. It was a stretch of pavement less than two lanes wide that traveled for a while. The road that led to that was two lanes that he could see getting attention in a snowstorm.

The start of the Razor reignited the pain in his head as its loud, unmuffled sound brought his headache back and the rich smell of exhaust worked to twist his stomach back into a knot. Janis put the Razor in gear then punched the accelerator. The rear wheels spun in the gravel before gaining traction to push Rowan's head back into his hard plastic seat. A quick look at Janis showed her focused on the drive ahead with an aggressive lean forward and determined look on her face.

The ride to the Red Sombrero was faster than Janis had represented. A cut through the trees provided the path from the back of her property onto the far rear of the Sombrero property, down behind its back deck. As the Razor emerged from the trees, Rowan looked around at the land below the building. It was a view that laid hidden in the darkness when he arrived. He was surprised to see people on the deck, already settled in for an afternoon of drinking.

"It's open already?" he asked as the Razor slowed to park on a grassy knoll.

"Opens at noon." Janis answered. "It's football season."

Rowan smiled at the comment that should have been obvious to him—although putting wine and football were his usual go-togethers for Sunday afternoons.

The parking lot was about half full as the two journeyed in from the parking area to the front door. Rowan smirked as he scanned the trucks and Jeeps to find his car, which should have stuck-out like a sore thumb. But its low profile was blocked by a newer, jacked-up Ford F150 that dwarfed the Audi in both height and overall size. The look of his car in the lot further cemented his thought of *what the hell am I doing here?*

As they walked into the bar, Rowan noted that it looked different from what he remembered. The artwork that hung on the wall was new to him. There were large, impressionistic oils that looked like the lower property they just drove through to get there. There were other pictures of people—some who were famous, some who were unfamiliar—painted directly on the walls as permanent fixtures.

The one o'clock game between the Cleveland Browns and the Houston Texans was projected on a screen behind the bandstand. The barstools were empty. A light crowd of Cleveland fans sat at a few tables close to the screen. Thinking through the geography of the area, Rowan realized Cleveland was as close to the Red Sombrero as Pittsburgh. The bar patrons' faces seemed more excited to be watching the game than he had seen in previous years at some Cleveland bars.

"Clark Kent lives," Lois announced from behind the bar. "Care for another round of kryptonite?"

Rowan smiled as he and Janis arrived in front of the bar. Of the three, he obviously felt the worst physically. Janis seemed to have a clearer head than when they met the night before. Lois was charged up for another day of slinging sweet wine.

"He needs to use your phone to call Pittsburgh." Janis said.

Lois exhaled with a huff to the request. A snarky expression hit her face as her eyes rolled back and forth between the two.

"That's long distance," she said. "It'll require the special operator."

Lois watched Rowan process her statement, which would have been true back in the nineteen fifties. He was afraid to ask for fear of offending her and losing the opportunity to use her phone.

"She's just fucking with you," Janis said. "Marnie, let him use your phone."

Lois' complete name change took the need to use the phone out of Rowan's head. He started to chuckle thinking about how the two country girls took him for a ride the night before. He then began to wonder if his American Express had been taken for one too.

"Marnie?" he repeated, while looking at her face, which showed disappointment that her charade was over.

"Only to my friends," she answered while giving a sneer to Janis.

"May I call you Marnie?" he asked to test the waters with the woman who still looked sexy despite the hungover state she was responsible for putting him in.

"We'll see," she answered, as she felt the heat of a blush fill her cheeks. "The phone is in the office over there. Excuse the mess."

Rowan remembered the urgency of his call. As he walked behind the bar, he noticed a considerable mess behind it. He wondered if the health department would find it up to code if they ever stopped by for a visit. That was one positive point about its location being so far off any beaten path.

As he was about to enter the office, he instinctively pulled his cell phone from his pocket.

"There's no cell service," Janis and Marnie reminded him at the same time.

Rowan lifted his hand holding the phone to acknowledge their statement.

"I need to get the number," he replied as he sat down at the desk.

Janis and Marnie looked at each other both surprised and annoyed that the other had interjected instructions to the man both found interesting.

"Where'd he sleep?" Marnie asked Janis in an insinuating tone.

Janis smiled, noting Marnie's jealousy. Marnie had refused to participate in the rocks, paper, scissors take-home competition because her ex-husband was present when they closed the bar.

"I think that's between him and me." Janis answered, as she adjusted her left breast in her bra.

"He's too highbrow for you," Marnie said with a laugh as she turned her attention to the bar. "Did you see his car out there?"

"No," Janis answered. "What does that matter anyway?"

"Cinderella's just a fairytale, Janis."

Marnie turned away to let her comment sink in. She knew her words would start to gnaw on Janis' mind as they always did, from high school until now. Janis was born, raised, and would die in the area without ever having left. Marnie had a broader experience and outlook. Although originally from the area, she was educated and lived outside of it while attending art school in California. She returned home when she was thirty-five and her dad became ill. He died soon after, leaving Marnie to care for her mother. That obligation kept her in Legend, Pennsylvania where she met, married, then divorced her husband while they developed the Red Sombrero Winery from a napkin idea.

"You just think your fancy California education and life makes you better than me."

Marnie smiled at Janis' accusation. She could have shot back a zinger to really plant her into the ground. But Janis was her best friend from high school and in life.

"He's not coming back, Janis."

# # # #

The office was nothing more than a small walk-in closet. It sat behind the kitchen, next to what appeared to be the production area for their house wines. Rowan was surprised to see stainless steel kettles and tanks instead of the more romantic stacked wood barrels he had seen in Napa Valley and France. Large, blue-plastic barrels that looked more like road barriers were next to the garage door he assumed led to a loading dock.

It was no surprise from the presentation of the bar area that the mess would flow into the office. Stacks of papers sat on every square inch of the small desk topped by unopened envelopes from vendors. Rowan made a special effort to not look at anything as he searched for the telephone that he expected to be somewhere on the desk. When that proved fruitless, he expanded his hunt to the surrounding surfaces.

Attached to the wall, he found a familiar looking plastic rectangle with rounded corners and a long, twisted, curly cord hanging down to the floor. It reminded him of his teenage years in the 1980s, before wireless phones with antennas and, later, cell phones changed the world. He lifted the handset from its nest on the wall, excited to see that the push-button pad hidden underneath still lit.

The tones that sounded from the phone as each button was pressed were louder than Rowan remembered. He thought about what excuse he was going to use with his client, and friend, that he was not going to be able to make the tailgate, game, and post-game he had been looking forward to for weeks. His anxiety dropped when Dorsey Schmitt's voicemail answered instead of the man himself.

"Dorsey. Rowan," he started, still processing the words he wanted to string together. "I'm sorry for this late call. I'm in northern PA stuck with car trouble, no cell service, and won't be back in time for the game. Please find someone to take my spot. I sincerely appreciate the invitation. Please text me back that you got this message. I'll call...."

The end-tone from Dorsey's voicemail stopped him mid-sentence. Rowan's chest tightened as he thought more about the potential impact of his late cancelation on the generous offer from his friend and client. He relaxed in the office chair as he closed his eyes to think. If there were ever a chance that God would step in to transport him from where he was to where he needed to be, now was a good time for that to happen.

"I'm sorry about the mess in here," Marnie commented, as she reached behind him for a three-ring binder. "Did your call go through?"

"Yes," he answered, as his eyes opened. "Thank you. The phone took me back to my teenage years, when you had to stretch the cord into another room for privacy."

Marnie smiled. She had the same memory growing up nearby in a farmhouse that had one phone in the kitchen. The cord was long enough to stretch into the front hall coat closet that was under the stairs. She used it for privacy often creating a tripping hazard for the rest of her family as the chord angled down from the wall down to go under the door into the closet darkness.

"The cord reaches the cash register and the vats," she replied. "I can't tell you how many times it has flown out of my hand when I'm talking to someone while doing something else. When the cord ends, it ends."

The expression on her face added to the funny visual she painted. Rowan could see her charging off to take care of something while talking, only to have the phone shoot back across the room as the cord coil reached its limit and retracted.

"They make cordless phones that you can take anywhere," he answered. "They'll even work in these dead zones around here."

The jab on the lack of cell service was clear. Marnie winced with a fake smile to acknowledge his attempt at humor without making any indication she thought it was funny.

"We've had those. They always get lost... or left outside in the rain."

Rowan thought about her comment as he looked around. Clearly, a wall unit was the best choice for keeping it intact and not get lost in the sea of paper on the desk. The cord was a tether that could not be disconnected without disabling the phone.

"The cord keeps it where you need it." he clarified.

"Within range. Plus, it always works."

Rowan stood, as it was becoming awkward for him to be sitting while she stood in the doorway.

"Thank you for letting me use your phone."

Marnie nodded as he worked his way past her. Her presence in the doorway made it necessary for him to turn facing her. Her elbow of the arm holding the binder rubbed against his chest as he passed by. As he returned to the small kitchen area, Marnie quickly returned the three-ring binder without having opened it. Rowan smiled as she looked away knowing she was caught checking on him while he was making his call.

As he walked through the kitchen back to the bar, he saw Janis sitting on a stool, looking at him with a sad face. A new round of awkward was approaching as it was time to say goodbye and get on the road back to Pittsburgh. Janis turned to face him as he approached.

"Janis," he said, exhaling his words. "Thank you so much for giving me a bed last night. I'm so embarrassed. I'd like to make it up to you. Can I buy you some wine...?"

Janis smiled knowing she was being blown-off. She had hope, and maybe some expectation, that the good-looking, city man, that happened upon her neck-of-the-woods, would hang around to give her a shot.

"Just come back," she replied. "Or stay for the game."

The last suggestion was hopeful to buy time she could use to advance her cause. Janis was not a football fan. But she knew enough from her time at the Sombrero that games were on Sunday. She also knew that Rowan was a big enough fan to go to the games. Her hope was that a few glasses of Sombrero red would keep him in there for a while.

"I'll definitely come back," he answered, looking around the place to grab a glimpse of Marnie, then back at her.

Marnie had moved from the office into the production area. He wanted to say goodbye to *Lois Lane* before leaving, to thank her for the use of her phone after getting him wickedly drunk the night before. But she had already intentionally disappeared to give her friend the chance she knew would end badly.

The easiest place to hide was the production room. Marnie made herself busy behind the vats, placing some empty blue bottles into a box for recycling. She could hear a murmur of conversation from the bar that sounded like Janis was having success.

When Marnie threw the box of empties at the cement floor, the sound of shattering glass echoed out the door into the kitchen, startling Rowan and Janis. When they entered the production room, they found Marnie sitting on the floor surrounded by shards of blue bottle.

"Are you okay?" Rowan asked, stepping through the glass to extend his hand to Marnie.

Janis followed him into the room. Her look of concern shifted to suspicion as she looked at the manufactured scene of her never-helpless friend sitting on the floor.

"I think so," Marnie said, exaggerating her shock and resisting Rowan's pull to bring her to her feet. "I tripped."

Although Marnie was looking at Rowan, she could see Janis roll her eyes behind him.

Marnie kept hold of Rowan's hand as she stood. Neither made a quick effort to release the other. As Marnie's eyes closed then reopened, she saw Janis flip her head into the air as she turned to leave the room.

"Thank you, Clark," she said softly with a smile.

"Here!" Janis declared as she returned to the room.

She extended a broom toward Marnie that Rowan intercepted with his left hand.

"It's the least I can do for you letting me use your phone."

Marnie released his warm, unusually soft hand as she smiled at him, then toward Janis. He started the work to pull the larger shards he saw into a pile. Their deep blue color against the gray cement floor made them easy to see. Marnie out of his way as Janis stood in the doorway watching her hopes fade.

As Marnie walked past her to leave the production room, she exchanged looks with her best friend. Rowan continued to sweep smaller pieces of glass from under the stainless-steel vats.

"Now that's how it's done," Marnie whispered to her friend as she passed by.

Marnie knew Rowan was interested in hanging around a little bit longer. All the other city boys who had come and gone through the winery left without a goodbye. Sometimes they even left without closing their tabs and collecting their credit cards.

Janis shook her head as she watched Rowan continue to sweep. She was mad at her best friend for making a play for the man she fairly won the opportunity to flirt with first. But she also knew that without Marnie's bold action, Rowan would have been on the road long ago.

# # # #

The Band-Aid she chose was the largest one in the first aid kit she kept in the office. The three- by five-eighths-inch wide strip wrapped around her thumb, with the padded middle sitting on the lower side of her thumb.

"What are you doing now?" Janis asked as she watched Marnie close the lid of the kit.

"Staging," she answered. "Just watch and don't say anything."

The adamant tone in Marnie's voice made it clear that Janis was to play along. Since growing up, Marnie was always the brain behind any operation they launched to accomplish the things they wanted to do. Marnie manipulated and positioned things to win boyfriends, prom dates, and even to get into college in

California as a marginal student from Legend, Pennsylvania. Janis never questioned Marnie's tactics. But that was always because they were going to deliver something she wanted. But this time, Marnie seemed to be working for herself rather than for the team.

"He's not going to care that you cut yourself," Janis replied while watching Marnie manipulate her hand so Rowan could not miss her wound.

"This is all we've got," she answered.

"That's not true. He'll come back because of last night."

Marnie paused as she listened to her friend's voice elevate while her nose pointed toward the ceiling. The look on her face showed that she was bluffing. Marnie smiled then returned to concentrate on her bandaged hand without saying another word.

"You don't believe me, do you?" Janis asked, irritated that her friend blew off her statement.

Marnie touched the bandage and started to look around the kitchen.

"Do you see the ketchup squirty thing?" she asked.

Janis looked to the doorway leading to the production area before replying.

"A little blood ooze should help sell this."

Several crashes of glass into the Rubbermaid garbage can clamored from the production room, giving the women final warning that the clean-up was about done.

"I'm going to tell him you're faking it." Janis stated in a strong whisper.

Marnie stopped, then wiped away the ketchup with a paper towel before pointing her index friend at her friend.

"You do that, and he never comes back,"

"He'll come back because of last night."

Marnie shook her head at her friend.

"I saw you two drive off. He was cooked when you left. Nothing happened, and we both know that."

Marnie's eyes stayed focused on the doorway as she kept her voice down to a whisper. She knew from the shuffling noise that showtime was about to start.

"If you seriously want him to come back then shut the fuck up."

Janis backed away to return to her stool. She knew Marnie was right. The only men who came back were the ones who lived in the area or hunted the area during the different seasons. The man sweeping the glass in the next room was neither a native nor a hunter. He was a keeper. Janis knew her best shot at Rowan was to let Marnie work her magic to get him to come back.

A shadow flicker in the doorway gave the cue for them to shut up and take their positions. Janis waved Marnie over and took her hand. If empathy was Marnie's tactic, then sympathy was going to be Janis'.

"All done," Rowan stated as he exited the room. "My wife has told me that I'm a lousy sweeper. So, if a rogue shard of blue glass shows up, it's because I missed it.

The girls looked at each other then to Rowan's left hand for a wedding band. As they turned, their staging collapsed, and Marnie's hand dropped to her side.

"Are you hurt?" Rowan asked, while moving his head for a better look at her hand.

"You're married?" Marnie replied without thinking.

The continued study of his left hand showed no ring. It was even absent of the ring mark that was easily seen on guys who would take off their wedding bands before heading out for a night at the Red Sombrero.

"Divorced," Rowan answered. "I mean, separated... I don't know, let's just say *not married*."

A noticeable exhale of relief exhausted from both women as smiles came to their faces. Rowan walked closer to Marnie, continuing to be intrigued by her hand.

"Is that a bandage?" he asked. "You didn't have that earlier."

The fact that Rowan made comment about Marnie's hand before the glass toss encouraged her as much as it infuriated Janis. The bandage was on her left thumb, two fingers away from her ring finger.

"It's fine," Marnie answered, as she lifted her hand to show him.

Rowan cupped her hand in both of his as he studied the bandage. Marnie glanced to Janis with a smile confirming that her strategy was working.

"You should probably wipe away some of that ketchup so that it doesn't infect the cut," he added, while rubbing the red stain lightly.

Janis immediately choked on her laugh when Marnie's face showed panic that she had been caught.

"Oh, that must have rubbed off when I moved the ketchup thingy back to the kitchen."

Rowan lowered her hand gently as he turned to walk back to the bar area.

"It'll be fine," he said, smiling at the half-assed attempt to show injury. "I'm sure it will heal to the point that you'll never know it even happened."

A quick look and wink to Janis told her he was on to them. Janis stood as he walked by, angling to follow.

"I do need to get going though. Thank you for a wonderful night."

Rowan walked toward Janis with his palms up to show he was going to give her a hug. A smile appeared on her face as she stepped to him. His embrace was genuine. He truly appreciated her kindness to let him sleep it off at her trailer. The feel of him in her arms gave her a new appreciation for him as she felt the firmness of his upper body, width of his shoulders, and remaining hint of his cologne.

"Give Travis a scratch for me."

Marnie started to migrate around the bar to stand next to them as their hug unfolded. Rowan moved his eyes from Janis to her as she stepped near then stopped.

"Take care of that thumb, Lois," he said with a snarky smile.

Marnie smiled at the ongoing back-and-forth teasing she had going with Superman. After an awkward few seconds, Rowan raised the palms of his hands to ask her for a hug. An uncontrolled schoolgirl look and stumble appeared as she moved toward him to say goodbye. Their embrace was no longer than his with Janis. But Marnie was the last to let go.

"Let me know if that dervish fellow gets out of hand. Once they start twirling, it's all over."

Rowan smiled as he waved and walked away. He was thankful to finally be separating from the two playful country women who he found amusing but would have walked by if the environment had been reversed. Had either of them shown at his place of work or his country club, he knew he would not have been so intrigued or benevolent to them as they were to him.

"Bye, Clark." Marnie called softly as he walked out the door.

Marnie exchanged a look with Janis who was waiting for her to say something more.

"He'll be back," Marnie said as she returned to the bar.

Chapter 3

The drive from Legend to Interstate 80 was shorter than he thought it should have been. His phone found a signal once he reached the two-lane road that was less than five hundred yards from the Red Sombrero. A series of audible pings announced the arrival of several messages and texts. His Bluetooth connected the phone to his car and he asked Siri to play his voice messages.

"Rowan, it's Dorsey. I hope everything is okay. We're in the B lot, section 18. Looking forward to seeing you."

Rowan looked at the clock on his dash. It read 3:10 p.m. He then looked at the time stamp on the message; it was 3:01pm. He had just missed Dorsey's call. But Dorsey should have received his message an hour earlier.

"Call Dorsey Schmitt," Rowan said to get Siri in motion.

The phone started ringing as Rowan thought more about the message he left. It was not unclear. The line from the Red Sombrero was fine.

FUCK, he thought. *Red Sombrero* must have appeared on Dorsey's caller ID when he saw the message. He probably deleted it before listening. Or if he listened, he probably knows Rowan lied about why he could not make the game.

"Rowan!?" Dorsey answered in a loud voice trying to drown out the background noise. "Did you get my message?"

"Yes," Rowan replied, uncertain on how to proceed. "Hey, listen, I'm not going to make it. I got stuck with car trouble up near Clarion. I'm just rolling now. I left you a message about an hour or so ago."

"I didn't get it," Dorsey replied, his annoyance clear in his tone. "How long you going to take to get here? I can leave the ticket at will-call."

Rowan looked at himself in the mirror. His hair was a reconfigured gel mess from a night on a pillow. He had not showered. And he was in clothes that were not only a day old in wear, but also not to the standard of a corporate box at Heinz Field.

"I don't know, man," he answered, still looking for words. "I broke down last night. I'm still in yesterday's clothes and honestly look like shit."

Dorsey laughed at the image that came to mind.

"You'll be fine. Stop and wet your hair, run a comb through it, and buy some breath mints."

Rowan knew he could not refuse Dorsey's modified invitation to the game. He agreed to show by halftime. His ticket would be waiting at will-call.

"Hold on," Dorsey said as his voice went faint.

After a few seconds, he returned.

"Is this *Red Sombrero* call from you?" he asked.

"Yeah," Rowan answered. "It was where I was waiting while they fixed my tire."

"Then yeah, I did get your message. I ignored it thinking it was a butt dial. No problem. We'll see you in a few."

Rowan smiled as he thought about Dorsey seeing the Red Sombrero appearing on his caller ID. He then thought about his first impression of the Red Sombrero from the street, his entrance, and after meeting Lois and Janis Joplin. There was a looseness there that was calming. It was funny that what he originally sought to find on his Saturday drive through nature ended up being a country winery in Legend, Pennsylvania.

# # # #

"You don't look as bad as I thought you would," Dorsey laughed, as Rowan walked into the plush corporate box.

Around him were fifteen, well dressed, properly attired executives, friends, and clients of Schmitt Development Corporation. Their Steelers apparel was not from the vendors from either around the stadium or the stadium's retail shop. Rowan bought a baseball cap and fleece pullover on his way in to celebrate his team and to cover his wrinkled clothes and crazed hair that was not to the standard he knew would be in the box.

Rowan worked his way across the box he had visited before. Its sightline stood on the twenty-yard line, away from the river. The views of the field, the city, and the confluence of the three rivers were all equally stunning, particularly when the sun was either setting or gone for the night.

"I had to Uber from the parking lot to get here," Rowan joked as he shook Dorsey's hand.

Dorsey smiled, thinking Rowan's walk was likely shorter and easier at halftime than when they entered pregame.

"Here," he said, as he handed Rowan a bourbon highball in a cut crystal glass. "This'll settle you down. The game is kind of a snoozer."

"ROW-an Delaney? How are you?" sounded in a nasally voice from behind him.

The voice was familiar. Rowan watched Dorsey's expression move to a smile as he looked over Rowan's shoulder then back at him. Rowan took a sidestep back to turn halfway to greet who he knew was there.

Nicole McCrady Schmitt smiled as she took a pull from the stemless wine glass overfilled with red wine. Her tall, slender body was covered from head to toe in excessive Steelers attire. Building from a hip-length black Steelers sweater that would have been considered bedazzled on any other woman, her black yoga pants continued her perfect lines down over her hips to her knees, where perfectly polished, black patent leather equestrian boots finished her outfit. Her hair was a perfectly set shoulder-length blonde parted on the side with the left side pulled behind her ear. The earring he could see was the Steelers logo created by a gold ring with different precious stones to create the three-star pattern in the middle.

"Nicki," Rowan said as he studied the expensive, manufactured look of a woman who likely could not tell anyone where the football field was.

Nicki loved Steelers games for the social event they always were. The corporate booth was special, and guests dressed and treated it as such. She avoided the tailgate, choosing instead to go straight to the company box where the food was good, there was ample booze, and there was an available proper, private bathroom. She rarely sat in the seats that gave the view of the field. She never watched the game.

Rowan opened his arms to invite a hug from the girl who haunted him through high school. Although two years younger, Nicki spied Rowan when he was a junior in high school. They dated for a year before he headed to Virginia for college. Nicki was not an academic, which limited her choices to the *acceptable* schools that Schmitt Development had relationships with. She ended up attending Bryn Mawr College near Philadelphia, finding her first husband at the University of Pennsylvania. They divorced after having three children who were now all out of the house, in college. Each one was expecting to return to Pittsburgh to work for Pap Pap's company and Uncle Dorsey.

Nicki's embrace was strong. It clenched around Rowan's neck and pulled him down as she elevated her five-foot seven-inch body to kiss him on the cheek.

"You going mountain man?" Nicki asked as she pulled away.

Rowan felt a twinge run through his body that Dorsey had told Nicki something that would get circulated throughout the city.

"What makes you ask that?" he inquired.

Nicki pressed the palm of her hand against his cheek. Rowan relaxed that her criticism was rooted in his unshaven face rather than his unexpected trek through Legend and the Red Sombrero.

"I like you better smooth," Nicki added, as she wiggled her hand on his cheek. "You need to take care of that."

Before Rowan could respond, Nicki was gone, off to her next conversation.

"She hasn't changed," Rowan joked, as he raised his glass of bourbon to his mouth.

The wash of warm, wonderfully sweet taste of Woodford bourbon eased his tension as it settled onto his gums with a slight burning sensation.

"That's my little sister," Dorsey answered. "God save the man she sets her sights on next."

The two men clinked tumblers before they took another pull from their glasses.

When the third quarter ended, it was clear the game was going to be a blowout. The box had emptied to a handful of people who appreciated football versus the social event that initially started in the cushy corporate box. Dorsey and Rowan had settled into the upper level of padded chairs that looked out over the playing field.

"So, where were you?" Dorsey asked, intrigued to hear the story behind the Red Sombrero.

"In a place called Legend, Pennsylvania," Rowan answered, working the truth as much as possible to ensure that anything deeper would not contradict something said earlier.

"Cook Forest?" Dorsey asked. "Clarion?"

"Yeah. I took a day drive to decompress."

"Did you really break down? Or did you have a breakdown?" Dorsey asked, knowing Rowan's situation and story.

"Let's go with both," he answered.

"So what is a Red Sombrero?"

Rowan smiled at the question as a vision of the haunted house out in the sticks appeared in his head. That vision quickly changed to the interior, with Janis, Cousin Dave, and Lois Lane. A smile came to his face as his vision zeroed in on Marnie's face right before he hugged her goodbye.

"I tell you... and you can't make this shit up either... It's the craziest place that I've ever seen."

Rowan started his story at Pennsylvania's Grand Canyon, which was several hours east of Legend. He wanted to build the foundation that he had ventured out to find some stress relief from his job and his separation. The two had known each other from the time Rowan had dated Nicki, Dorsey's older sister. They were neither peers nor friends during their childhood. They became friends in their forties, when Dorsey's father was still in charge of Schmitt Development and Rowan's job gave him the opportunity to pitch his bank to the company.

Rowan emphasized during his story that the search that led to him finding the Red Sombrero started with a desperate need to pee.

"Why didn't you just pull off and go in the trees?"

"I was afraid of getting shot," Rowan answered.

The description Rowan unfolded was not embellished because it did not have to be. He talked about the sight from the street, with a parking lot of pickup trucks, Jeeps, quads, and two-seat Razors. He described the sound emanating from the wood structure as a Siren's hum that pulled him closer, wanting to see more as well as go to the bathroom.

"I walk into this place and it's like stepping back to the nineties. Plaid everywhere. Crazy art on the wall. The freaking bathroom was in the middle of the room…. And it wasn't even a big room."

Dorsey smiled at the story, not thinking much of his description. To him, it sounded like a shithole.

"I asked a waitress where the bathroom was. Do you know what she said?"

"In the trees?" Dorsey replied with a smile.

"Yes!" Rowan confirmed, as Dorsey threw his glass up for a toast.

"But what about your car?"

Rowan's brain was running hard. He was queueing up all the different things that happened, which started once he decided to stay and found a seat at the bar.

"So I'm sitting at the bar and the bartender, who gave me all sorts of crap when I walked in, called me Clark."

Rowan gave a hand wave, as if it was not clear why she called him *Clark*.

"Clark Kent," Dorsey interjected. "Superman. I've always thought that. That you look like Clark Kent, that is."

Rowan took another pull of bourbon as he thought about Dorsey's comment. The image of various Supermans, from the sixties series to Christopher Reeves to Dean Caine, all appeared in his vision. Aside from the glasses, and maybe the hair, he did not see it.

The rest of the story flowed through meeting a cougar at the bar, Janis, and the sparky bartender whose name was Lois. Rowan decided to withhold the fact that it was a fake name intended to play games with him.

Rowan moved on to describe the wine as a funky sweet brew that had an unexpected kick at first taste. He then added that it mellowed once his taste buds aligned to a different expectation from a good cabernet or Merlot. He described the wine-making equipment in the back room as surprisingly sparse and industrial. The wood barrels in Napa were not at the Red Sombrero.

"Come to think about it," Rowan pondered, "I didn't see any vineyards anywhere."

"Did you see any big blue barrels?" Dorsey asked.

Rowan remembered the stack of blue barrels that looked like traffic barrels.

"They buy their stock then make adjustments to taste," Dorsey explained. "It's not uncommon."

As Rowan ran what he remembered through his head, the manufacturing and bottling system he saw began to make sense.

Rowan finished his story talking about the whirling dervish character they called *Cousin Dave*. He explained the outfit, from the thimble-shaped hat down through the flowing white jacket. Rowan was tempted to say that Cousin Dave reminded him of Nicki the way he worked the room, but he let his description end with a comment that the women loved him.

Rowan knew halfway through the whirling dervish description that Dorsey would want to know more about where he stayed and why. A flat tire seemed to be the best explanation. A nearby hotel was a better story than a tired trailer set back in the woods on a bed usually occupied by a hound dog named Travis.

"Tell me more about the two women," Dorsey asked as he refilled Rowan's glass to further loosen his inhibitions.

Rowan quickly formulated a description to include the funnier details while leaving out the awkward ones. He had to make up a few fillers that he could not remember due to alcoholic amnesia, which he had from the late evening up until the time that he woke to Travis's breath. The Sunday story captured Dorsey's interest as Rowan explained the two women's antics to keep him there.

"Thank God the guy fixing my tire got it done when he did," Rowan lied.

"I'm going to make a mental note of this place," Dorsey said. "Charlotte's been wanting to do a leaf tour up north. Maybe I'll make it part of the trip."

Rowan took another taste of bourbon as he thought about Dorsey seeing the Red Sombrero with his wife.

"I'm not sure it's Charlotte's kind of place."

"That's the point," Dorsey laughed as he put his glass to his lips to taste his final wash of bourbon.

# # # #

"No thimble cap tonight?" Marnie asked as Cousin Dave settled onto a barstool.

The four o'clock NFL games were ending. The crowd had expanded and contracted as it typically did throughout the afternoon. The joint pull of Steelers fans and Cleveland Browns fans kept the room active for the afternoon. The best Sundays happened twice a season, when the Steelers played the Browns. Fans on both sides showed up early to grab a seat and usually stayed long after to either celebrate or drown their sorrows.

"Not tonight," Cousin Dave replied as he stole a pour from an open blue bottle on the counter. "Not feeling it."

He looked at the label with a smile. It was a tribute he earned through both his eccentricity as the Whirling Dervish that showed up from time-to-time to amuse the crowd and for community buzz. Cousin Dave's antics bugged as many as it amused, and that split generally ran along gender lines. Marnie's ex-husband, Tom, was one of the many who did not find him funny.

"Hang in there, Cousin Dave," Marnie said, as she observed her friend slouch on the stool. "Life's too short to sweat the details."

"I'm getting old, Marn."

Marnie checked Cousin Dave's glass to see how quickly he was consuming his anesthetic.

"How about a dog?" she asked.

"Got one."

"A new quad?"

"My old one blows the new ones away."

"Jeez, Cousin Dave, what makes you happy?"

"Puerto Rico would make me happy. I think it has to do with the lack of sunshine here in winter. I always go dark when there's no sun."

Marnie continued to work her rag around the bar as Cousin Dave took another drink of wine. His image on the bottle's label made her smile until she looked at the disheartened real thing on the stool in front of her.

"How about just Florida?" Marnie offered. "You can go, tend bar, get sun, then come back when that season ends."

"Too many people," he replied. "I want seclusion. Maybe San Salvador."

Marnie stopped to look at him in disbelief.

"You work the crowd here," she said. "You love people."

"Eh, I love these people. The ones I don't like are like the guy you and Janis were fawning over last night. Mr. Pole-up-his-ass preppy…"

"Clark Kent?"

"Yeahhh, exactly…fucking Superman. People like him will ruin this place. Just like they did in the inner cities, pushing the poor out of their neighborhoods."

"He was actually quite nice…. Funny. You'd have liked him."

Cousin Dave took another pull of wine as Marnie closed out a tab for a waitress.

"You know, one of them finds this place, they have a good time, they tell someone else…"

"And business booms!" Marnie declared, happy to have such problems. "Rising tides lift all ships."

"That sounds like Republican bullshit that would've come from that dude last night."

"It's actually JFK," Marnie replied, waiting to see if this sunk in. "As in John F. Kennedy."

Cousin Dave started to think about a counterargument, then stopped. It was neither his business nor his place to advise Marnie how to run her business. He agreed that more customers would be a good thing. But only if those new customers continued to come without pushing out the existing base.

"I'm sure you're using it out of context," Cousin Dave said as he threw back the last gulp of wine. "I'm going to help you clean up."

He stood to straighten his pants, which had bunched as he sat on the stool. Marnie knew his routine and decided making her point was far less valuable to her than his help cleaning up the mess on the tables.

Cousin Dave's consumption of leftover wine never bothered Marnie. She never considered charging him for the wine that would otherwise go bad. She appreciated the value of the labor he provided without being asked. In her estimate, it far exceeded the inflated charge she would charge even an inebriated Clark Kent.

After a quick smile to mark the end of their conversation, Cousin Dave nodded and turned to walk to the covered porch. Bottles and glasses remained on tables from the afternoon crowd. The waitress either did not have time to clear them or was waiting for someone else to do it for her. Some of the residual mess was from the night before. The staff had either ignored it or was too tired to cart it back to the kitchen.

Marnie continued to watch Cousin Dave collect spent bottles, glasses, and several plates that delivered cheese platters or pizza. The menu was intentionally limited to just the foods required by the Commonwealth of Pennsylvania for the privilege of making and serving wine on the premises.

# # # #

A purplish-orange hue lit the western sky above the Ohio River as the midweek afternoon sun sunk down into the Ohio River valley. The view from the twentieth floor was a panoramic perspective over the older buildings that sat between Rowan's window and the confluence of the Allegheny and Monongahela rivers to create the head of the Ohio. Now three days into his work week, Rowan found his thoughts still drifting up north to the life he witnessed in the woods.

Rowan knew from Janis's trailer that the Sombrero's customers lives did not offer any of the luxuries he had at home or at work. Yet, they were a happy group of people. Loud in their approach to enjoying each other. Hands-on in their outdoor living using pickups, Jeeps, quads, and Razors to get around. He knew his mothership Audi sedan likely drew some looks from patrons leaving the Sombrero on Saturday night and arriving back for the Sunday NFL games. As he sat with his feet up on the air-handling unit by his window, the majestic sunset disappeared, replaced by a vision of the two funny women he met at the winery.

"Hey!" a voice called in from the door.

The unexpected call startled Rowan back to real time, causing his chair to teeter back then settle onto its four wheels. Leaning in was Roger Bailes, Rowan's protégé and a rising star in the commercial lending division of the bank. Roger had a wonderful knack for not just quickly seeing opportunities y in clients and projects but getting them onboard with the bank as their primary lender before anyone else could pitch a word.

"What's up?" Rowan asked, shaking his head lightly.

"We're having some people over to the house this Saturday, if you're available, for the game," Roger said. "I'm not supposed to add this, but Sandy has a friend she wants you to meet. So, feel free to say *no*."

Rowan smiled at Roger's caveat. He had no plans for the weekend, but his head was not in a place to be introduced to anyone new. His wife, Mindy, would certainly not find that funny either. Although they had been separated for over a year,

Rowan knew that it was best to keep his dance card clear in Pittsburgh. He had already been accused of dating Nicki Schmitt. He was determined not to go through that inquisition again.

"As enticing as that is," Rowan started, adding a smirk to his pause, "I do have plans this weekend. I'm heading north to Cook Forest to get some me time in the sticks."

"Sounds great. Can I go too?"

Rowan took a moment to picture Roger's response to the Red Sombrero. Roger was a social man. He could walk and talk with any man in any setting to get business done. But Rowan had his doubts about how Roger would handle the Red Sombrero socially. In particular, how he would handle the likes of Janis and Lois Lane. A smile came to his face as he involuntarily shook his head.

"What?"

"Nothing!" Rowan replied quickly, reaching into his lower desk drawer.

Two cut-crystal highball glasses with the bank's logo and a three-quarters-full bottle of Rough Rider bourbon appeared to finish their day.

"Someday," Rowan said, as he poured his protégé two fingers of heat-filled relief, "I'll take you up to Cook Forest. It'll blow your mind."

Roger toasted Rowan's proposition with a lift and clink of their glasses. Rowan savored the initial burn of the Rough Rider on his gums as a peace came to him for committing to returning to the funky place he found by accident a few days earlier. He made a mental note to find accommodations, thinking a rental cabin had to be available in the area. If not, Interstate 80 that crossed the northern tier of Pennsylvania had to have hotels for weary travelers seeking shelter. Peak leaf season made him worry that most good rooms may be gone.

After Roger finished his bourbon, he stood to show that he was one-and-done on the after-work drink with the boss. He repeated the invitation as open in the event Rowan's plans north either cancelled or washed out. Further insight into the matchmaking noted that the woman was Rowan's age, not his. And that she was his wife's work colleague and had been married twice before but never had children.

"Sounds perfect," Rowan joked as he rolled his eyes and waved good night.

The light emanating from the sunset was waning as Rowan turned to look again with a refreshed splash of bourbon in his glass. He laughed to himself as he took a light sip, trying to create a mental image of Roger and Sandy's match for him.

An audible ding followed by his phone's vibration against his desk's glass top, brought him back to real time. Maintaining his very comfortable reclined feet-up position with a view, he stretched to reach his phone, getting perilously close to falling backward.

Where was that Red Sombrero place you talked about? Going leaf watching Saturday with Char. May need medicated.

Fuck, Rowan thought. His plan just got blown up.

Char will hate it. Best to do with me another time before deciding to take her.

Rowan hit send on his return text, confident it solved the problem. Dorsey would be afraid to take his wife to somewhere seedy without having a special attribute that would make it *cool*. Rowan also knew that the likelihood that Dorsey would want to travel to northern Pennsylvania for any other reason than to drive through to ski in New York was minimal. The thumbs-up response from Dorsey confirmed he was right.

Rowan threw back what remained of the bourbon in his glass before standing to pack his briefcase for the night. He then sat back down at his desk to do a quick Google search for *Cabins for rent near Legend PA*.

# # # #

Tom rolled in the final batch of Dervish Red, which he had finished bottling earlier in the day. Marnie was getting anxious that her ex-husband was intentionally dragging his feet until Friday just to irritate her. He had a devious side that liked poking the bear just for fun.

"This should get you through the weekend," he said as he parked the hand truck loaded with stacked plastic milk crates that held the wine.

The milk crates were contraband heisted from the supermarket years earlier, when the winery opened. They were stronger than the cardboard boxes that delivered the empty wine bottles. Their initial runs lost several bottles of bad, first-generation wine when Tom tried to transport full bottles in boxes designed for empty ones.

Marnie started stacking the new wine toward the back of her shelf behind last week's vintage that needed to be sold first.

"We're getting low on juice," Tom added cautiously. "I can't make more to sell if I don't have juice."

"I've told you," Marnie started, with a stark, clenched voice, "that it's on-order. It'll be here when it gets here."

Marnie's blood pressure spiked with Tom's mention of the declining wine stock needed to manufacture her house blends. She had calls into her bank for another advance on her line of credit to pay down her account with the vineyard in Fredonia, New York. Up until Tom's mention, her head was in a good place, multiplying the bottles she saw by the fifteen-dollar average she got for each one. Tom's remark that their inventory was near depletion reminded her not only of the cost to replace it, but also the amount of money she owed for wine already sold.

"Hey, don't shoot the messenger," Tom replied. "I just need to schedule my time here with work. If I'm not making wine, I want to grab hours there."

Marnie gave a pained smile as she continued to place the fresh wine behind the earlier batch. It was her way of confirming that she heard him.

"I'm sorry," she answered. "I'll take care of it. Don't change your work schedule."

Tom smiled to give comfort to his ex, who he still loved above everyone else but knew he could never live with again. He opened his arms as he walked to her, giving her a bear hug as she stood stiff with her hands in her pockets. He knew Marnie was struggling. But he also knew her stubborn streak would not allow her to either admit it or ask for help.

"Let me know if I can help," he said as he kissed the top of her head.

Marnie remained quiet as she nodded to agree. To everyone around her, she was the California college girl who opened a successful winery business, and who was extremely artistic as seen through her paintings that both hung on the walls and were painted directly on them. Her time away in college and visible success with the Sombrero painted a false impression of her abilities and training. She was a creative who studied art, not business.

The Red Sombrero's seven-year survival was part of her legacy. It was a bigger story than a bar that had done well. It was a vision that was outside of the norm and that everyone ridiculed until it opened and had immediate success. That success created a cash flow that could underwrite a lot of business mistakes. But those mistakes had trailing effects, along with some unpaid payroll taxes and other personal and corporate tax levies that were catching up to her.

Marnie looked at the clock to see how much time she had before the happy hour crowd would start arriving. The band she hired was also scheduled to start at eight. A quick look around showed there was a lot of cleanup and setup left to do. She was afraid to check either bathroom for fear of what was growing in there. Seeing three o'clock on the wall gave her some reassurance she could get enough done to have her staff help finish before happy hour started.

"Get your shit together, Marnie," she mumbled as she headed out into the room.

# # # #

His approach into the eighteenth green measured about one hundred and twenty yards. Rowan played his second shot short of the creek that now crossed in front of him. He wanted to place his final full swing of his club into the sweet spot of his wedge for an easy two-putt to par.

Surrounding the undulating green were several shallow sand traps. Behind the green sat the grandeur of the clubhouse and his exit to his weekend. He took a moment to make sure his three playing partners found their balls before doing his final assessment on his approach shot.

Closing business on the golf course was a perk of his job. It gave him four hours of on-and-off conversation with his clients and prospects as they worked their way through eighteen holes. Depending upon the ability and integrity of his group, Rowan could adjust his game to theirs. He did not post his scores from client rounds for handicap. The competitive scores he would post set his handicap at four.

The three he invited to play with him were not good golfers. They were, however, a large, father-and-sons construction contractor that Rowan had been servicing on a growing basis for a few years. When their financing on a downtown building fell apart mid project a few years back, Rowan reworked their entire structure to not only get them to completion, but also at a reduced cost.

"Closest to the pin for a hundred bucks!" shouted Vinnie Giollota, who, at sixty years of age, stood just over five-feet-four-inches tall and nearly the same dimension wide.

Jesus Christ, Rowan thought. The round had already cost him over five hundred bucks in guest fees and lunch.

Vinnie's ball had carried the creek, putting him off to the right, about eighty yards from the pin. He was watching Rowan size up his shot with a recollection of Rowan's game through their round. Vinnie was confident that he could put his ball closer to the pin, given his angle to the green and being forty yards closer.

Rowan looked to Vinnie with a smile, then pointed his wedge at him to accept the challenge. As he set his feet for his shot, he looked at his ball knowing what he could do and what he had to do. He shifted his right foot back to push the ball right toward the traps. Hopefully Vinnie could place his simple half-wedge onto the green to win the hundred dollars.

The sound of the club swing grabbed his attention as he saw Vinnie holding his finish while watching his ball fly and drop onto the green. Its ending position put him within a respectable fifteen feet of the pin, which he should have be able to close out with two putts.

Vinnie's rude, me-first conduct and better-than-expected result changed Rowan's perspective. He shifted his right foot back to put the ball on the green. His hope was that it would fall outside of Vinnie's shot. But Vinnie's shot was good enough that he could claim luck if his final full swing of the round put his ball closer.

His swing felt perfect. The only sound he heard was the clubhead's wisp through the grass as the ball lifted cleanly and started its high, arching flight toward the green. The ball hit the short grass of the green within six feet of the pin and bounced past the pin. Vinnie's eyes lit as he watched it carry outside of the fifteen-foot radius Rowan needed to win. But as the ball settled on the green with its second touch, it appeared to die with a thud before immediately drawing back and past the hole as if pulled by a string. Its final resting spot was an easy three-foot putt for Rowan to finish the round with a birdie.

"Did you do that on purpose?" Vinnie asked as they came together to approach the green.

"No, just luck," Rowan lied. "I was in between clubs and muscled up on it to get it there."

Vinnie patted him on the back in appreciation for his effort and result.

"I would have answered, *yeah, do it all the time.*"

The laugh that followed reminded Rowan of Fred Flintstone. Vinnie had a similar stature. The fact that he just lost one hundred dollars on his challenge did not seem to bother him. However, Rowan did not expect that he would ever see the money.

Rowan checked the starter's clock that sat next to the first tee as they walked off the eighteenth green. In his head he was working through the timing of some nineteenth-hole refreshment in the men's locker room, a shower, then getting on the road to Legend to visit the Red Sombrero again. He had an excitement to return that he could not justify for any particular reason. He had fun there. That one aspect was new to him in itself. He was looking forward to going back, hoping not to be disappointed.

Vinnie's boys departed quickly to return home to waiting wives and children. Rowan invited the family patriarch up for some refreshment before heading home to the wife who, he complained, was also waiting for him. Vinnie laughed at his description, knowing it was an unfair representation of the love of his life. He was, however, anxious to have *a glass of* juice to finish his week, and to start his weekend.

"My father used to make his own wine," Vinnie said as he settled into his chair while looking at the stemless glass with the golf club's logo.

He swirled its contents to admire the color. But his face showed disappointment in the three-finger pour that was presented as a full glass.

"He drank it out of a jug…in a jelly jar glass…old school."

Rowan smiled as he watched Vinnie take a deep pull from his glass. He envisioned Vinnie's father as an old Italian man sitting in a simple kitchen on a wood chair. His jug wine would be sitting on the distressed wood top of the table where it was made. The pour in his jelly jar would be generous. The look on his face, peaceful.

"Sounds like quite the life," Rowan commented, to pull Vinnie back.

Vinnie's eyes were watery, having become emotional with the unexpected recollection of his father.

"Simpler, for sure," he answered. "I have some of his recipes. I just don't have the time. It's easier to just go buy a fifty-dollar bottle."

Rowan's eyes danced at Vinnie's bottle value. In his opinion, twelve-dollar bottles almost always competed with fifty-dollar bottles. He then wondered what Vinnie would think of the twelve- to twenty-dollar Red Sombrero wines.

"Everything's a lost art, Vincent," he added, to play to Vinnie's ear. "It's just easier to buy things that come from big manufacturers somewhere else."

"God only knows what's in it," he laughed as he finished his glass in one pull.

"That's the truth."

As Vinnie returned his glass to the table, he wiped his mouth on the monogrammed cloth napkin then stood to leave.

"Want to hang for another round?" Rowan asked, concerned he may have said something wrong.

Vinnie patted him on the shoulder to thank him for the round of golf and wine.

"No," he answered. "I just have this need to go home now. Flora will be waiting. I'll surprise her by being early."

Vinnie reached into his pocket for his money clip. He pulled a one-hundred-dollar bill off the top of many to hand to Rowan.

"Keep it," Rowan said. "We'll play again for double or nothing."

Vinnie bellowed another Fred Flintstone laugh that attracted attention from surrounding tables. He slapped Rowan on the back then pointed his finger at him to acknowledge the throw-down and accept the future round of golf.

"I'll walk you out." Rowan said, standing.

Rowan waved to the waiter that they were finished and made a scribbling gesture to show he would be back to sign his drink chit. The two men exited through the stairwell that led down to the pro shop and bag-drop area. Rowan was getting out of Pittsburgh an hour before schedule.

Chapter 4

The Friday afternoon crowd was light through happy hour, which began to concern Marnie as the band began to set up. Although not good with numbers, she knew that the cost of entertainment would be eating into her less-than-expected take from a usually heavier first step into the weekend.

Tom walked in still wearing his company gear that included gray work pants and a heavy denim shirt with an oil company logo above the left breast.

"Slow start?" he asked Marnie, who was in no mood to have it restated.

"Obviously," she answered. "Where the fuck is everyone?"

"Playoffs, I think." Tom answered. "Warriors…football."

Marnie winced.

"Who the hell cares about football?" she asked.

Tom laughed at the question. He could feel her pain in its absurdity.

"Obviously, they do," he answered. "But the good news is if they win, they'll want to celebrate."

Tom's observation perked Marnie up.

"And if they don't?" she asked.

"They'll want to drink!" they shouted together with electric smiles.

Marnie's attitude changed now, understanding her income for the night was not going to change. It was just going to come later.

Tom checked the supply of wine on the shelf, comfortable that there was enough to get them through the night. Inventory in the back would easily last through the Sunday NFL matchups that included the first of two Steelers–Browns-rivalry games.

"What can I do?" he asked, looking around to see that everything was in order.

"I didn't get to the bathrooms," Marnie answered, knowing he would blow that off.

Tom gave a thumbs up as he headed toward the table nearest the front door to settle in for the night. It was the perfect location to help control the crowd while also enjoying the band and his friends. As the weather got colder, he would move deeper into the room to avoid the wash of cold air that would enter despite a temporary, plastic-walled structure outside, with its own door to cut the direct arctic blast. The temporary structure, although effective, gave the building even less appeal than it already had.

# # # #

"Do you remember when football games end?" Marnie asked Janis, looking up at the clock on the wall.

"Nine? Nine-thirty?" Janis answered, having noticed the lighter than usual crowd. "I was wondering where everyone is."

Janis was seated on her usual bar stool three in from the end nearest the wall and the door. Like Tom, she chose it for the good vantage point to the door, to either scout new men or to leave unnoticed. As the weather got colder, she would shift closer to the kitchen where the draft was less and some heat from the ovens helped keep her warm.

Marnie tended to the business that was being presented as she watched her friend nurse her wine and continue to look at the door. A smile came to her face knowing exactly what Janis was hoping to see, and worried about closing time when it did not happen.

"What's so interesting about that door?" she asked, to poke her friend.

"Shut up," Janis answered. "It could happen."

Marnie continued to set up an order, having decided to let Janis's hopes hang. She had seen Clark's type come and go before. The unique environment was enough to get them to venture in. The novelty of the place was interesting enough to get them to stay. But, in the end, the simple nature of the clientele quickly lost its appeal to the lights and luster of the big city.

"Janis," Marnie said, now facing her friend.

"Marnie!" Janis answered sternly.

Marnie put her palms up to withdraw from the conversation. She knew that Clark Kent, like Santa Claus, was not going to show just because he was expected. Something had to happen to get him there again.

The crowd began to grow as the clock passed eight-thirty. The corner seat that Rowan had occupied the prior Saturday was still empty. Janis shooed some people away that she suspected would have been all-nighters had they settled in. Marnie did not say anything the first time. But the hour was getting later, and she could not afford to have Janis chase away any more refillable glasses.

"Next time, let them sit." Marnie said in a stern whisper as she leaned across the bar.

Janis's face had shifted from excitement to worry as she watched two hours tick away. The music was acoustic and comforting to the edge she was developing. She decided that maybe not watching the door, like not watching a clock, would produce better results.

Two songs ended the band's first set. Janis peeked a few times at the door to check on new arrivals. Each time she glanced over, she saw Marnie's Tom hosting a few friends and flirting with women they all knew from high school. He was happy to still be hanging with his old crew. She was happy that Marnie had finally decided to give him his freedom by throwing him out in the middle of winter two years ago. She still marveled at how much better they got along once they were apart.

The clock rolled past nine o'clock and, as expected, the crowd from the football game began to find its way to the Sombrero. The victory was apparent in their spirits as they walked in still on a high and ready to keep celebrating. Marnie began to calm, seeing dollars arrive as each person came through the door to fill the inside and back deck to capacity.

"Those two stools," she said, while looking a Janis and pointing to the corner. "Are first come, first served."

Janis's smile, which grew with the excitement that had arrived, drooped with the realization that her game could be ending. She thought about moving to the center of the three stools that sat between her and the wall. But doing that would add bad karma to her expectations. Everything had to remain the same as it was Saturday for it to happen again.

Janis watched Marnie work her way down the bar then disappear back into the production and storage area to restock.

She knew she could shoo away anyone that tried to occupy the stools while her friend was out of sight. Looking at the supply behind the bar, she expected that Marnie would be wheeling out a few milk crates of bottles. So she had a few more minutes of hope.

Then, as she had feared, a shadow passed in her peripheral vision to make its way to the open stools. Janis's immediate response was to lift her arm as a barrier to the person who was rude enough to think that two empty bar stools were an invitation to sit down. Her lift and throw of her arm hit the arriving patron in the stomach, which held firm and did not jiggle.

"Wow!" he gasped, as he pivoted to glide past her hand to his seat near the wall. "It's nice to see you again too."

Janis's breathing cramped to the sound of his voice as she kept her hand up. As she turned to confirm what she thought she recognized, Rowan was settling onto his stool while surveying the crowd and taking in his first few bars of music.

"Good crowd, great music," he said with a smile as his eyes reoriented to her.

Janis did not respond. Her mind was completely erased as she stared at Clark Kent in his surprisingly more country attire of jeans, flannel shirt, and dark-colored canvas vest.

"I should have been here an hour ago, but I got lost on my way to the cabin I rented." Rowan said, playing with some items on the bar. "Then my GPS got scrambled. I did the last few miles from memory."

Rowan looked to see if she was listening. Her silence made him wonder if she was even there.

"You're back," she answered in a quiet tone.

"Yup," he said while taking another look around. "Had too much fun last Saturday. Back to see if it was a one-off or something that could become a regular thing."

Janis unconsciously stood and moved to the stool that sat between them. As she did, Rowan pulled back and looked around her to the stool where she had been sitting.

"Anything wrong?" Janis asked, hoping his expected revisit to fun included her.

"No. I was just checking to see if your stool had a reserved marker, since it's the one you were on last week."

Janis winced a smile to acknowledge Rowan's poke. She liked the fact that he seemed happy to engage with her in a way that was flirty.

"It is my stool," she answered. "Everyone knows it."

Rowan nodded as he started to look around and recall a number of the faces in the crowd.

"Like that guy by the door?" he asked, remembering him from when Cousin Dave arrived in his outfit.

"Him? He's Uncle Tom," Janis answered. "He makes Marnie's wine. He's also her ex-husband."

Rowan was caught by surprise by Janis's placement of Uncle Tom in the Red Sombrero. After a moment, it only seemed right that Marnie would either be married or divorced. She looked to be in her early forties.

"That's interesting," he replied. "A real family business."

"Dysfunctional family," Janis replied with a laugh.

"Yeah, thinking the same, but wasn't going to go there."

Rowan watched Tom flirt with girls that were younger than Marnie. It was apparent why their relationship did not work. But the only thing those girls had on his ex-wife was that they were younger and maybe dumber. Marnie was prettier and was going to age well compared to what Tom was playing with now.

As he had the week before, the banker in him started doing the math of heads to dollars. He then wondered why the facility itself was not kept to a higher standard.

Rowan caught the attention of the bartender Marnie had left behind to order a bottle of Dervish Red. He reached into his pocket looking for cash, then decided to hand over his American Express again to open a tab. Janis smiled, taking that as a sign he was staying, then took hold of his bottle to both fill his glass and top-off hers.

Marnie appeared from the storage room pushing a hand truck that was stacked high with four milk crates of full bottles. She carefully navigated through the kitchen to the bar. The space was wide enough for the hand truck to pass, but she had to pay close attention to the turns so as not to pull things from the lower shelves when passing.

Rowan nodded to Janis to watch Marnie's meticulous approach to bring fresh stock to her bar. Marnie gave a quick look to the other bartender to give him enough warning to get out of her way while imprinting an image from her peripheral vision into her brain on where she wanted to go. Midway from the kitchen to where Rowan and Janis were seated at the bar, Marnie stopped, as if to think.

When her eyes lifted to confirm what she thought she saw, both Janis and Rowan lifted their glass to salute a greeting. Hers was to say *I was right*. His was to say *I'm back*.

"Look what the cat dragged back in," were the first words out of her mouth as she watched him take his first taste of wine.

Her smile showed she was surprised and happy to see him again. Janis knew the look from their past, when they were both interested in the same boy at the same time. The look on Clark's face also mirrored what she saw in the past, when she would lose to Marnie. A voice in her head was telling her to hold her ground next to him. There was a reason why she won rock-paper-scissors last week.

# # # #

Marnie continued to work the bar as the night passed midnight. She did her best to not look at either Rowan or Janis as they sat talking at the bar. The bartender that served Rowan when he arrived continued to pay attention to them as the night moved along.

"Looks like it was a successful night," Rowan observed as he watched the band start to break down their equipment.

The only conversation Rowan had had all night was with Janis. She was not aware of it, but he worked her through her life history, getting details on her life growing up in the area, then as an adult. Each time she tried to shift to collect the same information from him, he would craft a way to swing it back to her. That tactic was not to gather information. It was a process he used to engage clients in order to get them to like him enough to trust him and give him information he wanted and needed. People typically like to talk about themselves.

"So, tell me about this cabin you rented?" Janis finally asked, having waited for the right time.

"It's a one-roomer I found on VRBO... Vacation Rentals..."

"By Owner," Janis finished. "We go to the beach too."

Rowan smiled to apologize for assuming otherwise.

"It's up in Cook Forest. Lost my cell signal going in. I'll have to depend upon my memory to get me back there."

Janis saw his comment as an invitation to help. She looked for Marnie, to ensure she was out of earshot.

"I can help you get there," Janis said as she lightly brushed her foot on his.

Rowan's stomach clenched as he felt the pass, realizing he had left himself open to it. He later felt he should not have let it get that far, but there was too much fun in taking a different tack.

"How would you get home?" he asked.

"In the morning," flew from Janis's mouth before her brain had completely processed his question.

"It's a one-roomer," he repeated, hoping his implied message sunk in.

"I don't take up much space, Rowan."

Janis almost called him Clark. But she knew that would tie Marnie back into his thinking and likely blow her opportunity. Rowan smiled as he watched Janis's eyes stay trained on his.

"That's nice of you to offer," he answered, stopping to think about his choice of words. "I mean, to give me directions."

"Erections?" Janis answered, having chosen a time to get daring.

JESUS! Rowan thought again as he smiled and looked off into the crowd.

"Janis," he answered, working hard to hold back a light laugh. "I'm married."

"Separated," she replied, making him wonder what he'd said the previous weekend.

"Yes, separated," he confirmed. "I'm not in a good head space for a new relationship. I'm just here to get away."

"I'm not looking for a relationship either," she lied. "Can't we just have some fun?"

Janis worked her best angle, face, and expression to start Rowan's engine. Her awkward twisting started to become funny as seconds ticked by and she got no response.

"The hurt is just too fresh," he lied. "It wouldn't be good for me."

Janis finally gave in with a roll of her eyes. She looked again for Marnie as she thought through his pathetic excuse to blow her off.

"Clark," she said. "I'm good every single time. And I'd be good for you."

Janis knew her throwdown had to have a dramatic exit to make it stick. She immediately got to her feet and walked to the restroom. She knew, from history, that to look back would kill the impact of her message. She looked into the blurred reflections in the windows to the deck instead, to see if he was watching her.

# # # #

Last call sounded at 1:30 a.m. The music filling the room played from old stereo speakers that sat above the bathrooms. Rowan was alert and felt that he was in good enough shape to find his rented cabin. Janis had disappeared after her dramatic bathroom exit and extraordinary offer to be his tour guide; she never returned. "So, Clark, do you want one more? Or do you want to close out for the night?"

Rowan smiled that Marnie was now paying attention to him again. Both she and Janis had disappeared into the night, leaving him to make small talk with anyone who sat on Janis's stool and the one next to it.

"I think I'll close it out," he answered.

Marnie processed the American Express Platinum Card, exaggerating interest in its thickness and weight.

"What kind of limit do you get with this card?" she asked, as she put the charge down for signature.

"It has no limit. They just turn it off when they think you've gone too far."

Marnie looked puzzled at the possibility that any card would just let you go until they decided you have gone too far.

"Has it ever happened?" she asked.

"What?

"Gone too far?" she answered with a smirk.

"Not yet."

"That's good," Marnie replied, smiling as she wondered why the rich preppy dude was wasting his time in her country winery.

"Well, feel free to keep spending here, Clark."

"Thanks, Lois," he replied. "I added a nice tip for the attentive service."

Rowan doubled the bill on the final line of his charge. Marnie took a moment to think about his gesture before handing the bill back to him.

"We're not some country bumpkin charity," she said. "Fix this to what you would give back in the big city and that will be fine."

Rowan took back the mini clipboard holding the charge. He studied the amount before scratching over his tip and writing a new number into the space. Once finished, he covered the board with his hand.

"What are you doing tomorrow morning?" he asked, knowing she was anxious to see the new number he wrote.

"Between now and then? I'm sleeping alone in my bed...maybe with my dog."

An immediate image of Travis entered Rowan's head as he looked at Marnie.

"That's not what I asked. I also have a nice place to stay tonight... Minus the dog," he added. "I'd just like to get a tour of the area from someone who knows it."

Marnie felt tension build within her. Superman was asking her to spend time alone time with him. She found him surprisingly attractive when he first arrived, but she never expected him to return. His night with Janis was a knock against him even if he had to be all but carried out when they left together.

"Look, Rowan," she said, surprising him with his real name. "I don't think it's a good idea to spend time with you when my best friend in the world has a crush on you."

Rowan looked off to see if Janis was roaming anywhere nearby. Comfortable he could speak freely, he turned back to Marnie as he lifted the small clipboard.

"I just want to go see some pretty leaves with a pretty tour guide. It's kinda a twofer. I'll even buy lunch."

Rowan teased Marnie by extending the clipboard, then pulling it back.

"You're going to hold your charge captive to get me to agree?" Marnie asked, adding a smile while trying to keep from laughing.

"If that's what it takes," he answered. "Come on. What's the worst that can happen?"

Rowan handed the clipboard over as a gesture of good faith. Marnie kept her eyes locked on his as she accepted the board and revised charge slip. Her body relaxed as she lowered it to her side without looking at what he changed.

"Meet me here at 10 a.m.," she conceded. "If you want to see leaves, we'll leave from here."

Rowan smiled over the victory he thought he had won with the woman who had given him such a hard time when he first arrived. Janis's non-return to her barstool indicated she had moved on from her hunt to spend the night with him. Rowan lifted his near-empty glass of Dervish Red to toast his date for leaf watching.

"It's just leaves, Clark," she said, with a snarky smile. "Don't get any big ideas."

"I'm a simple man, Lois," he answered. "Pretty views, with pretty things to look at, are all I am interested in right now."

A warm wash flowed through Marnie's cheeks as he stood to make his exit. The man's body looked good in his jeans and flannel. A small wave was his only gesture as he turned to walk away.

"10 a.m., I'll be here," he said.

Rowan quickly disappeared out the door so as not to give Marnie time to change her mind. He felt an extraordinary vibe growing between them. In some ways, it was exciting. In others, it was frightening. He was growing anxious to see what Saturday was going to bring.

Marnie smiled as she watched Rowan make his exit. There was a warmth to him that she had not seen in any man since returning home to northern Pennsylvania. The feeling inside gave her a fresh renewal until she looked out over the mess left in the bar. There was at least an hour of work to clean up before she could go home. The better idea would have been to barter a leaf tour with Rowan to get his help closing the Red Sombrero for the night. Marnie set Rowan's charge board on the counter before turning to start cleaning. A quick glance, followed by a second look, showed the change he made to his one hundred percent tip added the same amount once again plus a smiley face.

# # # #

As he drove down the two-lane road from the Sombrero back to his cabin, Rowan's phone hit service, resulting in a continuous string of text tones. Nearing 2 a.m. and driving an Audi S8 on roads filled with pick-up trucks and horse drawn carriages, he resisted the urge to check any messages. He knew whatever messages he received could be answered in the morning.

"Hey Siri, directions to cabin," he said.

Rowan was surprised and happy that Siri and Google maps got him back to the driveway of his cabin. The rutted, dirt driveway was another five hundred yards of narrow road that he learned to take slow when his car bottomed out on the way in earlier. The total distance to the Sombrero was less than five miles with only two turns at easy-to-remember landmarks.

The cabin was dark when he approached from the woods into the clearing. Rowan flipped to high beams to better look around before stopping to get out of his car. The total blackness around the cabin gave it an eerie feeling that he did not sense when he checked in before the sunset.

Before closing his door, Rowan activated the flashlight on his phone to walk the fifteen feet to the cabin porch and front door. Complementing the eerie darkness was a dense silence that was periodically interrupted by a crack from deep in the trees. Rowan's heart began to race as he reached into his jeans pocket for the key to the door. He made a mental note to keep the porch light on for Saturday night, assuming he survived Friday.

The screen door slammed heavily behind him, adding more suspense to his walk into the cabin. He nervously reached for a light switch by the door, which he did not remember seeing during check-in. He found it, and turned on the overhead light.

With light filling the room, he saw his weekend bag set on the bed in the corner. The mattress was smaller than he was used to at home, but it was ample for just him and two nights in the woods. The rest of the cabin was rustic, but adequate. The kitchen was just big enough to cook breakfast and to want to go out for lunch and dinner. The wood-plank floor was covered with old, woven throw rugs Rowan believed to be Amish. He had seen similar rugs in Pittsburgh selling for over a thousand dollars. Finishing the furnishing was a two-person breakfast table that sat behind an old fabric-covered love seat facing the front door and windows. The cabin had no phone, no television, and no internet. He was officially off the grid, since he also had no cell service.

As he looked around, he wondered if taking Janis up on her offer was a missed opportunity. After a quick mental image of what that could have been, he was happy to just find some peace for the next seven hours before having to drive back over to go leaf watching with Marnie. That image was refreshingly good. He moved to the bathroom to get ready for bed.

The clock read 2:30 a.m. when he got into bed with just the bedside lamp on. Its soft glow was enough to light the corner of the cabin, leaving the rest dark. The still and quiet around him became more intense as he shut off the lights to the living area. There were no noises. And once he turned off the light by his bed, there was total darkness. This was a different experience from living in the suburbs of Pittsburgh, where streetlamps kept the darkness from completely taking over things while his neighbors and traffic kept complete silence at bay.

Rowan plugged his phone charger into the four-outlet wall socket that supplied power to the lamp and digital clock on the nightstand. As he moved about to get comfortable, he lit the screen to see texts from his wife Mindy and his daughter Claire. He was linked into a three-way texting barrage that looked to be over twenty messages long. Mindy and Claire had the typical, tumultuous oldest child, same-gender parent relationship. Although loving most of the time, things tended escalate quickly over issues Rowan thought were otherwise minor.

Someone hit my car.

was the first message that started the series. Rowan ran his fingers through his hair as he sat up to think whether it was worth reading Mindy's reply and the balance of the string. Claire was obviously not hurt and likely not in the car when it happened. The only questions to be answered were about the damage it sustained and whether or not she got the other driver's insurance information.

Are you ok?

was Mindy's reply that sat below Claire's initial message and could not be ignored. Rowan scrolled down for the answer.

I am fine. Car damaged on drivers side all the way down. The driver door won't open from the outside.

With two important questions answered, Rowan was now pulled into their conversation. To try to sleep would result in him staring at the ceiling wondering, which would only result in his reading the rest of the string five to ten minutes later.

Where was it parked?

Five Points.

Rowan knew Five Points from his weekends in Columbia, South Carolina for the Claire's first two college years of drops-offs, pick-ups and parents' weekends. It was a business district of mostly restaurants and bars frequented by students. Fridays in Five Points usually meant Ubering instead of driving because of drinking.

Were you drinking and going to drive home?

Mom, no.

Doesn't sound like it. You'll have to deal with your dad on that.

I'm going to the beach in the morning. It's an open weekend.

You'll just have to find another way to get there. Maybe your dad has ideas if he ever gets in this conversation.

Rowan checked the time of the texts. They started just before midnight. He knew Claire was headed to Charleston for the weekend. The South Carolina Gamecocks had an away game at Kentucky that they were expected to win.

The last text was from Mindy dissing Rowan for not being responsive to the chain. Claire was adding more anxiety to the mix, complaining that she would be stuck in Columbia over a non-football weekend without her car. The driver side of her two-door Mini Cooper hardtop would be difficult to climb into from the passenger seat. Although an automatic, the center console with the gear shift and parking brake would be an awkward, if not painful, barrier.

Without either cell or internet service, Rowan would have to drive back out to the road that had the cell service. He knew roughly where it started. Where it stopped was anyone's guess.

Rowan checked the clock again then shut his eyes. He knew that a text sent now would either not be read until morning or would stir the hornet's nest to cost him more time away from the sleep he needed. His phone was inaccessible now. He set its alarm for seven-thirty to get up in time to go out on the road to find service. He thought briefly about looking to find Claire a rental car until he remembered that he had no service.

The still-glowing phone provided the only light in the room. He set it on the nightstand then lay on the mattress with his head resting on the pillow. A mattress lump near his hip moved him to adjust his position to find something better. As his phone went dark, the room became black, still, and quiet. He would deal with things in the morning.

# # # #

Marnie parked her quad in her garage next to her Jeep Wrangler and Polaris Razor. Depending upon her mood and need at the time, one of the three vehicles worked better than the other two. The Jeep was almost twenty years old. She bought it new in California and drove it across the country when she moved back home.

The route she'd planned was roundabout, starting outside of San Francisco then down the coast of Big Sur before turning left to drive through Joshua Tree and the southern route back home. Her explanation to herself and friends for taking the long way home was to see as much of the West as she could before returning back home for good. She would later admit to herself that it was really to delay as long as possible returning to a simpler life and facing her parents in their fading years.

Marnie smiled as she thought about the snarky sparring she had with Rowan earlier in the night, along with the back-and-forths the previous weekend that got him to return. She wondered what it was that he was interested in finding in Legend. If it was just to have a good time with her then go, she was not going to bother with him. The fact that he would have any other interest just seemed beyond the realm of possibilities.

The clock in the kitchen read 3 a.m. Marnie's nature was to not need a lot of sleep. She did not drink any wine when working which enabled her to fall asleep easily and to stay asleep through the night. Her usual, automatic wake-up time of 8 a.m. would arrive soon enough. She walked to her bedroom to dial down for sleep.

As she sat on the edge of her bed, her last act after turning out the light and crawling into bed was to look out her window. Sitting across the valley, lit by moonlight, sat a camp in a clearing at the hilltop. The moonlight reflected off the gray aluminum shell of the Airstream camper to silhouette an old Dodge Dakota pickup and quad parked next to it. Starting at the camper and extending to a tree nearby was a concave dark line that was thin at the ends and thick in the middle.

"Good night Cousin Dave," she smiled, knowing from the thickness of the hammock that he was asleep inside its cocoon of thin fabric.

Cousin Dave's camper was used only in inclement weather. Otherwise, he liked to sleep outside in the fresh air with all of the other wildlife.

Chapter 5

The sound of his phone vibrating on the wood nightstand combined with the alarm tone to wake him to face the day. Despite the lump in the mattress, Rowan had found a position of comfort and slept soundly.

As his eyes opened to help guide his arm to the menacing noise and vibration, he felt a sharp pain in both temples that caused him to drop his arm to the mattress. His vision was blurry as his eyes began to focus on the table lamp then the room around it. He began for feel his mouth, lips and tongue all started to move involuntarily to clear a dryness that was pasty and uncomfortable.

As his phone lit, the time read 7:30 a.m. That meant he got just over five hours of sleep. He remembered his date with Marnie was scheduled to start at 10 a.m. at the Red Sombrero. He closed his eyes knowing he could grab an extra fifteen minutes without either showing late or missing the window to call Claire to take care of her car situation.

Rowan's eyes opened to more daylight. The traditional, white-face wall clock above the kitchen sink was the first thing he saw. A gasp filled his chest when the time on the clock processed through his brain that it was 9 a.m. He had one hour to get ready and to the Red Sombrero. He also needed to call Claire.

"Ah, JESUS!" he groaned as he sat up quickly.

The quick change in elevation filled his head with stars to make him dizzy. He was running the next sixty minutes in segments, allocating time for each aspect of his journey to meet Marnie on time. The cabin owner's warning that it took time for the hot water to appear in the shower was accurate. After standing naked in the cold air waiting patiently through hand-check after hand-check for warmth, Rowan finally decided he was out of time. His jump into the icy cold of the shower quickly woke him and removed the residual hangover effects from the night before.

The benefit of the cold shower was a motivation to get clean and out rather than to linger and soothe his body in a hot flow of water. As he turned the water off, the cold air he felt going in felt warm in comparison. He grabbed his towel to dry his hair first before working it the rest of the way down his body.

As Rowan stepped from the bathroom onto the wood floor of the cabin, his foot slipped, resulting in a quick twist and grab of the door to stay on his feet. A look at where he slipped showed a streak across the floor. The bottom of his foot was brown from the dirt that had accumulated on the floor over the years.

"For the love of..." he moaned as he took a step to feel a twinge in his lower back. "I need more TIME!"

Rowan had his outfit for the day ready to go. He did not know going into the weekend whether he would be sightseeing by himself or with a guide. He never expected Marnie to agree. Nor was he sure that he wanted to be committed to anything one-on-one with Marnie. As much as she intrigued him, she scared him.

His body started to warm as each item of clothing was added. His outfit looked the part, with his Levi's jeans and Ralph Lauren flannel over a thermal Henley shirt. His boots were Merrell's that his Mindy bought him to walk their Weimaraner in a local off-leash dog park that was just forested parkland. He threw a Patagonia fleece vest over his flannel to insure he had the layers he needed for whatever Marnie thought was good leaf watching.

As Rowan stepped through the cabin door into the open air, the cold hit his face and penetrated through his layers to give him a chill. He returned to the cabin to grab the L.L. Bean canvas hunting jacket he bought back in the early 1990s to have for the evening.

As he drove toward the tree gap for the driveway, he increased the temperature setting in his car to seventy-five degrees. He knew that the higher temperature would not heat the car faster, but he needed the psychological comfort in thinking it would so that he could concentrate on the next set of problems he had to solve. A look at his dash screen showed he was five minutes ahead of the schedule he created before freezing in the shower.

The Audi grounded a few times on the driveway as Rowan drove out faster than he wanted to. A quick left turn onto the two-lane road exponentially increased his speed to get to the Red Sombrero and to find cellular service. A series of text tones indicated that cell service was closer than he thought. It was just a few hundred yards away from the driveway to his cabin.

"Hey Siri, call Claire," he barked as he felt his car settle onto the two-lane road.

The road that was ahead of him could be seen for over a mile as it wound down into a valley then back up the other side. Approaching the crown of the hill on the front end, Rowan looked off into the farmland around him. The leaves beyond the farm fields were green with hints of yellow to orange to brown. The collage was a beautiful preview of what he hoped Marnie was going to show him.

"Dad! Where are you? I've been trying to get hold of you since yesterday!"

Claire's voice was high-pitched and demanding. Rowan took an intentional pause, just to take control of the moment.

"I'm in the country, sweetie," he answered. "I don't have good cell service."

"Well, we've been trying to get hold of you since yesterday," Claire replied in the same anxious voice.

What part of in the country with lousy cell service did you not understand? Rowan thought as his car started to cross the peak of the dip down into the valley ahead of him.

"Jesus Christ!" he yelled, as he swerved his Audi to the left into the oncoming lane before bringing it back into his lane. His eyes felt like they were going to pop from their sockets as his heart and breathing stopped.

"What's going on?!" Claire called into her phone. "DAD!"

Rowan settled as he took a deep breath and checked his rearview mirror to see what he'd left in his wake. The single horse-drawn carriage was continuing down the road at a trotting pace. Neither the horse nor the young Amish boy driving the carriage seemed fazed by the quick swerve of the full-size, German performance sedan that had just blown by them.

"Dad?!"

Rowan checked his speedometer to bring his speed back down to normal as he reached the bottom of the small valley.

"Sorry sweetie, I had to avoid a little something unexpected on the road."

Rowan looked back in his rearview to check again on the carriage. It was fading from sight as he started his climb out from the bottom of the valley.

"Did you... Mom said..." Claire responded, her voice interrupted by the poor cell service.

"Hold on," Rowan replied, to let his daughter know he was having problems hearing.

At the top of the hill, he pulled to the side of the road as his phone showed two bars of service.

"Your messages loaded last night as I was driving back to my cab...room. I don't have good service here. So bear with me."

"Jesus, Dad," Claire said with disdain in her voice. "Where are you?"

"I'm upstate, above Clarion, near Cook Forest."

"Never heard of it."

"It's not far from home."

Rowan was surprised Claire had never heard of Clarion. It was a small city, but it had a university that had to pull from her high school.

"Did you hear about the Mini?" she asked. "It's totaled. The door handle is gone. And I'm supposed to drive Josie to the beach this morning."

"And that's the greater problem?" Rowan replied sarcastically, feeling compelled to say it but then regretting that he had.

"Can you get me a rental car? I promised. Plus, it's the only open weekend I have before fall break," Claire pleaded.

Rowan looked at the clock. He had ten minutes to get to the Red Sombrero. He shifted his car back into drive knowing that continuing the call to solve Claire's problem was a crapshoot. He could immediately hear static indicating that his call was going to start breaking up.

"Claire, is the car drivable?" he asked.

"I don't know."

"Did you drive it home last night from Five Points?"

Claire paused, knowing that she had been forbidden, as a condition of having the car at school, to drive it to Five Points if she was planning to drink anything alcoholic.

"I just couldn't leave it there," she answered in a low voice.

"Did you get the name and insurance information from the driver that hit you?"

"I got...I don't...if he..."

Claire's voice broke and the call ended without notice. Rowan had lost the signal.

The turnoff to the Red Sombrero was less than five hundred feet down the road when the call dropped. Rowan looked at his clock. He still had seven minutes to arrive exactly at 10 a.m. He knew that to turn back to finish his call with Claire would take longer than that. He decided to keep driving toward the winery to make his appointment for his leaf tour.

Rowan saw Marnie at the front door of the Sombrero when he flew into the driveway. A bounce of his car's underbody on the gravel parking lot made his fast entrance regrettable. He swung wide left to make a counterclockwise turn to put his door on the side of where Marnie was standing.

"Good morning!" he said as his window rolled down and the Audi skidded to a stop. "Can you give me ten minutes to finish a call with my daughter?"

Marnie pointed toward the road with a smile, giving her permission while also letting him know he had to return to the main road.

"Thanks!" he yelled as he stepped on the gas again. "I'll be right back."

Marnie quietly laughed as she watched his window roll back up while all four wheels of his car spun on the gravel in her parking lot. His anxiety to have to ask was cute. She was looking forward to asking him about it and getting to know more about him.

When Rowan regained his cell service on the road, he had both a voice message and text from Claire. He knew that only being twenty-one years old, she would not be able to rent a car. Once the call connected, and he was able to see pictures of the damage, he knew he would be able to convince his oldest daughter that the car was not *totaled* and that it was drivable to the beach if she wanted to go.

Disappointment was evident in her voice as she accepted his opinion that she could get to Charleston safely in the damaged Mini. He was not sure if it was because there was not going to be a rental, or if she thought a new car was in her immediate future.

"Have a good weekend, sweetie. Just be careful," he said.

"I will, Dad. I'm just hours behind schedule," she answered.

"The beach will always be there."

"Not with global warming..." Claire interjected.

Rowan rolled his eyes at her immediate response. He shared her views on global warming and rising ocean levels, but today was time to just go to the beach to have fun. Just like he was going to do, driving through the leaves in the mountains. He looked around his front seat to make sure his car was presentable for his drive with Marnie.

"I'm not... that... be on the..." Rowan intentionally stuttered through to make Claire think their call was ending because of bad service.

"Dad, I know you're faking," she said.

Rowan smiled, knowing he was busted and willing to accept it.

"Okay, honey!" he answered. "Have fun."

Rowan pushed the button on his dash screen to end his call. He was happy Claire was going to have her beach weekend. He began to wonder if Josie was a girlfriend or a guy. That thought bothered him until he turned down the narrow lane that led to the Red Sombrero.

# # # #

Rowan looked for Marnie when he pulled into the lot. The entire parking area was empty. He thought, like Janis, that Marnie lived within walking distance and did not have to drive. His figured that with the time he requested to call Claire that she had gone inside to deal with some business. The main door was unlocked when he pulled on it to enter.

"Anyone here?" he called out into the darkness of the bar area.

"Back here, Clar..." Marnie answered, as she appeared. "Sorry, Rowan."

"I answer to Clark too." He smiled to soften the awkwardness.

"Daughter problem solved?"

"Yes. Thank you."

Marnie remembered the urgent calls she would make to her dad that, in hindsight, were rather mundane. But she also knew they were always very urgent to her at the time. Therefore, it was important that her dad give them his full attention.

"Do you want some coffee before we go?" Marnie asked, looking toward the Keurig that could make it in less than a minute.

"That's okay," Rowan answered. "I'm sure we can find some on the road."

Marnie smirked as she lifted her eyebrows to his comment.

"I wouldn't be too sure," she answered. "I've got some travel mugs somewhere."

Rowan watched quietly as Marnie disappeared behind the bar. A sound of things being moved around made him wonder how long the mugs had been in storage. And what condition they were in. A little satisfaction came with the thought that the steaming hot coffee would sanitize the container.

Marnie continued to mill around the bar, finishing details left undone from the night before. She sealed both cups and walked to the break walkway between the end of the bar and the bathrooms. Rowan started to step backwards as Marnie appeared near him.

"Where you going?" she asked.

Rowan nodded back to the parking lot.

"Back to my car," he said.

"I thought you said you wanted to see leaves."

Rowan paused to think about Marnie's question. He had seen most of the view and woods behind the Red Sombrero. Although pretty, it was not the views he was hoping to see with a local that knew the area.

"Follow me, Clark," Marnie commanded, falling back into her enjoyment of giving him shit.

Rowan cautiously started to follow Marnie to the back door and deck of the Red Sombrero. His first thought was that she was going to hand him the coffee, sit down, and say there is no better view anywhere, to fulfill her promise. She handed him his thermal cup as they walked through the door onto the slatted wood deck that looked out over the winery's lower property, overgrown grass leading up to a tree line of beautiful colors.

"Okay, Marnie," he said, as he stopped to qualify their plans for the day. "This wasn't what I expected. I thought we'd go for a drive."

Marnie smiled and continued to walk to pull him along.

"We're going for a drive okay," she answered as she stepped off the deck onto the stairs.

As they continued off the deck down to the lower field, Marnie's Polaris Razor came into view. It was bright red with a black tubular roll cage. It had a fiberglass body with a clear plexiglass windshield.

"Are those your clothes for the day?" she asked as she studied him from head-to-toe.

She had to clench her jaw to keep from smiling at his designer look that had to come from either Ralph Lauren or L.L. Bean.

"I've brought a change," he lied. "Why?"

Rowan knew what he had on was the best he had for the day. He expected Sunday to be less formal, leaving him with only the Steelers pullover he bought the previous weekend and another long-sleeve Henley to wear under it.

Marnie smiled as she pointed him to the passenger side of the vehicle. She knew he drove an expensive, high-performance sedan on the interstates and roads. She was not sure he was ready to handle her Razor up through the logging trails and powerline easements they were about to ride.

"No reason," she answered, looking away to hide her amusement. "Buckle up."

The seat of the Razor was surprisingly comfortable for Rowan's six-foot-two body. He snapped into the plastic-clasped seat belt system, wondering if either the belts or the plexiglass windshield would keep him from leaving the vehicle if it were either to roll or hit a tree. He looked at Marnie as she waited for him to finish. Her smile was reassuring that she was safety-oriented in making sure he was buckled in. The louder-than-expected roar of the engine that started behind him made him nervous as she shifted into drive.

Marnie leaned into the steering wheel as the engine wound to a high decibel and the buggy started to move. The open grass was an easy introduction to the ride. Rowan knew she was having fun with him as she accelerated heavily to fishtail toward the lower high grass then turned sharply left toward the tree line.

As the Razor accepted its new direction on the wet grass, it began to slide sideways. Marnie calmly counter-steered into the slide to maintain control, then punched the accelerator to gain speed out of the turn. A small window appeared in the tree line that had two ruts of matted grass to show it had been driven over before. Rowan took hold of a low handle on the right side of his seat to both show Marnie she could not scare him while also taking action to further secure himself to his seat.

Marnie looked to check on Rowan as they left the field to enter the trees. She knew a bump was coming that would give him the impression that they had caught air. But she knew, from experience, it was just a sensation. All four wheels usually stayed on the turf.

"Hold on," she yelled, just to get his juices churning faster.

As the Razor dipped then lifted over the bump, Rowan's left hand grabbed the roll bar above them to secure himself. The look on Marnie's face was pure enjoyment through the run of the trees. Rowan was not sure if it was because she was having fun with her machine, or because she was making him noticeably nervous. He glanced at the Razor's speedometer and saw they were going forty miles per hour before she slowed as she came to the end of the trail to turn onto a single-lane dirt road.

"They let you drive these on the road?" Rowan asked, yelling over the engine noise.

"Back roads, no one cares."

Rowan looked at the properties they passed as the road dipped down into a valley. There was a line of trees that sat between the road and the fields behind them. There did not seem to be any farming behind the tree line that opened into small fields before becoming thick forest again.

Soon a fork in the road appeared. The foot of the hillside was filled with dense pines that created a canopy above the confluence of two streams. A thick carpet of moss covered the ground and stones under the pines and along the streams.

"I bet this floods out in heavy rain," Rowan stated in a high voice, trying to sound environmentally smart.

Marnie pulled the Razor off the road up through a small incline that Rowan held no hope for clearing. As the vehicle slowed to a stop on the other side, Rowan looked back to revisit what the small ATV had just passed over as if it were nothing.

As he turned to look at his guide and their new surroundings, he noticed a majestic setting of lush green around him. It was nothing like the bold fall colors he expected to see.

"Where are we?" he asked, feeling like Alice after being pulled down the rabbit hole.

"This is a local wildlife club's property," Marnie answered, handing him his coffee that had been stowed in the cupholders. "I love coming here. There's a swimming hole on the other side where we used to, well you know, swim, among other things, when we were kids."

"Drink?... Party?" Rowan added, trying to impress his guide.

Marnie smiled at his naivete.

"Yes, Clark. That too."

Marnie's soft laugh clued Rowan into the skinny dipping and sex on the soft carpet. He gave her a smile to let her know he finally got what she was saying. She then flipped the lid of her thermal cup to take a pull of coffee.

"You probably have a lot of great stories from growing up out here."

Marnie nodded her head as she savored the taste of her coffee.

"Yes," she answered. "I thought I had seen just about everything until I opened the winery. That's created an entirely new series of stories."

Rowan could see on Marnie's face that images were running through her head about past shenanigans from her youth and current business. He turned to get a better look at the remarkable woman beside him who ran a winery and drove like a bat out of hell.

The snap of a dry stick startled Rowan as Marnie took hold of his arm to keep him quiet. His initial fear was that there was a bear nearby. He began to think about what to do if a bear appeared. His first thought was to play dead. He watched Marnie as she listened.

There was another faint sound and Marnie's eyes shifted toward the thick rhododendron that sat on the hillside. Expecting to see an animal, Rowan was surprised when a pale, upright figure appeared then settled into a pool of water in the stream. The naked male body looked familiar to Rowan as the man settled calmly into what had to be fifty-degree water.

"Holy ice bath," he mumbled as he watched the man disappear under the water.

Marnie smiled as she shook her head.

"Cousin Dave," she mumbled. "I honestly thought we were going to see a bear."

"He had to have heard us coming."

"I don't know," Marnie answered, still watching the pool. "Lots of quads run through here and never stop. Or maybe he's an exhibitionist."

Cousin Dave shook his head as he emerged from under the water. He ran his fingers back through his hair to push it from his face. As his eyes opened, he saw Marnie's Razor off in the distance, facing him. He could tell by her shape that Marnie was driving. He was not sure who her passenger was.

Marnie turned the key and fired up the engine as Cousin Dave waved. She was afraid he would stand and not be covered, which would have been embarrassing in front of Clark. It was not that she had never seen Cousin Dave naked. They all skinny dipped in that confluence from time to time. It just would have felt awkward when she was giving a tour to a refined city man that she had only known for a week.

"Time to go," she said, as the engine noise increased, and the Razor began to roll.

"No hello?" Rowan asked, to further the embarrassment he saw on her face.

"He'll be at the Sombrero later," she answered, turning the wheel back to the road. "You two can talk then. I have to work."

# # # #

Marnie drove the back roads for several miles before coming to a gated dirt road. There was an opening over a mound of dirt that rose quickly from the road then crowned in a manner that screamed rollover to Rowan. Marnie switched the Razor into four-wheel drive as she slowly approached the base of the passage.

Rowan was comfortable with her approach as she seemed to study the challenge in front her. He was impressed with her calm; it was the only time she had shifted into four-wheel drive since they had left the winery.

"Are you sure we can get over that?" he asked.

Marnie smiled as she turned to look at him. Her expression gave him combined confidence and fear as the engine noise elevated. The quick acceleration of the Razor pushed him back into his seat. He re-grabbed the handle and roll bar as the machine's front pointed toward the sky to climb the mound then drop straight down the other side.

"Jesus!" he cried out involuntarily as the Razor came to a stop on level ground.

"You want to drive now?" Marnie asked. "It's all logging trail from here."

Rowan looked back at the mound and the trail ahead. His face lit with the excitement of adding another level of experience to his leaf watching. Marnie put the Razor in park then hopped out. It was the first time Rowan noticed she was not wearing her seat belt. He fumbled to undo his belts as she stood next to him. A smile, along with a pat on his chest, gave him comfort that his nerdiness of wearing a belt and grabbing the handles was expected and okay.

"Let's go see some leaves," she added, rolling her eyes as she sat in his old seat.

Rowan hustled around so as not to leave Marnie waiting too long. He looked at her with a nervous smile as he put the Razor in drive.

"Seat belt?" she said, looking from his eyes to his crotch.

Rowan instinctively reached to clip the nylon belts as he watched Marnie's face light with a smile.

"I'm just messing with you," she said. "Your choice to wear or not."

Marnie giggled as she watched Rowan debate the decision in his head. His lift and drop of the belts showed he knew it was the right thing to do it for safety. But he also wanted to impress on his guide that he was no wussy.

"I won't think any less of you if you wear the belt," she added, continuing to amuse herself at his expense.

Rowan clipped the belt securely around his lap and shoulder using an I-don't-care emphasis. He pushed on the accelerator expecting the feel and response of his Audi. When the Razor exhibited a high tension of resistance and a slow response to revving the engine, he knew he was going to have to get used to a new feel.

The Razor pulled slowly from its stopped position. Marnie smiled as she put her hands behind her head to stretch. In his peripheral vision, Rowan noticed the push of her chest outward. When he turned to look at her, he saw the finish of a yawn. His initial thought was that she was bored by his driving.

"Late night, early morning," she said, as she stretched again by extending her hands forward. "Let's step on it a bit. I don't have all day."

# # # #

The climb up the old fire trail was more fun than scenic. The trees and views they were driving by were nothing more than what he saw on the drive on Friday.

"Where are all the great panoramic views?" he asked as they drove through the uphill, tree-lined trail of dense forest.

"Patience," Marnie replied, noting he was getting a little nervous being deep in the forest.

Rowan's focus was set farther and farther up the trail, more interested in what was to come than what he was driving by.

"Carpe diem," Marnie added, fully enjoying watching his intensity.

"Seize the day!?" he asked.

"Enjoy the moment."

Rowan's body relaxed as Marnie touched his right arm. Her touch and amused smile brought began to put him at ease as an opening to daylight appeared a hundred yards ahead. It was apparent to him that she had this part of the drive planned and timed to this exact response.

The opening at the end of the trees gave access to a mountaintop meadow. On the far side, it dropped severely to an immense valley of mixed browns, yellows, and reds. Marnie watched Rowan's eyes open as the view emerged in front of him.

"My wife would love this," he blurted out before closing his eyes in regret.

Marnie stayed quiet waiting for him to recover and look at her. She purposely had a sympathetic look for his faux pas, but now was uncertain as to why he asked her for a tour.

"I'm sure she would," Marnie answered.

"I'm sorry,"

"It's okay, really," Marnie said, studying his face. "It's not like this is a date...right?"

Marnie knew the question would embarrass him. She pointed to a spot at the far end of the meadow to park. Rowan let her question hang unanswered as he wondered to himself what the purpose of their day together was.

As Rowan put the Razor in park and turned the engine off, Marnie was already out unloading a cooler and bedroll from the Razor's rear storage area. A few steps behind, she threw him the bedroll and pointed to a small overlook fifteen feet away. She picked up the cooler with ease and walked with him to the sitting area. When Rowan tried to take the cooler from her, she shoulder-checked him away to let him know she could carry her own weight.

"Wow," he said, as he stopped to look at the 270-degree view of turning leaves across an expansive valley. "I've got to get a picture of this."

"It'll hold," Marnie replied.

"Well," he laughed, recalling his conversation with Claire, "Global warming."

Marnie dropped her cooler and looked at him.

"Please don't ruin *you* by telling me you're one of those far-left world-is-ending-types. You drive an Audi, not a Tesla."

"No," he answered, smiling at her concern. "But I do have my concerns."

Marnie relaxed to his confession. She knew Clark had to be a Republican from the way he looked, walked, talked, dressed, and wore his hair. His horn-rimmed glasses and look-at-me car completed his profile. Marnie was firmly a conservationist, just not an alarmist. She began to feel that even if she and Rowan were not in the same philosophical camp they were, at least, neighbors.

"You can spread that blanket out over there. I've brought snacks for brunch."

#

The panoramic option on his camera always gave him problems. The image on his screen would always start to build then stall as he panned his phone from left to right. This time, it seemed to be working. His effort to capture the entire swath of color and mountain-scape in front of him was going to be successful.

"It never gets old," she said as she walked to stand next to him.

"My God, I've fought NOT to come up here every time my wife wanted to."

Marnie smiled as she watched him evaporate into the emotion of the moment.

"Well," she replied, "you never would have seen this from the tourist sites."

Rowan gave a quick laugh and smiled at her.

"Yeah," he answered. "This is definitely not on the touring maps."

"Let's keep it that way, shall we?"

Marnie pointed back to the blanket. The cooler was set on the uphill corner to give them room to sit while having access to what Marnie packed for brunch.

The grass under the blanket gave the blanket a surprisingly soft feel. Rowan adjusted to the side to provide adequate room for Marnie to join him without them being too close to touch.

Marnie reached into the cooler to pull its contents. Rowan was not surprised to see a bottle of Sombrero wine come out first. She handed it to him with a corkscrew. As Rowan started to twist the metal screw into the top of the bottle, Marnie pulled a bottle of soda water from the cooler. She stopped when she saw him check the bottle of red then looked at the soda water.

"Trust me," she said.

Rowan continued his effort to uncork the bottle of red as Marnie returned to the cooler to pull a towel-wrapped loaf of bread and a foil-covered ball from a basket.

"What's in the foil?" he asked.

"Cheese."

The cork made a slight pop as it exited the bottle top. With the wine in one hand, Rowan picked up the bottle of soda water for instructions on what to do. Marnie nodded toward the cooler to look for cups that she had brought to mix the two together. After putting the bottles down, Rowan gave her an affirming smile as he twisted to grab two, tall, clear plastic glasses.

"What?" Marnie asked, feeling a little warmth in her cheeks.

"I'm impressed," he answered. "Spritzers!"

"Does the simple little country bumkin girl surprise you?"

"Yes," he answered, as he handed her his first attempt at a Sombrero spritzer. "Pleasantly so."

Marnie accepted the glass with a smile and waited for him to complete his pour.

"To fall leaves," she toasted, as their two glasses tapped together.

As they took their first taste, frowns appeared on their faces as they looked into their glasses. Marnie reached for the soda water to dilute her drink further. After two pours and stirs, she became satisfied with her final blend. She then took, and modified, Rowan's drink to the same mix. He smiled to show he liked it, even though he did not.

"Good cheese, and good bread too," he observed as Marnie broke a section of bread then spread some cheese on it.

"It's from the Amish, not the French," she said as she handed it to him.

Her initial thought was to feed it to him as a romantic gesture. But she still was not sure why he was there or how long he was going to hang around. It was easier, and safer, to hold her distance as she peeled away his layers.

Rowan's face tensed as he tasted the cheese and bread. He chewed to hold on to the endorphins his taste buds were delivering. Marnie laughed as his head started nodding before he swallowed.

"Oh my God," he said in amazement.

"We used to do the wine and cheese thing when I was out in San Francisco... Oakland, to be exact."

Rowan adjusted his position to keep his eyes on her as she started to give her surprising history.

"Why were you out there?" he asked.

"School. I was at the CCAC... California College of..."

"Arts and Crafts," he finished.

Marnie paused, surprised the preppie stiff sitting next to her had heard of her California arts college.

"You know my school?" she asked.

Rowan took another tear of bread with a generous smear of cheese. As his eyes closed to the taste, he nodded his head in agreement to both her question and the fabulous taste that was permeating his mouth.

"I do," he answered, while still savoring the taste. "My sister went there back in the late '90s, I think. Maybe later."

Marnie smiled at his confusion, knowing that she would have a hard time giving her graduation dates.

"We didn't overlap," she observed.

Both their glasses were soon empty and Marnie took his to pour a better first blend. As she poured hers, Rowan took a first taste and nodded approval.

"So, Marnie, I'm guessing your last name is not Lane."

Marnie smiled as she swirled her taste of spritzer in her mouth. She wondered if she should stay on first-name basis to keep him at arm's length. As his eyebrows lifted to seek her answer, she swallowed and waited, to maintain suspense.

"You know mine from my credit card," he added.

Marnie kept a smug expression as she tilted her head. Her eyes were locked on his, wondering why he was there and how she ended up on the mountaintop with him.

"I don't read the credit card names, Clark," she said, desperately trying to keep from smiling.

Rowan's silence added fuel to her fire, which made her explode in laughter. His smug look was inviting. She looked at his lips, wanting to kiss him. His innocent, quick touch of his glass to his lips that pulled no wine broke her resistance.

"Gardner," she replied in a heavy exhale.

Rowan smiled, then took a drink of spritzer.

"What?!" she declared.

"Garden-er? Really?" he asked. "Not wine-er-er? Or, grape squasher-er?"

His fumbled attempt at a joke fell flat. Marnie just stared at him.

"Those were my married names, until I changed them back," she answered, trying to salvage their elevated mood.

Rowan smiled to show his appreciation for her effort to play along. She was working to keep things on a flirty level that he both liked and appreciated. Her look, in her worn cowboy boots, blue jeans, denim shirt and vest, was not anything like he had ever gone for before. There was a freshness to her fifty-year-old persona that was overwhelmingly sexy. He was concerned that it was an attraction that would come and go quickly. He decided to dial back to keep it from burning bright, then out.

"Wow," he said. "You're quite something. Aren't you?"

Marnie felt a tightness in her chest that she had not felt in a long time. His eyes were cutting through her like butter. She felt like he could see and hear everything she was thinking and feeling. The city man was attractive to her in many ways. But he was also from a different culture than she had ever aspired to be part of. Marnie finished the last third of her glass of spritzer in one gulp before immediately turning to pack things up.

Rowan grew concerned that his comment was too forward. He took hold of her arm as she picked up the loaf of bread.

"Did I say something wrong?" he asked.

Marnie looked at his hand holding her arm. Her eyes did not shift as she thought about she wanted to say in response but chose not to.

"Nope," she answered, pulling away. "We just need to get rolling. I have to be back before two."

Rowan checked his watch, which read 11:30, as Marnie stood. They had more than enough time to get back. Marnie had the cooler repacked and was securing it to the Razor with bungee cords when he appeared behind her with the folded blanket. She shuddered as his hand took hold of her arm again.

Marnie took a moment to exhale, her eyes closed. She knew if she turned that the attraction would be too strong to resist. His hold was light but firm. He stayed motionless. But she knew he was there.

"Look, Clark," she said, using his fake name to separate him from the man she wanted. "This little country girl just isn't going to fall for your big city ways... So, let's just keep the tour guide, tourist thing going...if you don't mind."

Rowan's hand released as she finished her appeal. He had no thoughts or expectations beyond the moment. It just felt right. Too right. And Marnie was obviously misinterpreting everything. He knew she would never believe it, but she was the first woman he had met in years who truly fascinated him, and he did not want anything more from her than her attention and time.

"That's a good plan," he agreed, trying to calm the water.

Marnie pulled away from him reluctantly as he moved toward the passenger side of the Razor.

"Oh no," she said, hoping to recover and reignite the fun of their afternoon. "You drive. There's more to see."

Rowan smiled as he continued to walk around the front of the vehicle. Marnie tucked the blanket beside the cooler under one of the bungee cords. By the time she climbed in, Rowan was belted and waiting to go. She looked at his lap as she put her hand on his thigh. She held it there for a moment debating what she should do next. The firm squeeze that followed was all he needed to know that everything had returned to the fun they were having earlier.

"Take that trail over there, heading down into the trees," she said, pointing off into the distance. "Let's see what you have in you."

# # # #

The trail off into the woods took a sharp dive and turn after leaving the tall grass of the meadow. The canopy of leaves limited the light and visibility as the Razor made its way down a steep hill.

"FASTER!" Marnie yelled, holding onto the roll bar and seat handle.

She looked at Rowan with a devious smile that said she was enjoying the panic in his face.

Not to disappoint her, Rowan pushed the accelerator to wind the engine higher. The stiff suspension of the Razor transmitted each rut in the trail up through the seats and into their bodies. Rowan kept both hands on the wheel to both maintain control and stay in the vehicle.

"You're not going fast enough," Marnie yelled.

The trail began to narrow with no end in sight. Each bounce pushed the Razor to where a counter steer was needed to keep it under control. Rowan was growing concerned that his speed would send them into the trees if he hit a bump that was too much to handle. He looked at Marnie to make sure she was still comfortable. Her focus forward with both hands grabbing handles gave him little confidence that their ride together was going to end well.

As the engine wound higher, Marnie picked up her feet to put them against the dash of the vehicle. The decline of the hillside quickly leveled into a stream with water level and current that was moving from left to right.

"FASTER!" she shouted.

The Razor lifted off the lip of the shoreline to carry them out into the water before landing on all four wheels mid-stream, sending a monstrous splash of water in all directions. Rowan looked to her then to his feet as the stream began to fill the footwells through drainage holes in the floor.

"Don't take your foot off the gas," she said, looking at him with an excited gleam in her eyes.

Her feet were still high and dry against the dash while his were now soaked to the ankles with water now wicking down his socks to his feet.

"We're not going to make it," Rowan declared, as he felt the Razor lose momentum then start to float and drift to the right.

"Hold on," Marnie declared as he took his foot off the gas.

Marnie shifted the Razor into four-wheel drive.

"Turn with the current and punch it," she said, waiting to see if Audi-man could handle the task. "Then, straighten out until we get to that bend."

All four wheels began spinning in the water, creating rooster tails out the side as Rowan steered left and right to gain control. Marnie watched the concentration on his face as he worked through the effort to angle the Razor for the shoreline on the bend that was their exit.

As they approached the creek's bend that fell off to the right, Rowan turned the wheel to exit left using both the propulsion from the spinning wheels and their occasional bite on the stream bed to guide the Razor onto their desired exit. The Razor grabbed the gravel of the stream bed's far border and jerked upward as the tires bit into the shoreline to pull the buggy out of the water and onto dry land.

"Oh my God," he said, as he brought the machine to a stop. "I thought we were going to die."

He leaned against the steering wheel laughing as Marnie began to pat his shoulder.

"That's the most fucking fun I've had in decades."

Rowan could still feel his heart pounding as he sat back to savor the ecstasy of what he had just accomplished. The closest he could recall was doing doughnuts in his Audi in the golf club parking lot on a night it had snowed while he and Mindy were having dinner. Later she had chastised him for the juvenile stunt. He looked to Marnie to find a face lit with satisfaction that their ride had ended successfully, and that he was still having fun.

"And you wanted to go see leaves..."

Marnie shoulder-bumped Rowan to get him oriented to their next ride off into the woods. The bend was an open area that he was sure had stories from her youth. It was tucked deep into the trees away from any signs of life. It was the perfect spot for high school parties and other fun and trouble they likely found as kids.

"Feet wet?" Marine asked as the trail narrowed back through some thick brush.

The ground beneath the wheels was firm but wet. Rowan smiled to show that his wet ankles, feet, and boots were all good. A few puddles that sat hidden along the trail would splash muddy water off to the side when they passed through.

Rowan was growing confident with the Razor as he worked his way through the foothills. The terrain undulated up and down to push them toward the thick rhododendrons that filled the area. As he rounded a corner to follow the bottom of the hillside, the Razor dropped then elevated back up quickly as Marnie lifted her feet again.

The drop over the incline was more severe than Rowan expected. The Razor landed in a muddy bog dropping its speed by half in a blink.

"Don't stop!" Marnie instructed, holding her feet up.

That's what she said, Rowan thought with a snicker as murky, brown water started filling the footwells again. He stepped on the accelerator to keep the Razor from getting stuck. The smell of decomposition generated a gag reflex he knew he had to push back. Marnie leaned into him as the water rooster tailed up from the spinning front wheels that were turning left and right to find traction. She grabbed his shoulder to bury her face in his shirt, trying to stay clear of flying mud.

When she felt the front of the vehicle lift as the tires grabbed firm ground, she looked to confirm that Clark had landed in the right shoot out of the bog. A smile came to her face as she pulled away from him to check his expression as he brought the Razor to a stop.

"You drive like a champ," she said with a smile.

A clump of mud was stuck on the lens of his horned rim glasses. The look on his face shared some residual panic with the satisfaction of having successfully made it through the stream and bog.

"How am I going to tell people about this?" he thought out loud.

Marnie shook her head as she looked at the grown man with the little boy, amusement park response to a ride. His face showed pure joy and amusement. She could not resist the temptation to kiss him lightly on the lips.

As her lips touched his, he could feel her warm, sweet breath of life that said she was for real.

"Don't get any big ideas, Clark," she said, looking up at him seductively as she pulled away.

Several cute and clever responses came to mind, but the allure of her eyes was rich and fulfilling enough to savor as just itself. After a few moments passed, Marnie looked away and patted his thigh again.

"Let's see what's next."

# # # #

The final creek crossing lacked the excitement of the first two. Rowan could not decide if that was because it was now old-hat or if it was because he had mastered the all-terrain vehicle with the plastic seats, fiberglass body, and roll-cage.

Marnie lifted her feet again as the water began to enter through the drainage ports in the floorboards. Rowan barely felt anything now that his feet, boots, and pants were soaked and smelled of a rot he would rather not ponder. The clean stream water did provide a cleansing benefit to his boots that he was thankful to see.

Marnie pointed him toward the right side of an upcoming fork and instructed him to step on it. The hill climb she knew was coming was going to be disappointing for Rowan, who wanted to run more mud. She could see in his face that he was not done playing out in the forest. She hoped they would get more time to run more trails on other days.

The meadow reappeared as they left it thirty minutes earlier. As they reached the top of the hill, Rowan turned, then slowed to a stop. The majesty of the leaves that had grabbed him so completely when they first arrived still captivated his senses. He gave Marnie a quick glance with a nod back down the hill to get another go at the creek run.

"I can't. I have to get back," she apologized, leaving open a hope for what she wanted to hear.

Rowan's disappointment was written on his face, making her wonder if his desire to take another run through the woods was because of the Razor ride or her. She tried to think of a reason why a professional, straightlaced man like him would go for an artistic country winery owner like her. As her eyes regained clarity to look at him, she felt his lips touch hers. When he pulled away, her lower lip was clenched between his. She put her palm on his cheek for him to stop before kissing him lightly again.

"Thank you so much for this, Lois," he said, keeping his face close to hers.

Marnie shook her head in disbelief that she had just kissed the man she had found annoyingly attractive a week ago. She sat back to exhale and gain her thoughts. When she looked at him again, she found him focused on her with a big smile of satisfaction.

"I have to get back," she said, looking away to hide the smile that appeared as a warm, tingling sensation flowed up through her body.

The loud whine of the Razor's engine as they started their drive back did not pull her from the sensations she was feeling. She looked to him as they began rolling back to the road to the Red Sombrero. Marnie could not keep her eyes off of him until she noticed him look toward her. Her quick look away brought a smile to his face. It had been a while since he felt an inner warmth too.

Chapter 6

When the Razor emerged from the woods, the Sombrero already had a few Jeeps and pickups in the parking lot. A number of patrons were sitting on the deck overlooking the grassy knoll the Razor had to travel up to get to the service door on the side.

The production area for the winery fed off a garage bay and door that faced the road. Parked in front of the bay was a box truck with a vineyard logo and Fredonia, New York written underneath. Rowan remembered the Fredonia vineyards from trips his family would take to Van Buren Bay on Lake Erie. Their vacation spot was a small community of cabins that sat on the water, which was perfect for swimming and sailing.

"Fredonia," Rowan said. "I used to vacation near there as a kid. Van Buren Bay."

Marnie gave a puzzled look to the truck as Rowan's comment sank in. She knew Fredonia from her purchase runs to the area east of Erie to buy the juice stock they used to make their wines. She wondered what kind of vacations he used to take there as a child, as well as why the box truck was backed to her service-bay door.

When the Razor pulled up to the door, Rowan noticed the lumberjack man who yelled at Cousin Dave having a heated exchange with another man. Although about the same size and build, it looked like the two were a few words short of going at each other. Marnie jumped out of the Razor before it came to a complete stop.

"What's going on here?" she asked, fearful of what she was about to hear.

Tom looked at her with disbelief in his eyes, then at Rowan as he wandered up behind her.

"This man is here to take the equipment," he said. "He says you promised it as collateral for the juice and haven't paid."

Marnie's shoulders dropped with the news as she looked at Tom then back at Rowan. Every sense of joy she had from the morning had just been ripped from her in Tom's single statement.

"Marnie, this is serious," Tom declared to get her attention.

Marnie looked back again at Rowan, seeing concern in his eyes as he stepped forward. Looking at the ground, she thought through how much she had and owed. It was not enough to get the box truck to leave empty.

"Maybe I can help," Rowan said, stepping next to Marnie.

"Who are you?" Tom asked in an agitated tone, unsure of the man he recognized from somewhere but could not place.

"I'm your wife's attorney," Rowan lied, using a serious voice to make it believable.

The words caused Marnie's stomach to bind. She had no idea what Rowan did for a living. She wanted to stop him from creating a bigger problem if he was lying. But she was also confident that what he was doing could buy her time.

The man sent to collect the equipment looked at Marnie as she continued to stare at the ground. Tom could not figure out if, or why, the city guy with the wet feet and pants legs was actually telling the truth or lying to help his wife. If the latter, he was curious to know why.

"I was just sent here to collect the equipment that was promised," the truck driver said.

"You can't," Rowan answered. "You can't because this place is being put into bankruptcy tomorrow to be reorganized under the Chapter 11 statute of Pennsylvania law."

Rowan was pulling as much jargon from his head as possible. His bankruptcy knowledge was limited to graduate school and a business law class he had to take. He could not remember if Chapter 11 or 7 was reorganization. He was hoping that the truck driver did not know either.

"Look, I'm just here to do my job."

Rowan began to feel his argument slipping away. He was sure the man standing there was the supplier's enforcer who had heard every excuse possible from people who owed his boss money.

"I understand," Rowan answered. "Call your boss, let me talk to him. It'll save us all time. Or we can call the state police who will be here before you're done loading. I assume you have paperwork to show them?"

Rowan was bullshitting his way through the conversation. The driver's non-response told him that Marnie probably promised the equipment but never put in writing.

Rowan put his hand on Marnie's shoulder to pull her back into the conversation. Tom watched her shudder as his hand touched her back, hoping it was due to surprise. But his jealous nature made him think there may be more. Their eyes met as Rowan checked on the truck driver as he talked to his boss on his cell phone.

"What's going on here?" Tom asked with a whiff of hurt in his voice.

Rowan looked away, knowing it was best not to get into that discussion now. First, and foremost, he really did not know what was going on. Second, he did not want to add tension with Tom into the mix of tension with the supplier's collector.

"He wants to speak to you," the driver said, handing handed Rowan his phone.

Rowan knew he had to step up his game. He was becoming more confident that Chapter 11 was the reorganization bankruptcy and decided to run with it.

Marnie listened as Rowan exchanged posturing with the supplier's owner. Her senses were numb not knowing if Rowan was doing something to help or hurt her business. She trusted from her time with him, and his fancy, one hundred-plus-thousand-dollar car, that he had the business smarts to bullshit his way through it. Assuming he was not who he claimed to be. He did look like a lawyer.

Rowan handed the phone back to the driver. As the man turned to get his next round of instructions from his boss, Rowan put his hand on Marnie's shoulder and winked to give her comfort. He had bought her time from the repo of her wine production equipment.

The collector walked to the back of his truck and off-loaded their next order of juice. Marnie looked to Tom in disbelief as he directed the driver on where to put it.

"What the hell did you promise him?" Marnie asked, not sure if she wanted to know.

"We agreed that the repo of your equipment was pennies on the dollar for him," Rowan started.

Marnie knew he was right. She wondered how he knew.

"I told him it was high season for tourism and that if his guy left with the equipment, we would call the police to dispute this repo effort."

"Can you do that?" Marnie asked.

"I don't know. But it sounded good. And he bought it."

"So, what's next!?" she asked, thankful and wanting to kiss him again.

"You have thirty days to get through high-season and bring your account current," Rowan answered. "Can you do that?"

Marnie looked to Tom for confirmation. His expression did not offer much hope. But he did not shake his head no.

"We can only try," she answered. "Thank you."

Marnie put her hand on Rowan's shoulder then ran it down the side of his arm when she noticed Tom watching. Rowan's smile at her appreciation went blank when he also looked at Tom and saw his disdain for the two of them together.

"I'm happy to help. You two need to figure out how to make the money you need with what you have to square up that debt and stay in business."

The challenge appeared to break the angst as Tom returned to the production area and Marnie walked Rowan to the front of the Sombrero.

"Thanks for the tour, leaves...wine...bread...scary ride... and everything else," he said while fighting to hold back smirk, and looking to see if Tom was anywhere in sight.

"I think I should be thanking you," she replied. "I'm so embarrassed."

"It's okay," Rowan answered as he pulled her close for a hug. "It's just a hiccup. You'll be fine."

Marnie felt comfort in Rowan's arms as he held her close to his body. They seemed to fit together like puzzle pieces. There was a peace that flowed between them as she rested her head on his chest.

"Are you coming back?" she asked. "I mean, later?"

Rowan smiled when he heard the invitation that came as a question.

"I have to go change, maybe shower," he answered, looking at the swamp foul that was stuck on his boots and discolored jeans.

Marnie smiled, partially regretting having done that to him.

"I'll reserve your stool for you."

# # # #

Rowan ditched his boots in his trunk and rolled up his muddy pants legs before getting into his S8 to drive back to his cabin. There was a lingering smell of the bog decay that increased when his car door closed to trap it into the tight space. Dropping all four windows and opening the sunroof washed away the smell as the fresh, crisp autumn air quickly filled the cabin when the car started to move.

Rowan's phone connected to the Audi's Bluetooth and stayed quiet until he reached the point on the main road where cellular service bars appeared and messages could be downloaded. When the message tones stopped ringing, Rowan took the unusual step of not asking Siri to read them. He knew they could wait. He wanted to enjoy his drive down the two-lane country road in the middle of fall's beautiful foliage while keeping an eye out for slow-moving Amish carriages.

Off on the berm of the oncoming lane, a man appeared walking toward him from an abandoned quad. His gait was fast and appeared angry as he kicked at rock debris on the side of the road. His weathered face and brown curly hair seemed familiar from somewhere that Rowan could not immediately place. He knew his reference points in the area were few. That face had to be from the Red Sombrero.

Cousin Dave, Rowan realized as he stepped on his brakes to stop across from the man.

Cousin Dave noticed the expensive Euro sedan quickly approaching and expected him to blow by as they always did. When the car stopped abruptly , he expected to have to give some city asshole directions back to Interstate 80. Depending upon his mood, he would either gave them the easy two turn directions with landmarks, or he send them deep into the trees.

"Cousin Dave," Rowan shouted through his window.

Hearing his name caused him to pause. The car was unfamiliar, as was the darkened face of the driver hidden by sunglasses.

"Who's that?" he answered, hoping for clarity before walking over.

Rowan realized their familiarity was only one way. He was just a face in the crowd at the Sombrero a week ago, sitting next to Marnie and Janis, who were better to look at. Rowan checked the road in both directions to make sure staying stopped in his lane was still safe.

"Name's Rowan Delaney; I'm a friend of Marnie's," he answered. "Are you okay? Do you need help? Or a ride somewhere?"

Cousin Dave focused on Rowan's face, trying to place him somewhere with either Marnie or Janis. The face he was looking at, in the very expensive car, was not familiar. What was familiar was his concern that rich city folks would find their area, come in, and ruin it for the locals.

"I'm fine, sir," Cousin Dave answered, still searching his memory to place the man in the car.

"I'd be happy to drop you somewhere, go get gas," Rowan replied.

Cousin Dave was an intriguing piece of Legend and the Red Sombrero community. His impression from Marnie and Janis was that the quirky man across the street was not dangerous. Ordinarily Rowan would drive past a man walking down the street. Or, if he stopped, offer his phone for a call instead of a ride. But the man across the street, in trouble, seemed to be family to Marnie. So Rowan felt obligated to help him.

"Do I know you? Sir?"

The formality of his questions was amusing. Rowan was beginning to wonder if stopping to help was worth the effort. As he looked at the total image across the street, standing a lane away, he envisioned Cousin Dave in his white coat and thimble hat.

"We haven't met," he answered. "I was at the Sombrero last week when you came in. I was at the bar with Marnie."

Cousin Dave's eyes widened with his recall of the image of the two women with the city man.

"You're the city guy," he replied, pointing at Rowan.

Rowan did not know if being called a *City Guy* was a good thing, or not. Cousin Dave's tone had a negative connotation and bias.

"That's me," he answered, in a tone to blow it off. "I'd be happy to give you a lift. You out of gas?

Cousin Dave looked off down the road to where Rowan was heading. The distance back to his cabin was less than a mile. He would have to carry his gas can back. Accepting a ride from the city man would save him time. He looked harmless enough. And he knew Marnie.

"I'd appreciate it," Cousin Dave finally surrendered. "But it's about a mile back that way."

Cousin Dave pointed back toward the Sombrero. Rowan waved and smiled as he turned the wheel to turn his car around and pull next to Cousin Dave.

"I appreciate the lift," Cousin Dave said again as he opened the car door.

The dense sound of the heavy, insulated car door opening was different from the hollow rattle of his pickup's doors. The car's interior was plush, with soft leather seats and dense carpet on the floor. Cousin Dave looked at his boots to check for dirt and mud before climbing in. The electronic dash made him think of an airplane cockpit.

"Lots to look at in here," he commented as he clicked his seatbelt.

Rowan smiled, knowing that the Whirling Dervish in his car lived the simpler life of old pickups and quads. The dash in front of him with all its detail and information was mostly irrelevant to driving the car. The sophistication that surrounded him was beginning to make Rowan feel stupid for paying so much for it.

"Just tell me where to turn," he added.

The country lane back to Cousin Dave's property was a few hundred yards past the road that led back to the Sombrero. The access from the road was smooth and graveled. It quickly changed to a rutted dirt road that required navigation assistance from Cousin Dave after the Audi bottomed-out on an unexpected bump.

The final two-hundred-yard drive was under a canopy of dense, colorful forest foliage. It reminded Rowan of driving through the tunnels that led into the city of Pittsburgh from its south hills. The total encapsulation of the driveway kept his eyes forward to the endpoint that he could see coming. His expectation for what he was about to see would not be the magical Golden Triangle cityscape he called home. He was anxious to see Cousin Dave's view as a comparative.

As the Audi emerged from the tree tunnel, a mid-sized, shiny aluminum Airstream trailer appeared, sitting in a meadow next to the old Dodge pickup truck Rowan expected to find. It fit the setting, and the other vehicles that were parked at the Red Sombrero. Beyond the trailer and pickup was an expanse of color that looked out over miles of terrain and forestland. Cousin Dave directed Rowan over to a small shed tucked behind the trailer.

"Mind if I use your bathroom?" Rowan asked, feeling some bladder pressure.

Cousin Dave paused to think about his answer. Rowan saw concern in his face that suggested he may have been too embarrassed to let him into his trailer.

"I've only got two options depending upon your needs," Cousin Dave answered. "I got that outhouse over there or the woods."

Cousin Dave pointed to a small, single-stall outhouse that looked like it was taken from a bad movie. The sight of the wooden box filled Rowan's mind with all sorts of negative assumptions about the facility, which he knew he should avoid.

"I only have to pee," he replied.

Cousin Dave's eyebrows lifted as he took a deep breath.

"I suggest the trees then."

Cousin Dave laughed as the shoeless man with rolled pants legs walked into the trees and he opened his shed to find his five-gallon gas can. The debris on Rowan's legs answered the question that appeared in his head when he smelled a whiff of mud bog in the fancy European sedan that just gave him a ride home. He was the person with Marnie down by the creek.

As he entered the tree line, Rowan opened his trunk with the button on his key fob. He heard the popping noise it always made before turning to confirm it lifted as expected.

The two returned to the Audi at the same time. Rowan grabbed some hand sanitizer from his center console before walking to the back of the car. Cousin Dave placed his can down behind the car as he peered into the trunk.

As expected, a big bag of golf clubs sat in the middle of the trunk next to an emergency road kit of blankets, flashlight, and flares. Cousin Dave looked to Rowan, who had just finished disinfecting his hands, for instructions on what to do. His concern was that his dirty plastic gas can would permanently blemish the carpeting and golf bag.

"I don't want to dirty your trunk," he said.

"No worry," Rowan replied.

He reached into the emergency bag to get an old beach towel. After pushing his clubs toward the back of the trunk, he laid the towel down, then reached to pick up the gas can.

The weight of the can was unexpected, and Rowan appeared to struggle before lifting it into his trunk. Cousin Dave chuckled as he watched the city man work to lift something he himself could lift easily. They were about the same age. Cousin Dave thought the man in front of him should spend more time working outside than pushing paper.

"I appreciate the help," he stated again as Rowan pushed the trunk lid closed.

As they were about to get into the car, Cousin Dave looked toward Marnie's house across the small valley and pointed.

"Since you know Marnie, that's her house over there," he said, certain Rowan had seen his camp from her windows.

The house across the valley was small and modern. It had a Frank Lloyd Wright appearance, with stone pillars and glass exterior walls. Her California influence was clear in what she built to live in. He wondered if that house was at risk, with the Sombrero's financial problems.

"Pretty home," Rowan said as he continued to study her property.

"We keep an eye on each other."

Rowan smiled to acknowledge Cousin Dave's shot across his bow. He was now on notice that Marnie had a set of protective eyes watching her beyond those of the ex-husband, whom he had already met.

"Duly noted," Rowan replied, giving Cousin Dave the acknowledgement he was seeking.

On the drive back out the driveway Rowan focused on the avoiding ruts that could harm the low-profile car. When they finally reached pavement, Rowan punched the accelerator to childishly give Cousin Dave a taste of the car he was in. Then, as they approached the quad, Rowan regretted the action. He did not need to give Marnie's protector another reason to not like him.

"So, what's your plan?" Cousin Dave asked as Rowan swerved to the berm behind the abandoned quad.

Rowan looked at the weathered man whose tired eyes were now locked on his.

"I'll be at the Sombrero tonight. Then back to Pittsburgh tomorrow."

Cousin Dave studied the cavalier look on Rowan's face.

"You gonna bring some of your friends back with you?"

Cousin Dave's direction and concern were clear in his question. He wanted to uncover whether the city man was going to bring more tourism to disrupt the tranquility of his home.

"Tourism is great, right? I mean, they come, they spend, and they go."

Rowan tried to sell his point with a carefree wave of his hand.

"I'm not so sure about that," Cousin Dave replied as he opened his door. "That's not been my experience. Tourists come, spend, and change things for the worse."

Rowan decided not to debate the issue. He popped the trunk from a button inside the car as Cousin Dave closed the door.

"Thank you again for your kindness for the ride." Cousin Dave added, to close their conversation.

Rowan smiled as he watched him turn to fetch his gas can.

"I'll see you at the Sombrero tonight," he shouted, to finish their time with a friendly gesture.

The sound and feel of the trunk lid closing told Rowan that Cousin Dave had pulled his can from the trunk and that he was free to go. He checked his mirror for approaching cars before pulling out into the oncoming lane to head back to his cabin. Cousin Dave was already filling his empty gas tank as the Audi merged back out onto the main road. With his hands occupied, Cousin Dave looked and nodded his appreciation again for Rowan's kindness. A quick sound of his horn returned the send-off to the man he hoped to see later.

Chapter 7

The crowd in the Red Sombrero was as expected for a late Saturday afternoon. There were dueling tables filled with football fans watching the end of the Penn State and Ohio State football game. Penn State was closer to Legend than Columbus, Ohio but the two schools had equal representation in the area, since Legend was close to the Ohio state line.

Tom walked behind the bar to look for Marnie. She disappeared from her post when the bar stools emptied. The clanking of bottles coming from the production and storage room said she was filling milk crates to restock the shelves. He decided to wait for her to run into him instead of cornering her. What happened with the delivery man was scaring him. Being late on bills was one thing. Being to the point of repossession was another.

The squeak of the hand truck's wheels gave advance warning that Marnie had her bottles crated and was on her way back. Tom began to feel nervousness building in him. Marnie was a proud woman who worked hard to understand her business. The Red Sombrero was successful as a stand-alone. But the recent closing of Marnie's stab at a second location devastated her confidence.

While they were still together, Marnie and Tom debated expanding her success in Legend to one or more additional locations. Tom adamantly opposed the idea. Marnie believed she had the business down to a science she could duplicate. What she did not know was that diluting her attention across multiple locations was going to teach her a number of business truths that she did not experience at the first location.

The time it took open the second location was less than what it took to start the original. She had already gone through the trial-and-error of learning what to do, and what not to do. Some of those lessons were expensive, but manageable. The first location prepared her well to get location two open. It just did not prepare her well to run two locations at the same time.

Two lessons from the second location she did not anticipate had to do with customers and staff. The first was that some of her first-location customers found the second more convenient for socializing with friends. Her best guess estimated that loss at fifteen percent, just on familiar faces and head count.

The second lesson was the most impactful. Marnie spent all her time at the Red Sombrero tending to every detail. Her cash and inventory controls were rustic but effective, with constant oversight. When that oversight changed to splitting time between two locations thirty miles apart, cash receipts and deposits at both locations were less than expected. Dollars earned per bottle produced nose-dived. Both measures told her that cash was being pocketed and inventory was either being given to friends or taken out the back door.

The second venue closed without either warning or explanation. Marnie was the sole owner of the second Red Sombrero, so Tom never had any justification to ask her anything about it, outside of noticing that she was extraordinarily moody.

"You're here early," Marnie said, as she rolled the hand truck near his feet.

Tom stepped back with a glare as Marnie walked past with a sinister smile.

"Damn it, Marnie. I don't have my steel toed's on," he snapped, stepping back.

"Then keep your damn toes out of my path."

Marnie turned her back to him, knowing he was there to talk about the confrontation with the delivery man. She slowly pulled bottles of Dervish Red out one at a time, to buy time. Tom frowned as he watched. He knew she usually stocked them in pairs.

"Don't ignore me Marnie," Tom said, getting agitated with her antics.

"I'm not ignoring you, Tom. I'm just being careful."

Marnie's response angered him, and he started walk toward her. Marnie could hear her ex-husband move with his usual lumbering swagger.

"Marnie, we have to talk about the winery. The equipment. The juice."

Marnie stopped stocking to stare at the debris under the bar. A wash of emotion began to press on her eyes as she felt the touch of Tom's hand on her back.

"Marnie," he said, in his lightest voice, which she always found sexy, "tell me what's going on. Who that guy was. You don't need to sell yourself to right this."

Marnie's shame turned to anger as she processed Tom's accusation that she was prostituting herself with the city man in the fancy car to find money.

"Who the hell do you think you are!?" she asked, spinning to push his arm off her back.

Tom knew immediately he had gone too far in his speculation. The repo effort was first on his mind. But the convenient presence of her white knight bothered him too. The truck driver was not going to take the equipment. But Tom's approach would have been different from Rowan's. Rather than work a legal argument, he had just planned to fight him.

"Marnie," he replied, exhaling heavily in exhaustion. "You told me when you closed the Clayton location that everything was fine."

"Well, it was," she fired back. "It was over, done, and therefore...fine."

"You also said you got out of the lease and nothing else was owed."

Marnie looked in Tom's eyes, then away. She could feel tears building that she did not want to show. Her tried-and-failed solution for Clayton was killing Legend.

"I took all the money from here to pay off Clayton," she admitted. "I had to leave all the inventory, equipment, furniture, and even my paintings that I hung there that I was trying to sell just to get out."

"Well, the paintings never sold anyway," Tom joked, trying to pull her back.

Tom now understood the situation. He never knew why the second location, which mirrored the first, was a failure. Marnie took that as a personal failure she would not admit to anyone. But he now knew why the repo man showed up for the equipment.

"I can help you," he said.

"You don't have enough."

Marnie continued to stare at the floor until Tom found the courage to put his hand on her back again. His touch released her emotions into tears she needed to hide. Rather than run away, she turned to bury her face in his chest and shirt, holding him tight, so he could not see.

Tom wrapped his arms around his crumbling ex-wife to give her the reassurance that everything would work out.

"How much do you need?"

"More than you have," she answered.

Tom squeezed tighter to keep her from walking away.

"How much is more than I have?"

Marnie started to squirm to release from his hold. The more she squirmed, the tighter Tom held her.

"Okay," she decreed, in a shirt-muffled voice.

Her body went limp in his arms, showing she did not want to fight him anymore. As Tom relaxed with her, Marnie lifted her heel and slammed it down on his foot.

"Jeh...eeze...us, Marnie," he moaned, releasing her to bend over in pain. "I told you I didn't have my steel-toed boots on."

Marnie stepped away, feeling bad that she had to hurt Tom to separate from him.

"Geez, Marn," he groaned again. "Why'd you do that?"

"You're lucky I didn't knee you in the nuts," she answered.

Tom finally stood to look at her, still wincing in pain. He shook his foot hoping some blood flow would bring relief as the throbbing continued.

"You better not treat your moneybags boyfriend this way," he jabbed, knowing it would incite her.

"He's not my boyfriend," she answered, feeling strange to say it out loud. "He's just a guy that I agreed to give a leaf tour to."

Tom laughed. He thought about Rowan's wet boots and pants legs. He knew the only place that could have happened. The slight whiff of the mud bog when Rowan stood near confirmed it.

"Leaves, right," he answered. "Down by the creek. Can't think of anything you and I did there that would make me think otherwise."

Marnie's jaw clamped as her eyes squinted. Tom had just accused her of taking Rowan to the *love zone* after previously accusing her of prostituting herself with the city man for her business.

"You should go," she said calmly. "And, not come back tonight."

Tom leaned back against the bar and crossed his arms.

"You can't kick me out," Tom declared. "I'm too important to you. Who will make the wine?"

"You need to go, Tom," Marnie replied. "I can't have you here, staring at me, and do my job. I need to concentrate on making money tonight."

"It can't be that bad," he answered. "Let me help you."

Marnie looked straight into his eyes and smiled.

"Tom...it is...and you can't."

Tom's shoulders sank as he stood then turned to leave. Marnie stayed still. She watched him look back as he passed by her on the other side of the bar. She gave him a sad smile when he looked back one last time, before walking out the door.

"I'm sorry, Tom," she whispered.

As she thought about the damage she did with her ex-husband and current wine maker, she looked out over the crowd for any tables in need of more wine. The jingle of glasses being removed from the bar brought her back to the need to restock the bar for the crowd that always came on Saturday nights. A quick look to Rowan's spot by the wall gave her comfort that a friendly face would be there for her.

# # # #

Made it to the beach. Enjoy this video of me climbing to get out of my car.

Claire's text was the first of many Rowan saw as he walked from the Audi to the cabin. When he pressed to watch the video, a flowing swirl appeared to indicate the video was loading then quickly stopped to declare *no service*. The next text was from Mindy asking why he let Claire drive her dangerously damaged car to the beach. Her real complaint appeared deeper in her message when she said it was an embarrassment. Rowan was more concerned that it was unsafe.

When he checked his email, he saw that none had been delivered. That made him nervous to think about. But he knew he would have time on Sunday, when home, to go through everything, to be ready for Monday morning.

Once in the cabin, Rowan started thinking about changing for the evening. He took a moment to laugh at the fact that he felt more worried about dressing right for the Sombrero than he did for the symphony back in Pittsburgh. But back home, he was familiar with the norms and expectations for every venue he visited. The Red Sombrero was different. He did not want to look too *city*, while also not look like he was trying too hard to fit in. Why that mattered baffled him.

"Damn it," he moaned when he looked at his unfurled pants legs.

The release of the roll expelled a revolting smell of mud bog that brought tears to his eyes and made him gag. Rowan looked in his bag for other options. He found a pair of fleece-lined Adidas athletic pants from his coaching days that he intended to wear home on Sunday. He wondered if going athletic would be too much for the crowd he expected to see, and if Marnie would roll her eyes at his *look*.

"With the looks Cousin Dave gets wearing a white coat and thimble hat," Rowan mumbled to himself as he shook out the black, form-fitting stretch pants. "There's no freaking way I can wear these tonight."

Rowan knew he had no choice. There were no shopping options, aside from a Walmart Supercenter, that would be open, have what he wanted, and have his size. The lack of cell service added to his frustration because he could not do a quick search to see if Walmart was his one and only option. He was stuck with the Adidas athletic pants. His only hope was that other men would be wearing work pants instead of jeans.

He reached into the shower to start the two-minute process of getting hot water. A growl of his stomach reminded him he had not eaten. His recollection of how he felt on Sunday after his first night at the Sombrero told him he should eat before heading back to drink its sweet, red wine. He also knew the food served there was not what he wanted for his only big meal of the day.

Main Street, Clarion, Pennsylvania, looked like any other small city street in the northeast. The thoroughfare was lined with two- and three-story buildings with storefronts on the bottom and offices and residences above. It was obvious in some areas where new had replaced the old. Banks with drive-throughs and other construction that just did not fit the theme of the original town stood out from the old traditional structures.

Rowan's phone showed four bars of cell service as he drove through the heart of the town. He knew he had three hours to kill, needed to have a good, stomach-lining dinner, and would feel better if he could swap out his athletic pants for a pair of jeans. He fully expected that the college town would have a brew pub with good burgers and bar food. He did not expect to find a store like Langer's Clothiers.

The signs in the front window read like an REI advertisement. Patagonia, Merrell, and other higher-brow brands of outfitter wear were all represented on placards and window stickers. As he pulled his Audi to the curb near the door, he saw people walk in and out, indicating that the store was still open.

The wide, pine floor planks were worn and a step back in time. Their patina was dirty with obvious ruts and gouges from store traffic over the last century. The sign on the door said that Langer's had been in business for one hundred years. As he looked around, Rowan imagined the store as it started before the Depression. The racks on the walls looked original. Their chrome counterparts on the floor, which held the fancy gear, were newer.

The men's section was in the back. There were several displays of casual pants, jeans, and sporting pants. None of the gear was oriented to the traditional camouflage dress that Rowan expected to find in this type of town. There were also a number of choices oriented more toward fly-fishing, and the flash brands that tended to be all show and no go.

Rowan worked his way back to the jeans section to find a pair that was not relaxed fit. He used to wear that more-generous style when he was younger and heavier. However, pictures of him from back then, in those jeans, had reoriented his taste back to more traditional straight-legged jeans that fit tighter, and looked better on the thinner body he had now.

The brands on the table were unfamiliar. As he lifted a pair, the legs unfolded down toward the floor to give him a full view of what he would be buying. The color had a soft, washed look. There was no declarative stitching on the pockets. The size was the 36-inch waist and 34-inch length he wore. He decided to try them on.

"Finding everything okay?" a young male voice asked from behind him.

"Yes, I think," Rowan answered, turning to address the clerk. "I was really only looking for Levi's, or Wrangler jeans."

Rowan looked at the clerk, whose fit, mid-twenties body was a walking display for all the store's brands. His good-looking face, short hair, and cropped beard finished the advertisement.

"For those..." he paused for impact, "I suggest Walmart."

Rowan's immediate outward response was to smile at the kid's smugness. His internal desire was to punch him. The fifteen-dollar-an-hour clerk laying judgment on him was probably a college student he would be interviewing in a few years.

"I guess," Rowan replied, trying not to give it back as he checked the price of the jeans he was holding. "These would be working pants, not show. I'd rather not spend two hundred dollars on pants for that purpose."

Rowan reached into his pocket and pulled the Audi's key fob out. The kid had obviously prejudged him on the Adidas sports pants he was wearing. He turned to the window and pushed the button to lock the car again. The insignia on the fob caught the eye of the clerk as he looked to see where Rowan was pointing it.

"Excuse me a moment. I forgot to lock my car."

As the parking lights flashed on the S8 parked in the slot right beyond the front window, the brand-obsessed clerk slowly returned his eyes to the patron he misjudged.

"We do have more field-oriented pants over here in the fifty-dollar range," he offered. "They're not jeans, but they look good and work well in the woods."

As the young man turned his back to Rowan to lead him over to a display in the corner, Rowan smiled, feeling good that he had just educated the young lad about the dangers of prejudging. He thought that maybe bringing his golfing friend and client, Vinnie, to the store could be the boy's next valuable lesson.

Rowan left the store dressed in his new outfit. As the clerk mellowed, he was more helpful in finding attire that was suitable for the Red Sombrero without looking like Rowan was trying too hard to fit in. Their discussions led to where the clerk was from, what he was studying in school, and where he wanted to go in life. The young man obviously had higher aspirations than working in a clothing store.

When Rowan left, he handed the young man his card. Despite the awkward start, Rowan saw promise in him. He told him to reference the sales experience at Langer's when he reached out. There was a lesson there too. The first was to keep a common connection point for easy recall. The second was to remind him that he made a big error in judgement when they first met that he should not repeat.

As Rowan left the store, he continued to think about the styles and clothes Langer's offered. Like the clerk, he had completely misjudged the sophistication of the area. A college town would attract students who were more brand-conscious buyers. But the brands in the store window, along with the prices, showed there was also a significant pocket of wealth in the region that could afford to shop at Langer's.

# # # #

The microbrewery the store clerk recommended was five storefronts down from Langer's, on the corner of Main Street and South Fourth Street. It had a tired appearance reminiscent of an old diner, and not far off from the Red Sombrero. On the walls were various pieces of memorabilia that included national bands and brands that were local to Clarion and Pittsburgh.

On the back wall was a large chalkboard that listed all the night's beer offerings. The size and clarity of the lettering made the selections easy to read from anywhere in the restaurant. It reminded Rowan of the board behind the bar at Red Sombrero, but it had far fewer items. He sauntered past the beer list deeper into the dining area and he chose a booth by the window so he could watch events unfold inside and outside of the restaurant.

As soon as he was settling into his seat, the waitress appeared and identified herself as Maria. Both her dress and demeanor showed that she was college age, but Rowan could not tell if she was a college student. The tattoos on her arm and run of piercings up her ear made him think she was a local. But that was a prejudgment he was going to keep to himself and not ask to confirm.

Maria's working knowledge of the beers and their attributes was impressive. They had ten selections active on tap, ranging from a crisp pilsner to a coffee stout. Rowan asked about her favorite, which was a pumpkin-laced lager they had just brewed and that she recommended highly. After a short minute to think, he decided it was best to stay light to start his evening and chose the pilsner, which had the lowest alcohol count.

The menu offering was traditional, microbrewery food with a few attractive add-ons that included specialty-meat burgers and roasted Brussels sprouts and cauliflower. Looking around the brewery and back out onto the street, Rowan wondered who and where the patrons were that would buy this type of unique offering.

Maria returned with the twenty-ounce pour of pilsner that looked far bigger than Rowan expected. His first thought was that he would have to nurse his drink through dinner, which never happened on any other occasion. His second thought was that he needed a dinner that would soak up the beer. It had to be something that included a big piece of bread.

"Have you decided on your dinner?" Maria asked as she placed the beer down.

"I'll go with the moose burger, completely dressed with everything, including the mushrooms and bacon."

Maria smiled as she wrote his order on her pad.

"Want a fried egg on top of that?" she asked.

Rowan winced at the recommendation, then changed to a smile.

"No. Thanks." he answered. "I'm on a diet. I have to limit my calories and carbs."

Maria gave him a smile as she ran her eyes up and down his body. She nodded in agreement as she turned to walk away.

While he waited Rowan checked his phone for messages and emails. He watched the video of Claire stumbling in and out of her car several times. The hysterical laughter of both her and her friend behind the camera made the visual even better. He knew it would be story she would tell for decades. He also felt better to learn that Josie was a girl.

There were a number of messages from his Mindy that he decided to set aside. He expected they would be full of *how could yous* that he just did not want to ruin his evening. Another message from Vinnie to thank him for the golf reminded him of the comment he made about his dad's jug wine. He wondered if Sombrero wine would taste good to Vinnie's palate, which was now used to fifty- and one hundred-dollar bottles. Another message was from Dorsey asking if Rowan wanted to stop in to watch the game on Sunday with his family and Nicki's.

The final message was from his protégé, Roger Bailes, saying his wife, Sandy, was disappointed that she could not introduce him to her friend. After finishing the onslaught of messages, Rowan was happy to be at a table, alone, in northwest Pennsylvania, with a cold, fresh glass of micro brewed pilsner.

Rowan was about two-thirds of his way through his beer when his dinner arrived. The plate Maria set in front of him was nicely presented, with his loaded moose burger, cottage fries, and some ketchup and mayonnaise in small metal cups.

"Would you like another pilsner?" she asked.

Rowan smiled, thinking that it was best to not have another one. But he would certainly like one.

"No," he finally answered. "But I would be interested in taking some with me."

Maria nodded and said they sold both cans and sixty-four-ounce glass growlers. Rowan thought about what he had planned and keeping the beer cold. The growler sounded best. But he opted for two six-packs of twenty-ounce cans instead.

"Do you sell this anywhere I can find it?" he asked. "I live in Pittsburgh."

Maria looked to the back of the store before answering.

"We only sell it here," she replied. "I keep telling my brother that he needs to sell it in stores."

Rowan gave a puzzled scowl to her reply. He had seen the syndrome before with his clients. Founders of companies were almost always too mission-passionate to a fault. The positive was that it was a critical attribute for making a great product. But that level of focus also works against business and market development when the passion for perfection keeps the entrepreneur from either delegating responsibilities or taking advantage of opportunities to grow. The end result was always that the business owner tries to do everything, which usually ends with critical business parts being done poorly, if at all. This brew pub reminded him of the Red Sombrero.

"Interesting," he answered, still looking around, still thinking.

"It drives me crazy because we sell all these growlers," Maria said, in an exasperated voice. "People drive here to get them."

"That's good demand."

"He says to grow would ruin the *'art of his brew.'*"

Rowan smiled at the comment. Maria's brother was a perfectionist.

"That's admirable," he replied, trying to instill some comfort.

"Yeah, I guess. But I keep telling him Bud Light didn't go national thinking beer was art."

Maria's comment amused him. Her comparison of an internationally sold, low-margin, mass-produced product to their high-margin, niche product made her point. It also opened a segue to find out more. Rowan asked a few questions he did not know if she could answer. They were typical starter questions he would ask any business that came to him for money to grow. Maria's grasp on the business impressed him. Her ideas for branding, marketing and outreach were impressive and beyond what anyone short of a degree and several years of real-world experience would have.

Rowan left Maria a healthy, bill-doubling tip for her excellent service and insight. In two stops in the sleepy city of Clarion, he had met two impressive young people destined to be successful. He grabbed a paper menu on his way out for the itemized list of their beers and food. As he walked past the front window, he watched Maria check the credit card portfolio for his signature and his tip. Her eyes lit as she studied the numbers.

Looking outside to see him walking past and looking back, she waved with a smile of gratitude. Rowan returned her thanks with a thumbs-up, smile, and nod before he disappeared out-of-sight.

# # # #

Janis smiled when she saw Marnie look at the clock.

"That's the third time you've looked at the clock in the last fifteen minutes. You got a hot date?"

The look on Marnie's face told her best friend that she already knew the answer. After making her dramatic exit from her declaration to Clark about her being good for him, Janis stayed within eyesight, but out of his view, to see how he would handle it, her, and Marnie. It was apparent that his interests were elsewhere. It made her angry that Marnie won the boy again without much more than just being in the room.

"No," Marnie answered, in a snarky tone. "I'm working...not playing like those of you on the other side of the bar."

"Well, it's past seven o'clock, and your boyfriend is nowhere to be seen," Janis answered. "Maybe he came to his senses and hightailed it back to the city."

Marnie sneered at the comment as she wiped the bar in front of her friend.

"You're making a mess here, Janis."

Marnie's voice sounded agitated, which was the exact mood Janis wanted to put her in. At this point, she could both amuse herself by continuing to poke the bear and get some satisfaction that Marnie was not getting Superman either.

"What'd you two do today?" she asked, having watched them fly down the hill in Marnie's Razor toward the creek.

Marnie knew what Janis was insinuating. The pass down to the woods that hosted the creek exited out the back of the Sombrero property near Janis's camp and trailer. The creek was a popular spot for local high school kids to find love in nature, with its moss-covered banks that felt like thick carpet. If Janis took the time to look at the Razor when she heard it passing by, she was able to see who was in it and where it was headed.

"What are you asking me?" Marnie demanded, with a testy bite.

"I'm just sayin' that I saw you two heading out toward the woods and the creek area."

Marnie wiped the area again with a more aggressive swipe of her cloth.

"He asked me to show him the leaves," she answered. "So I took him there."

Janis started to laugh at Marnie's annoyed response. She took a drink of wine to hide her amusement.

"I'm sure you did," she mumbled.

Marnie heard the comment and was willing to let it pass. But when Janis added an eye roll followed by a full smile of accusation, Marnie leaned into the bar so that she could get face-to-face with her friend.

"And, it was great," she said with a tone of victory while looking into Janis's eyes.

Janis's smile evaporated with the mental vision of Marnie and Clark on the moss in the woods. She broke eye contact with her friend to look away.

"That's not nice, Marnie!" she declared in a soft voice.

Marnie pulled back as she wiped her hands with the rag. She could see that her comment hurt her friend, which gave her both a sense of satisfaction and empathy for Janis's disappointment. She knew Janis was more interested in Rowan than she was. Marnie did not want to deal with the drunk fool when he first showed and drank himself into a stupor. Janis spent most of that night with him to get to know him while Marnie butterflied in and out of the conversation as she tended bar.

"I'm sorry," Marnie added with an exhausted air. "Nothing happened. We just went for a ride."

Janis's drooped expression revived to Marnie's confession that their ride out into the woods was, at most, a first date. There was still some hope for her with the city guy they both seemed to find appealing.

"I don't care what you two do," she answered, trying desperately to sound over him.

Marnie's history with Janis, which included many spats over boys, including Marnie's ex-husband, Tom, told her that Janis did care, and that she was pissed that she was behind in the first leg of the race.

"Well, then," Marnie commented, chest tightening, pondering if she should really antagonize her best friend. "You should know I gave him the RIDE OF HIS LIFE... If you know what I mean."

Marnie's fist started punching up and down toward the floor as she walked away with a sinister smile and laugh. Janis gasped at the visual that reappeared in her head of the two of them down in the trees, on the moss.

"Fuck you, Marnie," she replied, before downing what was left in her wineglass. "Bitch."

Marnie stopped near the kitchen to pretend to set some things into place. Although funny at the moment, she felt bad that she had really stuck it to her friend. She knew Rowan would be appearing at some point in the evening. Given the conversation she'd just had with Janis, she was now concerned about her interest in a man ruining her lifelong friendship.

The early crowd at the Sombrero was heavier than usual. The faces that usually appeared around ten o'clock were in their seats by seven-thirty. Marnie looked at the clock on the wall to check the time before looking again at the empty stool in the corner she was holding with a cardboard box set upon it. Twice she had to shoo interested patrons away from the seat, saying it was being held to keep bar access open for the floor patrons.

Janis had disappeared into the crowd to make her rounds with friends. Marnie knew their earlier spat inflicted some pain that she would have to address to make better. The two had a history of going hard at each other, staying mad for a few days, then making up over a laugh. She was not sure if this would be that simple. When she married Tom, Janis stood with her at the wedding then disappeared for six months.

"This seat taken?" a deep, male voice asked from the other side of the bar.

Its sound and tone were familiar, causing Marnie's stomach to tighten and breath to momentarily stop. She hesitated before turning, trying first to regain an aloof composure she thought was right for where they were in their friendship.

"Oh," she stated, as she stood on her toes to look at the box on the stool, "No wonder no one has been sitting there. They left that stupid box."

"Then it's okay?" Rowan asked again.

Marnie was caught with an empty mind, numb at the sight of him.

"Marnie?"

The jerk of her body to his call made him smile. He could see she was flustered by the situation. The look on the faces of the people in the stools next to his said she had shooed away people and that he was the special snowflake with a reserved seat at the bar.

As Marnie's ability to think returned, she looked at Rowan as he reached to pick up the box that was holding the stool for him. His initial test of its weight gave him confidence he could hand it across the bar for Marnie to store.

"Barstools are cash flow," Rowan stated, as he sat in his reserved seat. "There should be a butt in each one, with a full glass in front of them."

Marnie replied with a smile that said she did not need a lecture from him. She then began to chuckle as she looked at her city man wearing his new clothes, that still showed their factory fold marks, settle into his reserved spot.

"I've been waiting for a big spender to show up," she replied, noting a small red sticker marked XL on his shirt pocket.

Rowan smiled as Marnie approached. He appreciated the gesture and was looking forward to the evening to both talk with her and observe the business she ran. His experience in retail lending was limited. Restaurant and bar lending were almost nonexistent at his bank. But he did know that any business that dealt with cash and goods that could be either given away or stolen out the back door had high risk for failure.

"Can I open a tab.... Please?" he asked, handing his platinum American Express across the counter.

Marnie smiled as she accepted his credit card, thinking this piece of what appeared to be aluminum could solve all her financial problems in one swipe. Its owner seemed anxious to help.

"You know, Clark," Marnie replied, feeling a bit flirty. "The processing charge on American Express is double Visa and Mastercard. You got something else?"

Rowan gave a puzzled look as he leaned forward to get his money clip. The silver monogrammed clip contained about ten folded bills with a twenty showing on the outside. It was attached to a small leather pouch with plastic showing out of one end. He pinched the contents and pulled out his driver's license, a card that looked like his health insurance card, and a Mastercard debit card. He handed the debit card to Marnie as she returned his American Express. The difference in weight between the two was considerable.

"I can also pay cash," he added, knowing there were no processing fees, and likely no taxes, on cash transactions. "But you'll have to trust me."

Marnie handed back the debit card with a determined sneer that said she was going to win the trust game.

"No can do, Clark. I know you big-city types," she said as she fiddled her hands below the bar as if doing something important. "I can take some of those bills in your clip and hold them against your tab. We can settle up at the end."

Rowan looked at the young couple beside him that had stopped talking to listen to his negotiation with the bartender. A lift of his eyebrows and nod was his request for their opinion on whether he should risk losing his cash and trust the feisty woman behind the bar.

The smile on the woman's face, combined with her boyfriend's nod to go for it, brought a smile to his face as he turned to accept her terms.

"You run a tough negotiation there, miss," he said, as he handed Marnie four twenty-dollar bills.

Marnie took the cash and, for spite, counted it in front of him.

"You don't trust me?" he asked. "I trust you."

Marnie stopped and looked at him. As she leaned into and across the bar, her hand approaching him, Rowan felt his breathing tighten. The touch on his chest, at first, felt like a snarky poke. But when he felt the fabric of his shirt pull away along with the sound and feel of a sticker being removed, he knew he had missed one of the labels from his purchases earlier.

"I'm still sizing you up," Marnie replied, as she stuck the XL sticker to one of the twenties. "Bottom line is that I'll still be here tomorrow, next week, next month. You, on the other hand, could disappear as fast as you came. I'm NOT getting stuck with the bill again by a guy willing to overpay for clothes at Langer's."

Marnie's message was clear. She had a wall up to keep from being hurt by a man who appeared from the darkness and could disappear again. She placed a bottle of Dervish Red in front of him along with a glass. Her first pour was a healthy five fingers. When she put the bottle down, she picked up his glass as if to hand it to him. When her lips touched its rim, she was looking right into his eyes. The Dervish Red was her favorite. She was still on the fence about Superman.

Rowan sat silent as Marnie returned his glass to the bar. In one swallow, she had taken half its contents as a throw down. Not to be outdone, Rowan picked up the glass without taking his eyes off hers. He pulled the remaining Dervish Red from the glass to confirm to her that he was not a fly-by-night, wham-bam-thank-you-ma'am visitor.

Marnie gave a half smile and nod to show her satisfaction with his gesture as he returned the glass to the bar. She knew others were waiting for bar service and that she had to leave. Both of them had lost awareness of the couple that was enjoying their dance as entertainment. A quick smile and turn sent her message that things were in a good place. Rowan spun in his chair to survey the crowd as she walked away. He accepted and laughed at a fist-bump from the man next to him as congratulations for a game well played.

Janis became jealous as she watched the banter between Marnie and Rowan from outside the glass windows to the back deck. In her mind, she should have been next to Rowan, with Marnie somewhere off in the distance. The lights on the tables near the glass that separated the deck from the bar area kept her in the darkness with a clear line of sight to the bar. She thought his new look, trying to fit in, was cute and fun. That only added to her fury that Marnie could win his attention just by being there.

In situations past that involved a common interest in a man, Janis would just walk away. Marnie always got what she wanted; there was no hope in challenging her. All of the others were not worth a fight. Marnie's ex-husband, Tom, was a perfect example. They were both interested in him when Marnie returned from California. All she had to do was smile at him and the game was over. But Rowan was different. They both could sense it. She, therefore, could not just give in.

"Hey stranger," Janis said, as she appeared next to Rowan from behind.

"Janis," he replied. 'Where have you been? You disappeared last week and never came back."

Janis gave a look of disbelief to the honesty in his statement. He obviously had not missed her after she left. The fact that she took care of him the first night, when he drank too much, meant nothing.

"I've been around," she answered. "I just try to be where I'm wanted."

An immediate feeling of guilt hit him as he thought back through their last time together. Rowan knew he was not interested in Janis, and this was not based on her appearance. Janis was an attractive woman. Her level of sophistication compared with any other woman in the bar, including Marnie. But Marnie had a special spunk and spirit that he wanted to feed on. It was free and untamed. Janis's fire seemed constrained to always having been there, in Legend.

"You must really think I'm an asshole," he stated, knowing the answer and wanting to see if she would confirm it.

Janis smiled at his self-accusation. He was more aware than she expected he would be.

"Don't mess with me, Rowan," she said. "I'm not in the mood, and it's clear to me who you're interested in."

Rowan involuntarily looked to the kitchen for Marnie. She had left the bar to go to the production area minutes earlier. Rowan expected her to return with another hand truck full of wine.

"What do you think makes one person more attractive than others even when you don't know them?" he replied. "I mean, have you ever walked into a room and been totally captivated by someone across the room just by their look? Or by the way they look at you?"

As she watched him take a drink of wine, Janis thought he seemed to have impressed himself with his ponderance. She knew who he was talking about. She saw it in his face the moment he sat on the stool and started talking with her and Marnie for the first time, a week earlier.

Janis decided it was better for her to let Rowan's question stand unanswered. After a short smile to show she both heard him and knew she had no chance, she lifted her glass of white wine to her mouth and looked off into the crowd. It was her hope that looking away would not show the welling she could feel building in her eyes. She prayed no tears would run.

"Oh, there's Lauren," Janis lied, as she sat taller to look into the crowd. "I have to talk to her. I'll be back."

Janis collected her drink and her clutch bag. Had Rowan been interested in her, her quick departure with her wine glass and clutch would have said she was not coming back. Janis gave a quick look back with a toast of her glass before weaving into the crowd. In a matter of seconds, Rowan lost sight of her, then he turned back to look for Marnie.

"City man," a familiar male voice stated a man sat next to him on Janis's stool. "I think I owe you a glass for giving me a ride today."

Rowan recognized the voice before focusing in on the figure beside him. Cousin Dave had a twist in his accent that was distinctly his.

"So, you like my Dervish Red?" he asked, pointing to the bottle.

The blue bottle was distinctive in itself. But the labeling added flair. Although printed, it looked to be handwritten in a sub-par calligraphy effort around a fuzzy photograph of a man in a white suit and funky thimble-shaped hat.

"That's me," Cousin Dave stated, placing his index finger on the label's picture. "It took a long time to get Marnie to put me on the bottle."

Rowan looked at the label, then at Cousin Dave. He was out of uniform, sitting in an equally interesting camouflage coverall. A thought came to Rowan's mind he had to express.

"Dervish Red is a red wine," he said, then stopped to let this sink in. "Your Whirling Dervish outfit is white...with a canvas-colored hat."

"And that bothers you?"

"No," Rowan replied. "Just the symmetry between it all seems a little...whack."

Rowan was puzzled by his own word choice as it came out his mouth. Although representing what he wanted to say, he thought it was a little bit harsh and not his usual vernacular.

Cousin Dave nodded to Rowan's observation as he looked at the chalkboard wine list.

"The entire universe *is* whack. It's bound up too tight in structure." he started, still staring at the wine list before turning his eyes toward Rowan. "Asymmetry, now that's how you make it interesting...and healthy. You don't always have to go with the flow."

The look on Cousin Dave's face showed that he was coming from a deeper stream of consciousness. But he was right.

Rowan's life conformed to the norms of the cultured world. As a result, he was very successful and had two wonderful children. But in retrospect, it seemed kind of empty as he thought through the wonderful, but generic, times he had now with his kids, wife, and friends. The most exhilarating moments he could recall were skiing down a Colorado mountainside, wanting to push harder before pulling back because of a fear of falling and injury; and running in the Razor with Marnie less than twelve hours earlier.

"Starting with a blue bottle of table red that carries a label of a man in a white costume?"

"It's not about changing the outside. It's about being fulfilled by what's inside and around you."

Rowan immediately looked off down the bar toward the production room for Marnie. He found her stacking some new inventory behind the bar on the far end. Within a second of his watching, she turned to look back at him, and her face lit up. As her eyes fixated on his, she smiled briefly before returning to finish her work.

"I don't know, Cousin Dave. Life's obligations make living an asymmetrical life seem impossible."

The next fifteen minutes was a one-sided conversation as Cousin Dave worked through his theories supported by his own life history as to how he ended up in Legend. To Rowan's surprise, Cousin Dave disclosed he was from a mill town area of Pittsburgh. He grew up in a stable home, His father worked in an office job at the steel mills while his mother worked in a local store.

Rowan's first impression of Cousin Dave was that he was the local crazy, born and raised within a quad ride of the Red Sombrero. He was right in his guess that Cousin Dave was about his age, despite the fact that his weathered skin made him look older. Cousin Dave was married and divorced early, and said he regretted never having children. Rowan chuckled at that comment wondering what Cousin Dave's children would be like.

Cousin Dave's word choices and observations suggested that he was either a well-read or well-educated man. Rowan was not surprised to hear that he had not only earned a bachelor's degree from the University of Pittsburgh, but he also possessed a master's degree in special education from nearby Slippery Rock University.

"You were a teacher?" Rowan asked, seeing a quality in Cousin Dave that he remembered from his favorite teachers as a child.

"Special ed," he answered. "Loved every part of dealing with the kids."

"But..."

"The fucking ladder-climbing administration, the mountain of bullshit paperwork, and the overdemanding, ungrateful parents who wanted everything to happen in a snap, killed it for me."

Cousin Dave smacked his hand on the bar. Marnie looked over to see what caused the noise, then at Rowan. Her concern told him that he had to be careful.

"But the kids?" Rowan offered as an open question to redirect Cousin Dave's thinking.

"The kids," he answered, nodding his head as a smile appeared. "With all their demons and problems, they were amazing. It was just all of the fucking do-gooders, with all their systems and structure, that wanted to get them to 'fit'... TO CONFORM... to their norms that created all of the problems."

"Square pegs into round holes?"

"Exactly."

Cousin Dave returned to a peaceful state as the city man began to show understanding of his objections to the career it seemed he abandoned. Marnie checked on the two men from a distance to ensure things did not get out of hand. The hand slap was alarming. But she knew Rowan's problem-solving nature would allow him to listen to Cousin Dave's rants without inciting anything.

"So you moved here…"

Cousin Dave finished his story. He retired from teaching early, having had enough. He said he missed the work with the troubled children he served but mentally, he had to get away. Legend, Pennsylvania was not the destination he chose when he decided to separate. Rather, it was a place that found him. A weekend visit to a family camp nearby to celebrate a graduation introduced Legend to him. Outside of a few trips back to Pittsburgh to move and visit family, he never returned to the city he left. His new identity was forged that graduation weekend when his cousin, who owned the camp, introduced him to his friends in the area as his *cousin Dave*. The name stuck.

"Cousin Dave," Marnie said, approaching behind the bar. "I don't know what you two are talking about, but don't scare him."

Marnie's eyes shifted from Cousin Dave to Rowan as she finished her declaration. A slight smile appeared on her face as she leaned into the bar.

"I'm glad to hear that I'm liked and that you want me to hang around," he whispered, as if sharing a secret.

Marnie pulled back from her lean. She was trying to be coy. But through that, her underlying feelings began to show.

"You pay cash, Clark," she replied, in a snarky voice. "Cash customers are gold."

"And?" he said, egging her on.

Marnie looked at him, puzzled as to what he wanted to hear. She realized that she had never really thanked him for his successful intervention in the repossession effort. She knew Tom's tactic would have been more physical than Rowan's. As a creative soul, Marnie could not decide which she found sexier.

"And...for your help in solving unexpected problems."

Unexpected? Rowan thought. There is nothing unexpected when the repo man shows up.

"And..." Rowan said with a sinister smile, tilting his head. "The ride in the quad."

Marnie smiled as she shook her head. His face looked too cute, and too attractive, not to want to kiss.

"Jesus," she finally gave in. "It's a Razor. A quad is a four-wheeler motorcycle."

Rowan's quick tweak of his head asked for more.

"You were a competent driver," Marnie finally surrendered.

Rowan smacked his hand on the bar as he leaned back to the point of almost toppling off his stool. He quickly looked to Cousin Dave to see if he was still listening, then back at Marnie.

"And?" Rowan asked again, egging her on further with a big smile.

Marnie exhaled as what he was looking for came to mind. Her smile was half appreciation and half embarrassment to mention in public.

"You're a good kisser," she mumbled, trying not to see if Cousin Dave was paying attention.

Rowan slapped both hands on the bar then backhanded a soft slap on Cousin Dave's arm. Marnie's expression showed both embarrassment and relief to have confessed her physical attraction to the city man.

"Damn, boy." Cousin Dave shouted. "Marnie's in love! Let's celebrate."

Marnie gave a brief chuckle as she squinted in disbelief. Cousin Dave's glass and Rowan's bottle of Dervish Red were empty. She knew Cousin Dave was using the situation to get some free wine.

"Let's do that," Rowan said, loving Marnie's appreciation for his kiss, as well as the opportunity to pump more cash into the Red Sombrero. "Take it out of my cash reserve behind the register."

Rowan looked at Cousin Dave, knowing he was fishing for a free bottle of wine. As Marnie reached to blindly grab another bottle of Dervish Red, his eyes shifted back to find her still looking at him. Rowan's smug face showed he knew he had hooked her.

"What's going on here?" Janis asked, reemerging from the crowd.

Rowan's face went flat as she ran her eyes through the three people in the conversation she had just entered. The panicked look on Marnie's face told her everything she did not want to hear.

Janis's smile dropped along with the rest of her posture. Marnie slowly placed Rowan's fresh bottle of wine softly onto the bar. Her eyes stayed locked on her best friend's hurt stare back at her.

"What'd you do, Marnie?" Janis said in a soft, angry voice. "What'd you two do down in the trees?"

Rowan stood to take hold of Janis's arm. He felt stuck in an awkward crossfire that was about to erupt between two lifelong friends. He was beginning to wonder if he was even interested in hanging around for any length of time. More than that, he began to wonder if his interest in Marnie was just curiosity, or if it had a deeper connection to it.

"Janis," he said. "Nothing happened between me and Marnie."

Janis jerked her arm away from his hand.

"What makes you think I care about anything between you and her?" she asked, obviously hurt. "You'll just come and go, like all the others."

The jab was as much to put Clark in his place as it was to sting Marnie back into reality. Marnie continued to stand still as her eyes stayed locked on her friend.

"Janis," Rowan said. "Take a stool. Sit with us. We're all just friends."

Cousin Dave stood from his stool and backed away. He took the stool next to his, which was empty, and repositioned both to a good social distance between friends.

"Come on, Janis," Marnie implored.

Marnie's request and eyes were her way to seek forgiveness. Janis had seen it before from high school up to the time she married Tom. Janis could feel the pressure of tears building behind her eyes. She knew she did not want to cry. It would be embarrassing in front of Clark. Worse, it would give Marnie a higher level of victory.

"Do I get a glass?" she asked.

Her question put a smile on Marnie's face as she reached back for a glass. Rowan eased back onto his stool to create room and to invite Janis to sit with them. Cousin Dave watched as Marnie filled Janis's glass with a healthy four-finger pour. Before she set the bottle back down onto the bar, he pushed his glass forward. Marnie laughed as she looked at his eager face. Cousin Dave's eyes were focused on the glass, waiting for his portion of sweet Dervish Red.

Chapter 8

"Marnie?" Rowan called from the bar area.

Marnie stood silently as she finished an informal count of what she had left for the weekend. Concerned about her waning supply, she ran her fingers through her hair.

"Marnie?" Rowan called again. "Marnie?"

"What!?" she called back, knowing it was Rowan but irritated that he kept calling for her.

Marnie's glare back out into the kitchen fell away when Rowan appeared in the doorway. His presence helped move her angst away from the dwindling supply around her.

"Janis needs to go home," he said. "I'm going to drive her to her trailer and come back."

Rowan was uncertain how Marnie would respond to that gesture. She knew Janis got handsy when she was drunk and certainly had an interest in Rowan. But even with the threat that her jealous friend might make a pass at him, Marnie just stood in the middle of the storeroom. Her mind was more captivated by her wine problem than her concern that Rowan might be persuaded to stay with her best friend.

"Marnie?" he asked again.

Marnie gave a flustered shake as she came back into the moment. She looked to see Rowan staring at her. She knew he was looking for permission for something. She just could not recall what it was.

"That's fine," she finally answered, hoping that was the right thing to say.

Rowan smiled to see she was comfortable with him taking Janis home. He then watched as she evaporated back into thought.

"I'll miss you," he said glibly, to invite a smile.

Marnie did not respond. Her eyes were glossed over as she scanned the boxes around her.

"Marnie?" Rowan called again, to bring her back.

Marnie's eyes closed as she took a deep breath.

"Is something wrong?" he asked.

"No," she answered. "Just go do what you need to do."

Rowan walked toward her, curious to get a better look and to lend some support. When he reached to touch her arm, she instinctively pulled away as she mentally dealt with the issue of the rest of the weekend with a limited supply of wine.

"I can help you. I want to help you."

Marnie smiled as she listened to his uninformed offer.

"Can you make five cases of wine?" she asked. "We're going to run out. And that means..."

"...a big hit on sales and cash flow." Rowan finished for her.

Marnie's eyes began to tear as she stared at half the boxes that should have been there.

"Let me take Janis home. When I get back, we'll figure this out."

Marnie allowed Rowan to put his arm around her. As he pulled her in for a hug, he felt the tension in her body hold then release. The heat from her body felt good against his. He stroked her hair as she buried her face in his chest. Rowan finished his comforting with a light kiss on the top of her head.

As he released Marnie and turned to walk toward the door, he felt guilty about leaving her hurting. But he knew taking Janis out of the picture would help Marnie work with a clearer head while getting Janis home safely.

"Drive her back in my Razor," Marnie said, as he walked through the doorway. "She can walk back for hers tomorrow."

Rowan smiled to confirm her suggestion. The image of Janis walking back through the trees, suffering with the effects of *wine flu*, with her hair tousled, was too much to keep him from a light laugh. He pointed his finger at Marnie to thank her for the amusing thought before disappearing back through the bar.

# # # #

Janis was standing, ready to go, when Rowan appeared.

"Marnie give her permission?" she asked.

"Yes," he answered. "And the keys to her Razor. She said you can walk back for yours tomorrow."

Janis's shoulders were feeling heavy from the wine. Her mouth felt numb and was concerned that her speech was slurring.

"OR!" she declared. "We could take mine...and you could walk back tomorrow morning."

Janis leaned into Rowan as she made her proposition. Rowan looked at her current state, thinking *She will be asleep the minute she hits her bed.*

"Let's go Janis," he said, putting his hand on her shoulder to turn her toward the door.

As they headed out, Rowan surveyed the tables to find Tom staring at him. There was a look of disapproval in his eyes that said he thought Rowan was leaving with Janis to cheat on Marnie. Tom stood as the two approached his table by the door.

"Hey, Tom," Rowan said, seeing Tom move toward him. "I need to talk to you when I get back."

"Tonight?" Tom answered, moving his eyes back and forth between Rowan and Janis.

Rowan rolled his eyes as he smiled.

"Five minutes," he said.

"You can last longer than five minutes, can't you?" Janis asked as she leaned into him.

Tom's face showed he found no humor in her comment. Rowan shook his head quickly to confirm he would be back at the Sombrero in five minutes.

"Come on, Clark," Janis said as she grabbed his hand and began to walk toward the front door.

Tom stepped aside to let them leave. As Rowan passed, Tom did a quick scan of Rowan's clothing. He could tell by the pressed appearance of his shirt and pants that they were new. The city dude was trying to fit in, which he appreciated. His concern, however, was how his presence was going to affect Marnie.

# # # #

The Razor started with a louder engine noise than he remembered from his afternoon ride. Neither Rowan nor Janis bothered to belt themselves in for the short drive back to her trailer. The moonlight offered some assistance to the limited headlights on Marnie's buggy.

"You remember where I live?" Janis asked.

Rowan smiled at the memory of her humble abode in the trees. He shook his head to the recall of her dog, Travis, climbing up into the bed he had slept in.

As they arrived on the gravel driveway that circled in front of the trailer, Rowan guided the Razor toward the front door, guided by single, yellow door lamp Janis left lit.

"Only one light?" he asked.

Janis put her hand on his right shoulder as she leaned into him. Rowan could feel her breasts rubbing against his arm.

"What are you afraid of? BEARS!?"

Janis's quick elevation in voice startled Rowan. Her laughter at his reaction told him that he had to walk her back carefully, without putting himself in a position for her to make any moves on him.

As they walked to the door, Janis leaned on him for balance and guidance she did not need. It was an old trick she used to get men from their car into the trailer. Once inside, she would ask them to just help her lie down in bed. Most often, if she got that far, she won the battle and had a breakfast date.

"Rowan," she asked. "Can you help me inside? The steps are loose, and it's dark."

Rowan had planned to escort Janis to the front door to ensure she got inside her home safely. She played the role of the helpless damsel perfectly as they took each step through the driveway then up onto the porch. Rowan was surprised that Janis's trailer was unlocked as they walked in.

"Aren't you afraid of someone stealing anything? Waiting for you?"

"Nah," she answered. "I'm more concerned with them..."

Janis stopped her comment. Finishing with *getting away* would clue Rowan into her tactic to steal him from Marnie.

"Can you help me back to my bedroom?" she asked.

Rowan gave her an uncertain look as he redirected them down the hallway.

"Wait!" Janis exclaimed, stopping next to the bathroom. "I have to pee."

Janis started laughing with her confession. She slid through the half-opened door and closed it behind her. Rowan's first thought was that it was a perfect opportunity for him to leave.

"Don't you leave me, Rowan," she called out, as he heard her peeing into the toilet. "I don't want to fall in here and get stuck all night."

Rowan knew she was playing him but felt guilty to think about leaving. The sounds behind the closed door went silent. He waited to hear the water run as she washed her hands, brushed her teeth, or finished her day with some other noise-generating bathroom activity. But after waiting for another minute, he began to grow concerned and knocked.

"Janis?" he called out, to get no reply.

After another minute passed that included two more knocks and calls, Rowan turned the handle on the door to check on her. His fear was that he was going to find her naked waiting to throw herself on him. He was pleasantly surprised when she came into view, passed-out on the toilet with her yoga pants and panties down around her ankles.

Rowan's first thought was to leave. Janis was adequately propped up between the wall and the side of the vanity. She was slumped forward into a position he knew would be painful in the morning. A little bit of bobbing up and down showed that she was still breathing.

As he started to close the door on the problem, guilt came over him. He could not leave her asleep on the toilet. He slowly reopened the door to check out the figure that remained as he had left her.

As Rowan stepped close to her, he debated whether it would be best to wake her or to pick her up. Each had its plusses and minuses. Waking her could reignite her. Her pants were already down to her ankles. She could step out easily and make a play for him.

The other option was to lift her. Looking at her, he concluded she was chunky but not heavy. Rowan felt he could lift her the way he used to lift his kids without waking them. The size difference created problems for the door and hallway. He knew it would be easier with her yoga pants and panties either pulled up or taken off. He thought through the possible complications of doing both.

"Janis!" he said sternly, while shaking her shoulder.

Janis woke with a snort to look at him adoringly.

"Clark," she answered, with a twinkle in her eye, before falling back asleep.

Clark shook her again with no success. He knew his question about how to move her had just been answered.

Rowan took Janis's left ankle in his hand and lifted her foot to remove her yoga pants. He was afraid that his kneeling position in front of her while she was asleep on the toilet would raise serious questions with unbelievable answers if she were to wake up. After putting her foot back onto the floor, he waited to see if she was waking. A quick snort and adjustment of her head gave him a firm indication she could sleep through much more. He repeated the task with her left leg getting no reaction. He did a double check to ensure she was still breathing.

The lift from the toilet seat was going to be dicey. He needed her upper body to nest into this right arm and chest as his left arm cradled her knees. He started to giggle as he positioned both arms just before the initial lift.

Janis was lighter than he expected and lifted easily. Her upper body rolled into his as her knees became awkward to hold. He could feel her smoothly shaved leg with his hand as her naked bum pressed against his crotch with each step he took.

Please don't wake up was all he could think as he made his way through the bathroom door and down the hall.

The doorway to the bedroom swung into the room toward the front wall of the trailer. Janis's head was leading her body as Rowan sidestepped down the hall. He knew he would have to pivot her through the door to avoid both the door frame and dresser that he could see. His fear was waking her by a knocking either her feet or head into the wall. He started to laugh as he studied his options to get her into the room.

Rowan could feel Janis slipping in his arms as he backed into the room, concentrating on each move to ensure neither her head nor her feet hit anything. When he turned to face the bed, it was just as he expected. The cover was old, white, and flowery. The head was loaded with pillows of various sizes, shapes, and colors. Each pillow had a mate. Rowan shook his head in disbelief as he started to lower Janis onto her bed.

The transfer from his arms to the bed was always a problem when Rowan would put his kids into their cribs. There was a point where he had to remove his hand from behind their heads that always ended with eyes opening and tears flowing. He thought about that upcoming dismount for Janis so that he could exit safely.

The first point of contact went without issue as her naked bottom landed on the bedspread. Her next touch point was her feet, leaving her knees bent. His kids never had that challenge. The final task was to place her head on a pillow. He slowly bent as her body relaxed onto the bedspread. After carefully pulling his arms away, Rowan stood upright to stretch his back. The task was completed successfully.

The warm grab and pull on his hand startled him. When he looked down, he saw Janis's eyes half open looking back at him. In his head, he started counting down from five. At three her hand let go and fell to her side. By one, her eyes were shut again. Rowan took a blanket from the foot of the bed to cover her. As he positioned the blanket under her chin, he ran his hand over her hair and gave her a light kiss on her forehead. She was going to feel like shit in the morning. And it was time for him to go.

# # # #

The parking lot was clearing out as Rowan brought the Razor back through the trees to the Sombrero. He'd lost track of time while dealing with Janis and getting her to bed. He knew it was either nearly closing time or that closing was happening as he arrived.

The brighter lights turned on after closing hurt his eyes as he opened the front door. Despite having downed nearly three bottles of Dervish Red with Cousin Dave and Janis, Rowan was feeling close to sober as he walked back into the bar.

"Five minutes, huh?" Tom said, as he sat by himself at his table.

Rowan turned to his question with a puzzled look.

"It took longer than I expected," he answered. "Janis was really drunk."

The sound of the wood legs scraping across the wood floor sounded louder than they should have. Tom stood slowly, keeping his eyes on Rowan. The look in his eyes was signaling that he was going to inflict some harm. His clenched hands, along with the three empty blue wine bottles on his table, told Rowan that Tom's target was him.

"What's going on here Tom?" Rowan said, while starting to drift back and raise his hands. "You know Marnie and I are just friends, nothing more."

"This ain't about Marnie," he answered. "It's about you disrespecting the women here."

Tom's comment confused Rowan. He knew he had to think quickly to solve Tom's fury before it erupted on him.

Tom and Rowan stood about the same height. But Tom's physique was thicker, stronger, and more tested in physical confrontation than Rowan's. Rowan started to think of questions he could ask to defuse the situation before Tom landed his first punch.

"Help me out, here, Tom," he started, still sifting questions in his head. "I'm trying to be helpful. Helpful with the vendor today. Helpful to get Janis to bed..."

Rowan stopped midsentence, having realized the cause of Tom's anger. The city man had arrived to distract the women with sophistication and money while, at the same time, two-timing both of them without the other knowing.

"Tom, Janis passed out in the Razor on the way back to her trailer," Rowan lied. "I tried to wake her up. But she would have slept in the thing had I just walked away."

The mental image of Janis passed out in Marnie's Razor stopped Tom's forward motion.

"What'd you do?"

"You mean after taking five minutes to think about what I could do?" Rowan replied, trying to fill time in the timetable but regretting leaving open the possibility of Tom thinking anything sexual. "I carried her into the house."

Rowan could see Tom processing his story. He knew he was thinking through what it would take, and how long, to get Janis into her trailer.

"Where'd you put her?" Tom asked.

Rowan started to reply that he had just put her into bed. But as he started to compile his word, he remembered that Janis was now asleep in her bed without pants and panties. Janis was a talker. Although she would have no recollection of anything from the bathroom to her bed, she was going to wake up half naked, wondering what happened and how she got there. Janis would want answers. Marnie would be her sounding board. And Tom would certainly hear through the grapevine.

"Well, and this is kinda funny," Rowan answered, hoping to lighten the tension. "As I carried her from her living room down that tight hall, her dog ran by causing me to stumble…"

Rowan paused to see if his story was sinking in, and whether Tom was buying any of it.

"Did you fall?" Tom asked, still processing the vision of what had happened.

Rowan laughed, as he continued to compile his story.

"Just into the wall, which woke Janis," he answered. "That was when she said she had to go to the bathroom."

Tom's posture began to relax as Rowan told his story. He was content to listen to the play-by-play as Rowan carried Janis into her trailer until he realized what he thought happened still had a chance to happen.

"And…" Tom asked, throwing his hands forward to demand the rest of the story.

"I took my opportunity to leave," Rowan answered, thanking Tom in his head for the easy out to the story. "I called through the door to say I was leaving. She said good-night."

Janis surrendering a man she wanted in the hallway to her bedroom was not something that seemed believable. Tom was beginning to think Rowan was bullshitting him.

"I had to get out of there, man," Rowan pleaded. "I was heading out the door when she stumbled out of the bathroom. I didn't look back."

Rowan's sincerity sold Tom that he was telling the truth. Both men knew that Tom's protective instinct kicked in because he thought Rowan's intentions with the women he loved was improper. He knew he and Marnie were over. She threw him out. And he was not looking to go back. But he still loved her deeply. He knew she would find someone he would have to accept. Rowan's background and timely arrival seemed suspicious. Tom exhaled and closed his eyes to relax.

"I'm sorry, man," he said, embarrassed and shaking his head.

"Don't stress over it," Rowan answered. "I'm kinda thankful you're watching over the girls. God knows they both need it."

Tom smiled at Rowan's compliment.

"Ain't that the fucking truth," he answered.

As Tom made his way for the door, Rowan turned to go find Marnie. After searching the bar area, he moved outside to the deck, where he saw tables full of uncleared glasses, bottles, and debris along with a familiar silhouette sitting in an Adirondack chair by one of the still-burning fire pits.

Rowan walked quietly, to sneak up on her from behind.

"I couldn't deal with it," Marnie said into the air, when he was within two steps of her.

"How'd you know I was back here?"

Rowan threw three pieces of wood onto the fire. He knew they would be there for a while. After positioning the wood to burn, he extended his hand to Marnie to ask her to stand. After shaking her head no to his offer, he reached to take hold and pulled her to her feet. As she shuffled to gain her balance, he took her place in her chair then tapped his lap for him to join him.

"What are you doing?" she whined, wanting desperately to cuddle with him.

"Just sit with me."

Marnie made a small move toward him then pulled back. She was wondering if he was serious about being there for her or just trying to take advantage of her in her moment of weakness.

"I've got to finish cleaning this place up. Then figure out what to do with the wine shortage. And the money shortage."

"Where's the wait staff?" Rowan asked, choosing the smallest issue to distract her.

"I sent them home. You know...wages?"

Rowan nodded, agreeing with Marnie's decision to send the wait staff home instead of paying them to stay. Cash was a scarce commodity at the Sombrero. He appreciated the fact that Marnie was now recognizing that fact.

"Leave it. I'll meet you here tomorrow morning around ten and we can knock it out before you open. The rest is all solvable."

Marnie felt a warm relief wash through her body. Not only would she have help to clean up the mess that was going to ripen overnight, but Rowan implied that he was heading back to his cabin to sleep. Marnie reached for his hand, which was laying on the arm of the chair, as she moved to sit on his lap. The warmth of her body radiated into his as she settled her head on his right shoulder.

"Thank you, Clark," she said, with a slight smile he could not see. "You've really been my Superman today. Although I wasn't quite sure if you were going to survive Tom."

Rowan adjusted his body as Marnie finished her observation.

"You watched Tom coming at me? And did nothing?"

Marnie reached to pull him closer to her.

"I did...through the glass. Heard everything too."

"Seriously?" Rowan asked. "Did you not see that he was about to kick my ass out the door!?"

"I was actually hoping he would," Marnie confessed. "I mean, you were gone a long time. What was I supposed to think?"

"I don't know, Marnie," he moaned, irritated to think what she was willing to let happen. "Maybe *what a great guy he is to help my friend*?"

Marnie squeezed tighter to hold him closer.

"That trip takes five minutes," she answered. "You were gone over twenty."

Rowan shook his head in disbelief that she was keeping tabs on his whereabouts. The woman he pursued to spend the day with, kissed, and helped with her business problem, had just accused him of getting a quickie with her drunk best friend. He was seriously reconsidering his offer to help clean in the morning.

"What do you think of me, Marnie?" He wanted to take her temperature on where she was in their evolving friendship and relationship.

"What do you mean?"

"What did you think of me when we first met? City stiff? Arrogant asshole?"

Marnie smiled as she relaxed in his lap to think about his question. She could not answer it honestly. That would open too many additional things she did not want to have put on her plate. She could not think of a good answer to his question.

"What did you think of me?" she asked, to have him open up first. "Country bumpkin barmaid?"

Rowan took a deep breath as he smiled and put his arms around her. He knew she was dodging his question which is what he had to do with her, for the same reason.

"I thought you had a nice bum," he whispered, tightening his hold on her.

Marnie's body straightened as her belly laugh echoed out into the valley.

"That's funny," she replied as she sat up. "I thought you had a nice bum too."

"And that's not even my best feature," he answered with an insinuating smile.

Marnie smacked her hand lightly on his chest as she nestled back onto him. Their fire was fading from its initial roar and they both fell silent to enjoy their confessions while watching the flames dance.

"I'm really glad you're here," she whispered. "I thought you were just hitting on me to get me into bed."

Rowan tightened his arms around her as he thought about how to reply.

"Well, I'm not going to lie," he answered, making Marnie begin to stir, expecting to hear something bad. "I have thought about you...and me...and that... But..."

Rowan paused, unable to finish his thought.

"But, what?"

"If that happens with us, I want it to be really special...not just some romp to regret later."

Marnie could feel her eyes start to well as she worked to hold off a smile. He said what she was feeling perfectly. She snuggled in a bit more to make sure he was real and could not go anywhere.

"Me, too," she answered.

Her confession to him released all her tension to a comfort she just wanted to ride as far as it would carry. He was the first man she felt would be honest with her, respect her, and understand her for who she was. She wished she had a blanket by the fire so they could just stay and sleep there together until morning.

Chapter 9

A morning mist had settled around the Sombrero and flowed out into the fields that held the fire pits. Seven hours earlier, Rowan had said goodnight to Marnie in the parking lot. Both were showing signs of not wanting to leave the other. But they both wanted to hold true to Rowan's wish. Doing so meant their first night together would have to be on another night. Their last touch was a hug in the parking lot. Rowan gave her a kiss on the top her head that was less than gratifying for both of them. But it was right for the moment.

Rowan pulled his Audi to the front door to take the best parking space he had since he started patronizing the Red Sombrero two weeks earlier. The fresh dew that rested on the front doorknob caused his hand to slip when he pulled to find it still locked. It was unlike Marnie to be late. But recalling the mess they left on the back deck and presumably around the firepits, Rowan knew he could get started on the outside while waiting for Marnie to arrive to open the inside.

The outside service and prep area on the covered porch were left open. Rowan found large black plastic bags to carry around as he picked up debris. What was left around the firepits was not as much as he expected. The covered and adjoining open deck was another story.

Rowan smiled as he looked at the trash that was around the chair where he and Marnie had sat. His memory of a clean, healthy, and romantic setting evaporated after looking at a scene that was a few beer cans short of a landfill.

"Good morning," came from behind him as he was picking up some spent wine bottles.

Her voice was raspy and tired. Despite her obvious exhaustion, Rowan could see a warm glow in her face that said she was happy to be there and, more so, happy to see him.

"How do you feel this morning?" he asked as he approached her.

Marnie straightened her back and squinted back at him.

"I feel like I need a hug," she answered.

Rowan slowly dropped the bags he was holding to walk to her. As he took her in his, her arms stayed at her side until they slowly lifted to return his embrace. As they separated, Rowan moved to kiss her on the cheek. Marnie misread his attempt and moved to meet his mouth with hers. The awkward shuffle of lips and mouths ended badly, with a sloppy kiss they both laughed about. Rowan pulled her close again to enjoy the feel of her body next to his.

"Time to get to work," Marnie finally declared, as she playfully shoved him away.

Rowan returned to his bags and she walked up onto the deck to open the building. As she crossed the open area overlooking the firepits, she called out a small detail that could help him.

"There's a garbage cart in the garage."

Rowan gave her a look of relief. It made the mountain of debris that was forming less threatening. With a cart, he knew he could be inside cleaning within thirty minutes.

# # # #

Tom walked into the front door of the Sombrero as Rowan emerged onto the back deck after disposing of all the bagged debris from the firepit. He was carrying a large Rubbermaid dish tray filled with wine glasses that had been carried off to the firepit areas despite the Sombrero's plastic-cup rule once off the deck. Marnie had cleared all the tables on the deck and wiped them down with a disinfectant to reclaim the shiny lacquered finishes from the patina of Dervish Red and other drinks.

"Marnie!" Tom yelled toward the production and storage room.

His voice had anger in it that was clear but not uncommon to anyone who knew him. Rowan stopped to watch Tom continue back toward the kitchen, wondering why he was there.

The clinking of bottles told Tom where he could find his ex-wife. He followed the noise back into the storage area.

"Marnie?" he called out again.

As he approached the double door to the storage room, Marnie appeared with a hand truck full of milk crates that each held nine bottles of Red Sombrero wine. Her jump and gasp at the unexpected sight of Tom showed that she did not hear his calls. Two wires hanging from her ears that fed into her shirt told him why.

"Jesus H. Christ, Tom," Marnie proclaimed, as she pulled her earphones out with a single yank on their main cord. "You almost made me dump the cart. And that would've been really bad for today's football games."

Tom was still holding his hands out in case any of the top milk crates decided to topple. He took a slow breath to recover from his unexpected fright while also trying to remember why he was there.

"What!?" Marnie demanded.

Tom broke into a smug smile he knew would irritate her. He never arrived at the Sombrero before a kickoff on Sunday. The clock in the storage room showed two hours earlier than he would have been expected to be there.

"Shoot Marnie," he said, starting to laugh at her annoyed face. "I thought I'd come by to help clean up from last night."

Marnie wheeled the hand truck over the spot where Tom's toes were before he pulled them back. He was not anxious to repeat the pain he had felt the last time. "Since, when?" Marnie was exhausted, thinking he was too late to clean the tables and main bar area, and just happened to arrive after she had finished the hard job of pulling inventory to put behind the bar. "What's the matter? You jealous of Clark Kent out there?"

Tom looked puzzled.

"You mean, that Rowan guy?" he asked.

Marnie lifted her eyebrows in the affirmative before turning to continue her trek to the bar area.

"You know damn well who I am talking about," she answered as she started to aggressively clank bottles onto the shelf. "Why is it that you always fucking come catting back around each time someone takes an interest in me? Then go totally zombie when no one's around."

Rowan could hear the muffled sounds of their animated conversation as he moved to find a better vantage point without being seen. As much as he did not want Tom around Marnie, he was enjoying his jealousy and anxious to hear how Marnie would defend him.

"That's not true," he answered. "I see you almost every night."

"It is true, Tom. And it's been happening since before I opened this place."

"We," Tom corrected.

"No, ME," she replied. "I want, and need, you in my life. But would you please just leave my love life alone?"

Tom felt the weight of her words hit his chest. He was happy to let Marnie butterfly around as a single. That enabled him to do the same without concern that he had let the best thing that ever happened to him slip away.

"So you're interested in this guy?"

Rowan could hear better from his new position by the deck's service access to the storage room. It had a window that was used for both ventilation during production, and for passing wine and empties back and forth when the Sombrero was in full swing. The window was open, often forgotten and left open at closing. The Sombrero's attention to locking down for the night was always sloppy.

"I guess," she answered. "He's smart, good looking, educated..."

"Rich, rich, and rich," Tom added to keep the attributes flowing.

"Really?" Marnie replied in a condescending tone. "I hadn't noticed."

Marnie dramatically turned away from him as she finished her thought. She did not want him to see the panic she knew she was feeling by admitting to her ex-husband her interest in a new man from the outside.

"Does he like you? I mean, as in like-like as a person?"

"Instead of what?" Marnie answered. "A quick go, off in the trees? On the moss? By the creek?"

Tom knew he had overstepped. Marnie's fire seemed to extinguish as she had to continue the awkward self-realization with her ex-husband.

"I just don't want you to get hurt," he said. "Do you think there's hope with this guy?"

Marnie did not answer the question. Its insinuation was that she was foolish to think that any rich, cultured man from the city would fall for a country bar owner. Turning to look at Tom, she could see his concern and adoration for her competing in his eyes. He was obviously hurt to think that Rowan could not only be a serious relationship, but also give Marnie far more than he ever could.

"Whatcha listening to?" whispered a familiar female voice from behind him as Rowan felt a hand touch his lower back.

Rowan's head jerked up in surprise and banged on a shelf that crossed mid window, a platform to place glasses and bottles to either send out to be sold or take back to be washed and sanitized.

The sound of the collision rattled through the open window into the bar, startling Marnie and Tom so they both stopped talking and started toward the back deck without a second thought.

Janis's smile told Rowan that she was no longer a threat to his interest in Marnie. It was playful and light, totally enjoying the pain her question inflicted.

"Jesus, Janis!" Rowan complained, as he rubbed the back of his head. "How about a little warning?"

"I thought about goosing you. But I didn't want to give you a heart attack."

Janis had a gleeful bounce in her disposition that showed her delight to have him to herself.

"Well, thank God you're so thoughtful," he replied. "I probably have a freaking concussion."

"Oh, don't be such a pussy."

"Pussy? Really?"

Rowan's face showed continued pain as he rubbed the throbbing at the back of his head.

"So, where'd ya go last night?" Janis asked, showing she felt some symptoms of wine flu from the night before. "Last thing I remember is driving back to my house with you."

Janis leaned toward Rowan to insinuate a romantic connection.

"I just dropped you off," he answered, hoping she was unconscious through his having put her to bed half naked. "We said goodnight in your living room, just before you headed to the bathroom."

Janis's brow furrowed as she attempted to recall what had happened. It made sense from the trail of clothes she left in the bathroom that he was telling the truth. Half-naked would not be how she would have ended an engagement with Clark. The look in his eyes told her he was telling the truth. She was disappointed with that reality.

"Well, perhaps, another time...maybe," she whispered.

Rowan smiled, without saying a word, at her proposition. He could see she was embarrassed and somewhat hurt. He knew it was not fair to either give her false hope or a complete rejection.

"What the hell is going on out here!?" Marnie asked, annoyed.

Marnie expression showed surprise at finding Janis next to Rowan, and him rubbing the back of his head. The sight of the two completely washed the noise that pulled them outside from her active memory. Tom's suspicions began to rise again. But this time, he was more happy than mad because Janis could pull Rowan's eyes off of Marnie.

"He banged his head on the shelf above the sink," Janis answered.

Marnie looked at the sink, noticing the open window. She then looked at Rowan, knowing he was eavesdropping.

"If you want to hear what we're talking about, just come in," she barked at him. "And you! If you want him, you can have him."

Janis smiled to the offer as Marnie turned to walk away. The combination of the jealous husband, sneaky new boy toy who she thought was a friend, and her friend she now caught with him was too much for Marnie to handle. She knew she had work to complete before the staff arrived fifteen minutes before the Sombrero was scheduled to open.

Marnie slammed the door as she re-entered the building. After connecting eyes with both Tom and Janis, Rowan turned to walk toward the backyard while still rubbing his head.

"You want him too?" Tom asked Janis.

"He is a nice piece of ass," she replied.

# # # #

Rowan let Marnie burn off her anger. He was not sure if she was truly mad or acting out because of something that happened either at the Sombrero or somewhere else. One thing was certain: she needed to cool down before anyone approached her.

Tom and Rowan finished cleaning the tables and bar area. Although they worked in the same area, each worked as hard to stay away from the other. Janis disappeared as quickly as she came. Once she saw Marnie was in a bad mood, she knew that any fun with her or opportunity to flirt with Rowan was over.

"What was Marnie so pissed about?" Rowan asked quietly, looking to the storage area to ensure she was out of sight.

"I don't know," Tom lied. "She's just moody like that. Happy, then in a blink, a tornado."

Rowan's eyebrows raised as he turned away to think if Marnie was worth the trouble. He knew she had a lot on her plate and was too proud to accept any help. He decided to find her to see if he could calm her down before the rowdy football crowds appeared.

"Marnie?" he called out, before looking into the storage room.

"What do you want Rowan?" she answered, seeming still troubled by his presence.

Rowan paused to think about her response, which inferred she did not care if he was around or not.

"I'm going to be heading back to Pittsburgh," he lied, hoping she would ask him to stay.

Marnie did not respond as she continued to pull bottles from the wood tables to put into the stolen milk crates.

"Marnie?"

"Clark," she gasped, "go, stay, I don't care. I have work to do."

Marnie's indifference was hurtful. Her exasperation with her situation was overwhelming her.

"Marnie, let me help you."

Marnie moved the last milk crate onto the hand truck then turned to look at him. Her expression showed she had lost hope.

"Help me?" she asked. "You barely know me... and believe me, you're better off keeping it that way."

Rowan stepped close to her to take her hands into his.

"Let me help," he offered, again. "I'm a fresh set of eyes. Maybe I can help you figure things out."

Rowan realized with that statement that Marnie knew very little about him and his background. He was just a preppy city stiff to her. She never asked about his family or what he did for a living. It was the first time he realized that and began to think it was strange.

"You can't."

"Try me."

"You got eighty thousand dollars!?" she demanded.

Rowan did not answer her question. The smirk that appeared on the corner of his mouth said enough. But he also was not offering any money.

"Of course, you do," Marnie gasped, exasperated by the unfolding scene. "Your car is probably worth eighty thousand dollars...and paid for."

Rowan's smile grew as Marnie looked at him in frustration. He squeezed her hand to get her attention, and for her to know he was not letting go.

"It's fixable," he offered. "You just need to have a plan to get it done, then stick to it...the latter part being more important than the first part."

"It might as well be a million dollars," Marnie answered, tearing up. "We have no juice so we can't make any wine."

"No wine," he corrected, smiling while moving in a hip-hop rhythm. *"We got no juice so we got NO wine."*

It was an attempt at humor that used to irritate his ex-wife and embarrass his children. Marnie smiled at his goofy move and expression.

"Seriously," she added.

"Okay," Rowan said, as he stopped with a smile and one last dab of his head and shoulders. "I work in finance. I can go through your books and see where you're leaking money and can make some."

Marnie looked off to the far corner of the room as she explained her business. The Red Sombrero was a bar. It had two registers. One for the accountants and government. The other was for her personal account under the guise of *tax avoidance*.

"What?" Rowan asked.

When she did not respond, he exhaled in exasperation because his task just got harder. He began to think about how he could measure her bottle volume, prices, and margins to get a revenue number. Although the Sombrero did serve food, it was a minor source of business that he was not going to attempt to quantify.

"Don't bother," Marnie implored. "I'm fucked."

A smile appeared on Rowan's face as he looked at the beautiful woman who greeted him so harshly his first night and wondered how she could be so submissive. He felt that any other time, he could have responded coyly to her last statement to get a laugh and punch.

"Marnie, I'm going to help you," he said again, moving his head to gain eye contact with her.

"I can't take your money," she answered.

"That's good," he answered. "Because I'm not offering you any. Give me a week to pull something together. We'll talk again next weekend. I just need your juice order history to see what volume you buy. From that I can roll out the numbers to solve your problems without investment."

Marnie was excited to hear his confidence and believed he could help her. But the current reality facing her was a diminished supply of inventory to sell. The process of turning vineyard juice into any of their wines took four to five days. She barely had enough inventory from the last delivery to get *to* next weekend, let alone *through* it.

"We need juice now, the finished stuff that just needs flavored and sweetened, to be served by this weekend," she stated, knowing he was completely aware of their diminished inventory.

"I know," he answered. "I've got a plan for that."

"It's more expensive."

"Always is," Rowan smiled. "Time is money."

Marnie knew that anything short of buying juice with cash was not going to work. But she felt a twinge of confidence that what she did not know about Rowan likely had some magical way to get juice to the Sombrero in time for a Thursday all-nighter to bottle and label inventory for the weekend.

"I don't want you to spend your money on my business," she said, taking hold and now squeezing his hands. "Just promise me that."

Rowan smiled at the lovely image in front of him. Marnie's eyes showed a warmth he had given up on finding. Her face nested beautifully in the frame of her gray hair. She had a confidence about her that was intoxicating, and weaknesses he just wanted to coddle.

"I promise," he answered. "But I have to go to get this done."

Rowan wanted to be out of the Sombrero when he made his calls. He did not want either the distraction of the people or to have Marnie listen in to disrupt either his thoughts or his opportunity to swing some deals in her favor. Marnie disappeared for a moment to reappear with a thick file labeled *Novinci Vineyards*.

"The paper clipped ones in the front are the past-dues."

Rowan thumbed through the ten-sheet-thick pile of overdue invoices going back two months. He noticed that there were two delivery addresses. One was to the Sombrero, the other was to the closed bar in Clayton.

"What's Clayton?" he asked.

"A bad memory," Marnie answered, not wanting to show another failure to him.

"History?" Rowan qualified. "Not breathing? Dead?"

Marnie was getting irritated but could not hold back a smile to his obsession with the status of the Clayton Sombrero.

"This is it," Marnie replied, getting tearful to the thought that she may lose it too. "This is all I have left."

Rowan released her hands to give her a bear hug. Marnie was sad, but not in a mood to be hugged. She kept her arms at her sides as she reluctantly accepted his warm gesture, only to give in when she felt the heat from his body permeate hers.

"This place will rock again," Rowan said, kissing the top of her head.

As Rowan released his hold on Marnie, he stepped back to look at her face. He was hoping to see a new light of hope in her expression but it remained still, her hands dropped to her side.

"I'd like to take two bottles of Dervish Red with me," Rowan said, grabbing them from the cart.

Marnie's expression showed she saw money walking out the door in his hands. Rowan saw her concern and responded by pulling a one hundred dollar bill from his wallet.

"You can add this to my tab, and give that hot bartender a generous tip," he said, smiling.

Marnie accepted the bill while trying to fight a smile.

"How do I know it's good?" she asked with obvious sarcasm.

"Of course it's good," he answered. "I'm a banker, and bankers print their own money."

Marnie started to put the bill into her jeans pocket, then stopped. Rowan knew that meant that she was going to put it in the cash register for sales they did not report to the government. Marnie's puzzled look showed she was now gaining hope that good things would come again.

"What?" he asked.

"I would have guessed you're a doctor...like a brain surgeon."

"Sorry to disappoint?" he pondered out loud. "Put that bill in the legit cash register, not in your pocket."

Marnie grabbed Rowan's shoulders to pull herself up to give him a kiss on the cheek. A quick smile and pat on the file full of receipts was Rowan's announcement that he had to go. For the first time, Marnie was excited to see him walk out the door. She knew he had a renewed purpose and two bottles of Dervish Red to set up his week. She slipped the hundred dollars into her pocket.

"There's good karma in this room," Cousin Dave said from the storage room's exterior door, which had been left ajar. "I feel good energy building here."

"Well, how about harnessing some of it and taking a walk through to straighten up anything not where it's supposed to be."

"Don't worry Marnie. The forces of the world are coming to help you."

Marnie gave Cousin Dave a smile to acknowledge his sentiment. She did feel the return of a positive vibe for the business. As she saw Rowan's car drive past the open door, she began to well with tears she knew she had to hold back. He was going to help her solve her problems and keep the Sombrero from shutting its doors.

# # # #

The large cyclone fence that surrounded the Giollota Construction Company was capped by three strings of barbed wire. Inside the perimeter was an array of sporadically placed pieces of equipment, some pallets of bricks and cement blocks, and a small white building toward the back with a sign bearing the company name. An arrow pointed to the office door. Anyone entering the property would not believe it was an eighty million dollar a year development company.

Rowan looked at the two large gates that sat propped open by two cement blocks at their base. It always amused him that despite all of the flash and cash Vinnie had, he was an old soul for simplicity when it came to his company.

The property appeared empty as he pulled to the building to pick Vinnie up for lunch. A text on his way home from Legend on Sunday to inquire about his availability Monday got an immediate response. Rowan knew Vinnie was always up for lunches, which usually took over two hours. He wondered if the hundred dollar, closes-to-the-pin debt he was owed was going to be remembered and used for the lunch bill he knew was going to be large.

The office interior mirrored the outside of the building. Aside from the dull beige computers sitting on the old metal desks, the office was completely absent of anything contemporary. Vinnie's strong Italian influence could be felt through the dark artwork and a setting that resembled something from *The Godfather*.

Vinnie's office manager, Louise, showed an immediate smile when she saw Rowan. Her matronly attire and poufy hair completed her 1950s look. Her enthusiasm at meeting him was always rooted in her interest in introducing him to her niece Gina, whose husband mysteriously disappeared years ago, without warning.

"Vincent asked that you give him a moment to finish a call," she said, looking at the two bottles of wine he was holding.

"Is one of those for me?" she asked.

Rowan smiled. He wanted Vinnie to taste the Dervish Red to qualify an idea he had for the Sombrero. But Louise was more to the age, and cut from the same cloth, as Vinnie's dad. She would be a perfect addition to his focus group.

"Maybe," Rowan answered. "I'd love to have your opinion too."

Rowan handed her the bottle. A confused look appeared on her face as she spun it in her hands to study the label.

"I've never heard of this," she said, her eyes shifting from the label to him. "What's a Dervish Red?"

"That's what I'm hoping to find out," he answered, now looking for Vinnie to enter the room.

Louise studied the blue bottle for more details.

"Why a blue bottle?" she asked.

"I'm not quite sure about that either."

"Pretty. It reminds me of the old country."

Rowan checked the box in his head to confirm market appeal. He was concerned about the use of a blue bottle to host red wine. People like to see what they are buying.

Vinnie appeared irritated when he entered the room. He gave Rowan a pat on the shoulder as he charged past him to a long row of file cabinets.

"Rowan, my boy." Vinnie said, as he thumbed through a long line of green hanging file folders. "I may have to ask your indulgence to reschedule our lunch."

Rowan smiled to see the small man stand on his toes to look into the top drawer of the cabinet. He would never admit it, but he was glad to hear Vinnie cancel. It opened time in his afternoon to call the juice manufacturer in New York and confirm completion of their deal to get the Sombrero more supply.

"Not a problem, Vinnie. But I do want you and Louise to each take a bottle of this wine I found and give me your opinion."

Vinnie stopped his thumbing when he heard the word *wine*. He immediately spun to walk back to his waiting guest and office manager to see what Rowan had brought.

"Why wait!?" he said. "Louie, sweetie, find us some cups."

Vinnie checked the label with a questioning scowl. Checking the top of the bottle for a cork, he pulled open the center drawer of the desk sitting in the reception area. After moving his hand back and forth to move things around, he stopped to grab something in it.

Louise returned with three Styrofoam cups as Vinnie began uncorking the bottle.

"With the day I'm having, Mother, God, and Jesus must be sending this."

Rowan smiled to see Vinnie excited about the reprieve he had just delivered. But he was concerned that the Dervish Red would fall short of the wine Vinnie remembered from his dad. It certainly had no chance to compete with the high-dollar bottles Vinnie drank now.

Vinnie poured a sample into each cup, then looked at the bottle again. He then waved his hand across the cups, inviting Rowan and Louise to join him in a taste.

As Rowan waited for Vinnie to raise his cup, he searched for an Italian drinking toast.

"*Salute*," Vinnie offered raising his glass to his banker and office manager.

As his focus group participants took their first sip, puzzled looks appeared on their faces. Rowan watched both of them closely while they processed the flavor. He then tilted his own cup just enough to let the Dervish Red touch his lips before allowing it to recede back into its Styrofoam holder.

Vinnie remained silent as he moved his mouth, still processing the wine's taste and texture. His head started to bob up and down as a smile appeared on his face. As Vinnie tuned back into the room, he looked to Louise, who was also nodding.

"In my dad's day," he proclaimed, "they called this Dago Red. *Mmm, magnifico.*"

Vinnie lifted the bottle to add a generous pour into his cup while offering more wine to both Rowan and Louise.

Rowan felt a wash of excitement fill his body. Like the brewery close to the Sombrero in Clarion, he knew that for the Sombrero to be successful, it needed to serve a larger demographic, beyond the locals and lucky tourists in the area.

"I had no idea what to expect in sharing this with you." Rowan said, taking his first legitimate drink of wine.

"Where is Legend, PA?" Vinnie asked, spinning the bottle in his hand.

"It's up north, by Clarion."

"We could sell this." he offered, with a twinge of excitement in his voice.

Rowan kept his eyes focused on his friend and client as he responded *amen* in his head.

"I have an associate who is in the liquor business," Vinnie added. "Let me take this to him to see what he thinks."

Rowan smiled in agreement, then looked at Louise to tell her that her bottle was being rerouted.

"I'll get you another bottle," he offered.

Louise nodded her thanks. She could read the excitement in Vinnie's face, which was a dramatic mood shift from fifteen minutes earlier. For that alone, she was willing to surrender her bottle of red.

"And, I think we'll have to come up with a different name." Rowan laughed while glancing back and forth between his impromptu Italian focus group.

Vinnie smiled as he added more Dervish Red to his cup to wrap up his taste test. He quickly drank what he poured, then threw his cup into the waste can. As he turned to leave, he patted Rowan on the shoulder and grabbed the second bottle to take back to his office.

"Rowan, my boy. You just changed my day from chickenshit to chicken salad."

The door to his office swung closed behind Vinnie **as he** left the room. Rowan turned to Louise, who had her cup elevated to offer a toast.

"Mine too," she said, as she tapped her cup to his.

Rowan smiled to think about the possibilities the wine had within the old Italian community through Vinnie. That thought, however, was short-lived because he realized that possibly had just created a demand that the Sombrero could not fill.

"What have you done!?" she shouted through the speakers of the Audi.

"Hello to you, too," he replied, knowing she was pissed and why.

"I told you I do not need your money, or your help."

Rowan could hear in her voice that she was not going to be reasonable. She also only told him she did not want his money. But it was a twenty-minute drive back into the city so he decided to give an explanation a shot.

"First, you don't need my money to fix anything," he said to be agreeable and to calm her down. "But you do need my help."

Marnie gave no immediate response. She was relieved that he had not paid any of her debts or for the new product that was scheduled to arrive later in the afternoon.

"Then how did you get me more juice?" she asked.

Rowan paused to think about an answer that would be true but not infuriate her.

"I didn't pay for it. I just guaranteed it would get paid."

At first, Marnie felt fine with his explanation and effort on her behalf until she realized that he just added the pressure of their relationship to her personal anxiety about making the Sombrero work.

"You had no right to do that without talking to me first."

Rowan closed his eyes briefly. He exhaled slowly to find some comfort and peace of mind. Making this level of decision, even to create a good for her, without talking to her about it first was one of the principal relationship blocks that wrecked his marriage. If Marnie had been Mindy, Rowan would have become defensive and say it made financial sense and that time was limited. But six months of marriage counseling that ultimately ended unsuccessfully taught him that apologizing then keeping quiet was better than giving reasons when seeking forgiveness.

"You're right," he replied, letting a silence fill the air.

Marnie's nonresponse gave him hope that he was making headway.

"Live or die," she replied in a calm, but angry, voice, "this is my business. If I need your help, I will ask you for it."

Rowan felt some relief from her reply. He knew she was a proud business owner who wanted to make her idea work. His only concern was that her way was leading the Sombrero to doom. He thought about Tom's squaring off with the repo man, and that his likely resolution tactic would have involved fists and a lawsuit when the driver sued. Expanding her market share was not in Marnie's line of thinking, outside of opening another brick-and-mortar drinking location. Getting juice to supply her drinking establishment was the second time he had stepped in without first asking.

"Marnie, I want to help you. This is what I do. And I'm good at it."

Marnie looked down the bar to the spot where Rowan had taken residence over the past few weekends. She ached to just touch him.

"Just talk to me first...before doing anything."

Rowan knew that was a one-way declaration. Marnie was going to do what Marnie wanted to do. He decided that it was probably not a good time to mention his success with Vinnie.

"I should probably not surprise you with an order for bottles either," Rowan said, working hard to hold back a laugh.

Marnie shook her head at the news. But she knew the wine had to have containers to be sold.

"You're coming up this weekend, right?" Marnie asked, to avoid dealing with his confession.

She wanted to confirm his arrival and opportunity to discuss business, and to have time with him.

"I'll be there," he answered. "I have my cabin rented and everything."

Marnie felt both relief and an aching sensation at his words. She wanted to offer for him to stay at her house with her but knew they needed more time to know each other better. They both were divorced, which meant that they both had baggage and expectations of what would happen next.

"That's great," she answered in a calm, quiet voice. "We can talk then."

"Or sooner," he added. "We don't have to wait for the weekend."

Marnie gave a light laugh to his reply. She was excited that he wanted to talk with her on an ongoing basis.

"Call me when you can," she answered, to test his desire.

"I will... You too... Bye."

Rowan waited through a few seconds of silence for Marnie to respond. His dash display showed she was still connected.

"Marnie? You can hang up."

"You hang up," she answered with a slight giggle.

Rowan smiled to the high school antic of back-and-forth demands for the other to hang up first. He started to laugh as the silence grew in his car.

"Okay," he finally responded. "I'm saying goodbye."

"Okay."

"Marnie, just hang up...please!"

"You hang up."

He could hear Marnie's laughter through the phone.

"Okay..." Rowan replied as he placed his thumb onto the end-call button. "I'm hanging up now and... I miss you too."

Rowan pushed the button as he finished his comment. He knew not giving her an opportunity to reply would infuriate her while also not giving either of them the opportunity to say something the other was not feeling. He also was relieved she was over the juice order and could ramp up production.

For the remainder of his drive into the city, the Audi's stereo remained silent. He was enjoying his thoughts back through their phone conversation, how fun, refreshing, and *high school* it was.

Chapter 10

The cargo truck from the vineyard that delivered the juice and had tried to repossess the Sombrero's wine-making equipment two days earlier was bright purple with the vineyard logo in white on its sides. It could be seen from a mile away when approaching on the highway from the opposite direction.

Tom was adjusting the radio station on his 1998 Ford F-150 pickup truck when he sensed something odd in his peripheral vision. He was on his way home from a long day of work, anxious to take a hot shower and relax with a beer. The impression bothered him as he worked through the static to find the country station he wanted. Without looking, he knew what he had seen as it passed by him heading toward the Sombrero.

The F-150 fishtailed and the wheels screeched as Tom stood on his brakes to stop. His fear was that the vineyard owner had played Marnie's new boyfriend to think the Sombrero's wine-making equipment was safe when he was just planning to circle back on another day to grab it.

The purple truck was out of sight when Tom finally got turned around. A big plume of blue smoke blew out of his exhaust pipes as he accelerated from a dead stop to eighty miles per hour to catch him.

Marnie gasped as she saw Tom's truck flying down the road past the trees as she helped guide the backing purple panel truck to the production room garage bay. Keeping one eye on the truck to guide the last few feet for her delivery, she strained to keep the other on Tom's hasty arrival, wondering what news he could be bringing that was so urgent.

"Lady, I don't know how you did it," the driver said as he walked back to start the unload, "But, you have enough juice in here to light up half the state."

Marnie looked puzzled as she waited for the man to open his back gate. In the confusion, she had never asked Rowan how much juice he had actually ordered.

Tom's truck came to a skidding halt next to the purple panel truck. He threw it into park and jumped out in one motion. His face looked like he wanted to kill something as he approached her and the back of the van.

The driver was preoccupied with his clipboard as he used muscle memory to step down from the back of the truck. He had made the trip up and down so many times, he never had to either think or look. Marnie turned her head to greet Tom as he arrived. She could still not figure out why he was on a possessed charge.

"Tom," she said in her normal voice before repeating in a shout, "TOM!"

Tom's punch dropped the delivery driver to the ground. His clipboard flew up from the force and toppled under the truck. Marnie ran to grab Tom's arm before he could strike the man again. She was afraid he would kill him.

"TOM, STOP!" she yelled, jumping onto his back.

His arm was too strong for her to stop its forward motion, but she was strong enough to slow it the point that Tom might stop on his own to ask why.

"This son of a bitch ain't going to take the equipment!" Tom shouted in winded excitement.

Marnie struggled as Tom tried to buck her off his back. He spun a full three hundred and sixty degrees with her arms strangling him and her legs squeezing his middle. His aggression subsided as she refused to let go, and his energy fell flat. As he came to a stop, Marnie hesitated before dismounting to make sure his calm was not just baiting her to get her off him.

"Are you calm?" she asked while still holding on.

Tom began to realize he had misinterpreted things. He exhaled and closed his eyes to reach complete calm.

"Good," she answered as the delivery man began to stand. He appeared to be unhurt but held his jaw to manipulate it left and right to ensure it still worked.

"I'm good, Marnie," Tom finally said. "You can get down."

Tom's instruction to get Marnie off his back was painful. He treasured the touch, the pressing of her body to his. Although not a hug or any type of affection, it was still physical contact. He bent his knees to let her drop off him easily.

"Hey, man," Tom said, as he turned to the driver. "I'm sor…"

Tom's first look toward the driver saw his fist about ten inches out on its approach to his face. The landing was solid to his left eye. It made no sound that he could remember. He fell to the ground like a tree falling in the woods.

"Jesus Christ!" Marnie yelled as she looked at the driver.

He was rubbing his fist, satisfied that he had dropped the man who had harassed him over the weekend when he tried to reclaim Marnie's equipment.

"Your boyfriend has to keep his head up," the man said, shifting his eyes from Tom to Marnie. "Now, where do you want this juice? I've got a two-hour drive back."

Marnie pointed to the usual delivery spot inside the garage bay. She stepped toward Tom, who was now moving and groaning. As she touched his chest to offer comfort, Tom reacted with a swing of his arm that swept hers away. At that point, she was willing to let him suffer.

Marnie sat back onto the gravel as she watched the delivery man climb back into the cargo area of his truck. She placed her hands on the ground behind her to lean back and shifted her attention to Tom as he began to sit up, holding his eye.

When the power lift started to whine, Tom looked toward the truck. On the lift sat three fifty-five-gallon plastic containers of juice.

"What...the...heck?" he mumbled, turning to Marnie for answers.

"Don't ask," she said, in a slightly disgusted voice.

"You can't afford to buy that!" he said.

The comment caught the attention of the delivery man, who nodded in agreement. Things had changed too dramatically since Saturday.

"Your boyfriend bailed you out, didn't he?"

"No, Tom, he didn't," she answered. "He also is NOT my boyfriend. So please just chill...out."

"Then what's happening here?" he asked. "I'm also guessing that you'll want me to start making wine tonight to have for the weekend."

"That would be helpful," Marnie answered, failing to hold back a laugh.

Tom, still seated on the gravel, rubbing his eye, looked like a little boy in a sandbox after being taken out by the playground bully. By the time he had the strength to stand, the delivery of twelve containers of juice had been completed.

"Four white and eight red," the driver said as he handed Marnie the delivery order to sign. "That's a big order for you going into November. You usually get four and four."

Marnie handed the signed delivery order and clipboard back to the driver. He tore the bottom sheet of the three-paged, carbonless form to hand to her. He then reached his hand out to help Tom to his feet.

"Couldn't let it go unanswered," he said. "We good?"

Once standing, Tom continued to rub his eye as he worked to balance. The driver offered his hand to Marnie to bring her back to her feet too.

"Yeah," Tom answered. "I thought you were circling back to get the winemaker."

The driver gave Marnie a smile and wink before turning to leave.

"I hate repossessing equipment," he said. "It makes one less customer to deliver to. Don't screw this up. I'm rootin' for you."

The man was in the truck before Marnie could answer. She put her hand on Tom's shoulder for balance and to comfort him. The sound of the truck starting startled Tom.

"Jesus!" he cried out.

Marnie pulled his arm to direct him to the production bay. She told him that he needed to get away from the noise and dirt of the truck. Her real reason was that he had to get to work. She was now excited that Rowan had done what he did. Although she was never going to tell him that. She held Tom's arm and leaned into him as they walked together back into the Sombrero.

# # # #

Rowan pulled into the garage of his condominium building in a hilltop community overlooking Pittsburgh. The building's panoramic view covered the confluence of the city's three rivers, with sightlines up each valley. The view of lights, colors, water, and architecture was an aesthetic he found calming at the end of long days. More nights, than not he would either sit on his deck or at its window just staring off at the view as he pondered problems and worries. But this week, so far, had gone well. Although, after two days, he had not heard from Vinnie.

Rowan checked his phone as he walked into his condo. He had over sixty emails waiting in his personal gmail that were likely advertisements or people asking for money. Some lights were on as he meandered through his front hall, placing his keys on a table before continuing into the living room.

"Hi Daddy," a familiar voice called from the couch.

Rowan stopped to think before shifting his eyes to look at his daughter.

"Claire," he said, not hiding his surprise.

Claire stood to greet her dad with a hug as he circled around the couch to greet her.

"What brings you home?" he asked suspiciously, thinking he may have forgotten something.

"Fall break."

As Rowan released his oldest daughter, he looked puzzled.

"I thought your weekend in Charleston was your fall weekend."

"That was just a no home game weekend, Dad."

"Do you even go to school?"

Claire pushed away from her dad, disappointed he apparently did not have her on his calendar for the long weekend.

"Don't change the subject," she said in disgust. "You forgot I was coming home this weekend."

Rowan took a deep breath, thinking through Claire being home and his need and desire to be back in Legend at the Sombrero. The cabin had adequate space for two people, but its accommodations and privacy were well below what Claire would accept. He would have to call Marnie to cancel. That made him nervous, given the guaranty he had given on the juice and bottles he had just purchased.

"I did not forget," he replied. "It just slipped my mind...which may be problematic."

Claire stepped away from her dad as she let him think about his comment.

"I can go stay at Mom's. But she's at the beach...so, I'll be alone...for the weekend."

Rowan started to smile as his daughter did her best to throw the guilt. Thinking through the weekend...he could drive north to Legend on Saturday. Leaving early would give him enough time to gather the details he needed from Marnie to possibly structure a loan for the complex. He also wanted to introduce the idea of private labeling of the Sombrero wines if Vinnie followed through on his interest.

"How would you like to go quad riding on Saturday?"

"Quad?"

"Or Razors," Rowan answered.

"Who are you!?"

Claire's look at her dad told the whole story. The most outdoorsy thing he had done since she had been born was walk the dogs in an off-leash park near the home where she grew up. Up until now, his version of a quad was a golf cart. And four-wheeling involved fairways.

"Come on," he said. "It'll be fun. I'd like you to see this place."

Claire sighed as she gave in.

"Mom said you were going to some secret place. She heard it from Mrs. Schmitt."

"Nicki," Rowan mumbled.

He tried to recall what he had told Dorsey. Nothing came to mind outside of the first night at the Steelers game.

"What'd your mom say?"

"Nothing," she answered. "Just that you found some winery up north that Mrs. Schmitt wants to visit."

Rowan chuckled at the thought of Nicki socializing at the Red Sombrero. The thought of her using its ladies room made him laugh harder.

"Yeah," Rowan started, then paused. "That's the place. But I don't think it's Mrs. Schmitt's type of crowd."

Claire watched her dad disappear into his own head as he thought about the place. She was intrigued to see this new find that got him to start *quadding*.

"I'll go, if we can go see if I can get my car fixed," she replied.

Rowan paused to make Claire believe that he had to think about her proposition. The Mini Cooper had to be fixed. He knew it would take a week in the shop to be repaired and painted. He had already planned for this for either the week of Thanksgiving or during Christmas break. But it could also be done back at school in Columbia. Leaving the car damaged was how he was punishing Claire for driving it to Five Points instead of taking an Uber. The car was still safe to drive; she could exit easily from the driver's door. Getting in was just a hassle through the passenger door and over the gear shift.

"Okay… But you can't tell your mom about it."

Claire smiled about the potential to have something to hold over her dad.

"Deal."

# # # #

A cryptic voicemail from Vinnie inviting Rowan to his home to *discuss business* had him thinking about all of the *Godfather* and *Goodfellas* movies he had watched as a kid. Vinnie's home was dramatically different from his office. It was an estate framed by a brick wall topped by ornate wrought iron. It had a complementing driveway gate with a call box. Rowan knew from Vinnie's finances and visible projects around town that he was legit. Vinnie's lifestyle led Rowan to believe there might be other sources of income.

Vinnie's housekeeper met Rowan at the front door and escorted him back to Vinnie's study. The wood-paneled room was elegant, hosting a large mahogany desk and a sitting area that included a leather love seat and chair. Vinnie was waiting at the door when Rowan entered. A guest stood from the love seat as Rowan walked in.

"Rowan," Vinnie said enthusiastically. "Welcome."

Rowan shook Vinnie's hand with an accompanying pat on his back as he walked into the room.

"This is my good friend Salvatore Roberto. He's in the liquor business."

"Sal," the man said, reaching to shake Rowan's hand.

Rowan looked at Salvatore Roberto as he felt the oversized hand engulf his own. Sal Roberto stood at least six foot five. He had a thick flow of slicked-back black hair. Not more than forty years old, he could have played either side of the line for the Pittsburgh Steelers, but his hands were soft to the touch. He had a gentleness in his eyes that said he was a sincere person.

"Sal's father is a good friend of mine," Vinnie said. "Sal played ball with my boys in high school."

"Football?" Rowan clarified.

"Soccer," Sal answered as Vinnie held his hands out to question if there was any other football worth playing.

"Gotcha." Rowan answered. "Me too. But our *futbol* back then was pretty ugly. Ten-year-olds play a better game today than we did."

"I agree," Sal replied. "My son, Carlo, he's on a team here that plays amazing."

Vinnie smiled, seeing the immediate kinship between Rowan and Sal. His purpose for the meeting was to introduce the two about the wine Rowan had shared with him. Vinnie waved to Rowan to take a seat next to Sal as he sat in the adjacent chair.

"I wanted you to meet Sal because he and I shared your bottle of wine and discussed some opportunities for it."

Rowan shared a look with Sal before shifting his eyes back to Vinnie.

"It's good." Sal declared. "I don't mean as a wine-competition type thing. But more for a market we've been looking to serve with a dedicated product line."

"Yeah, us old dagoes," Vinnie laughed.

Rowan smiled and laughed nervously at Vinnie's ethnic joke. From anyone else, it would have been offensive. But Vinnie was an old-school Italian. He loved his heritage as much as he enjoyed making fun of it. It was part of his self-deprecating humor. Similar comments on the golf course with his boys would bring scowls to their faces as he laughed and moved on.

"Right," Sal answered enthusiastically, pointing to Vinnie for emphasis. "We're looking for an inexpensive jug bottle we can sell for around fourteen, maybe sixteen bucks. That means we'd be looking to buy it for about six or seven bucks."

Damn it! Rowan thought. This proposal was way ahead of his thinking. He had no idea of either Marnie's production costs or freight to get it anywhere.

"Delivered?" he asked.

"Yes," Sal answered. "Here, in the Burgh."

Rowan nodded his head to give Sal and Vinnie hope. He knew he could not make any deal without Marnie's input and consideration.

"Any idea on volume? That affects pricing abilities."

Rowan was delaying. But he also needed that information. Too little volume would increase costs for shipping. Too much volume might surpass production capabilities. Both could easily be solved by either more equipment or outsourcing. But he wanted to have the details to take with him to Legend on Saturday.

"Let's start with two thousand bottles to test it." Sal answered.

Rowan's brain switched into math mode as he calculated the initial twelve-thousand-dollar deal for Marnie. If two thousand bottles was a test, the rollout could be hundreds of thousands of bottles.

"What states are we looking at here?" Rowan asked, trying to think of potential.

Sal looked at Vinnie, who nodded.

"Right now, we're looking at Pennsylvania and New York. But we're thinking national, to all the hot Italian markets."

Rowan felt a twinge of excitement build in him. He visualized a large distribution facility in Legend to produce and send the sweet red wine out to all fifty states and beyond.

"I think this is really possible," he answered. "It's certainly more than I expected to hear tonight. I do have to talk to my partners who, I expect, will be very interested in working with you."

Sal smiled as he listened to Rowan. He gave Vinnie a quick look to thank him for the introduction. Vinnie's slow nod of approval accepted his gratitude.

"Labeling?" Rowan asked, to clarify.

"Private," Sal answered. "We're thinking…"

"Dago Red," Vinnie interjected in a loud, declarative tone.

All three men laughed.

"Vincent, I think you guys are the only ones that can make that name fly." Rowan replied.

"You produce the wine. We'll do the branding and send you the labels," Sal added.

Vinnie stood to declare the meeting over. As Rowan and Sal joined him, they exchanged cards. Sal looked surprised as he studied Rowan's card.

"You're a banker."

"He's my banker," Vinnie answered. "I told you that."

"Yes," Rowan replied, somewhat concerned that Sal needed a favor. "The winery is owned by a friend."

Sal nodded to his answer.

"Well, good to know that you're a numbers man," he answered. "Some of these small deals get screwed up by well-intentioned artisans that don't pay attention to the money."

If you only knew the truth, Rowan thought as he smiled in agreement.

"I see it every day," he answered.

"Even more comforting." Sal replied, now confident that Vinnie's banker was not presenting something that would get *fucked-up* downstream.

As Rowan drove back out through the gates, he wanted to call Marnie with the news and to ask all the questions he needed answered. That thought quickly became overwhelmed with concern that calling was a bad idea. Marnie would have too many questions. She might even be mad he'd shopped her wine without her permission. Saturday was two days away. He knew he could lay out a proposal to her in person that would make sense as well as gather all the cost information he needed. He also knew Tom would have to be there as her wine maker to determine what was necessary to meet production needs.

# # # #

When they separated, Rowan switched his wife's ringtone to the Wicked Witch sound from *The Wizard of Oz*. It was audible warning of who was calling, in case he answered without checking. It was also an audible piece of humor that would lighten his mood, as he usually tensed with anything Mindy might call him about. Those calls were never social. And with Claire home in his condo, it was good that his ex-wife caught him in his car.

"Mindy!?" he forced out in his most welcoming voice.

"Rowan, we've got to talk," she answered. "Claire's car has to be fixed. That's your lane. You need to deal with it while she's home."

Rowan cocked his head as he listened.

"We've dealt with it," he answered. "When was the last time you spoke with her?"

Mindy paused. Her last conversation with Claire had been the day before. She knew about the visit to Mini of Pittsburgh to get the repair estimate. She did not like that Claire would be driving her damaged car nine hours back to South Carolina after break.

"I spoke with her yesterday."

Rowan shifted his head again, puzzled that it was after they had visited the dealer.

"Then you know it's taken care of."

"That's not the point," Mindy replied. "She can't be driving her wrecked car back to school."

"That's where it's getting fixed," Rowan replied. "It's safe. She can get out from the driver's door in an emergency. She just has to climb in through the passenger door...assuming she doesn't leave her door open when she stops at a rest stop."

"It's unsafe."

Rowan was beginning to get frustrated. Mindy was using the car to take out her anxiety on him.

"It's perfectly safe...BMW safe...and she'll be fine on her drive back to school."

"Well, I disagree,"

What else is new? Rowan thought.

"Well, it's fine," he answered, thinking his only other option would be to give her his car to drive back "She's having a nice visit. Tomorrow we're going quad..."

Rowan paused with the slip that came through distraction.

"Quad, what?... Quadding?" Mindy qualified. "You're taking our child quadding?"

Rowan smiled at the mental image of Mindy's ears steaming. She had an exaggerated fear of any vehicles that offered less protection than a car. The Mini took a sales effort because she thought it was too small for the long drive to South Carolina.

"Yes. We're heading up north for the day to quad with a friend," he answered, leaving out that the friend was a *she*, pretty, and an interest.

"Who?"

"A client," he answered, stretching the truth to make it fit.

"That's dangerous," she replied. "People die on those things."

"We'll be safe," he answered, visualizing the race down the tree shoot that ended in the creek. "It's not really quadding. It's a Razor. A two-seat dune buggy with a full roll cage."

"Oh my God, Rowan. A DUNE BUGGY?" Mindy answered, before going silent to think. "Well, okay...as if I have anything to say about it anyway."

BINGO! Rowan thought, elevating his hand to claim his prize.

"It'll be fine..." he answered. "Just like the roller coasters at Kennywood."

Rowan knew the reference would spike Mindy's blood pressure. But she was at the beach. She could take a walk to either calm down or overthink it. Either result was acceptable.

"Rowan, be careful with Claire. She still is not over us splitting yet."

Rowan's glee subsided at the thought of his daughter's despair. Although who Mindy was with at the beach was secret.

"I know, Mind. I'll take care of her."

"Do that."

Mindy disconnected before Rowan could answer. It was her way to be in control of their conversations. She decided when to start them, and when to end them.

# # # #

Friday night was particularly busy. The turning fall foliage was waning to barren trees so the last tourists were scurrying about the region, with many finding the Red Sombrero to end their day.

In anticipation of the tourist rush, Marnie had contracted an acoustic duet she knew tourists liked and the usual crowd tolerated. They were inexpensive locals who did not approve of alcohol but were willing to make exceptions to get a gig.

"Where's Superman?" Janis asked, noting that Marnie had said nothing, and that Clark was not in his usual spot.

She was still pondering the night Rowan took her home and her waking pants-less. Rowan's story that he left her on the couch seemed to make sense. She found her pants in the bathroom. And, once down, she could kick them off easier than pulling them back up before falling into bed.

"His daughter is home for fall break from college," Marnie answered in a snarky tone. "He's coming tomorrow with her and some exciting news."

Janis smiled at Marnie's cold presentation of Rowan's plans. Marnie was clearly upset he was only visiting for the day. But she also knew she had no reason to complain, given that they were not in a relationship, and that he had to pay to stay at the local cabins, which were renting at premium rates.

"College daughter?" Janis asked, with an exaggerated clenched jaw.

"Don't start," Marnie replied adding a glare to reinforce her message.

"I'm just saying that you're dealing with an educated group there."

Marnie scowled at Janis.

"I have a degree," she said.

Janis laughed. She remembered the comment a tourist made who got into the same discussion with Marnie about degrees, particularly art degrees.

"You have an associate's degree."

"Stop right there!" Marnie declared, knowing where Janis was heading.

"What!?" Janis laughed harder. "It only means you can *associate* with people who have degrees."

Marnie slammed her hand onto the bar as Janis curled into a belly laugh. She looked left and right to see other patrons laughing with her. They had obviously tuned into their conversation having none of their own.,

"Fuck you, Janis." Marnie declared. "At least I have one. I'd also have my bachelor's if my dad hadn't gotten sick."

Janis stood from her stool to straighten her top. She walked off to the ladies' room to give Marnie time to cool down. Her collective joy from both Rowan being absent and being able to jab Marnie with her worthless degree had to be savored.

As Marnie's glare followed her best friend off into the crowd, she wiped the bar by Janis's stool.

"A bottle of your finest red," came a voice that brought a smile to her face.

"Cousin Dave," Marnie spoke without a confirming look. "Anything else?"

Cousin Dave settled onto Janis's stool knowing he had ten minutes to sit before she returned from peeing and socializing.

"Is there anything else?" he answered.

"Not here."

Cousin Dave nodded as he surveyed the bar area. He noticed an unfamiliar face sitting on the corner stool where Rowan had been roosted for the past couple weeks.

"Where's our friend?" he asked, hoping he had not ended his visits.

"Don't you start too," Marnie answered.

Her voice was declarative, but her tone was seeking sympathy.

"Something happen?"

Marnie's smile was pained as she looked back into eyes.

"No," she answered. "He'll be here tomorrow...for the day...with his college daughter."

Cousin Dave's eyes lit at the news.

"Meeting the kids...that's a big step."

Marnie's heart skipped a beat with the different perspective from viewing it as an obstacle. She would have to present better to his daughter, who was likely one of the typical, snooty, city down-lookers who usually visited the Sombrero.

"I hope not," she replied, with an *Oh my God!* look on her face.

"It's all good," Cousin Dave replied. "It'd be worse if he was hiding you from them."

Marnie responded with a puzzled look.

"What makes you think there's anything going on? Because there isn't..."

"Yet," Cousin Dave answered. "Karma, Marnie. Karma."

Cousin Dave raised his fresh glass of Dervish Red to toast the concept. Marnie sneered as she picked up his bottle to clink his glass. She then lifted it to her mouth to take a swig before returning it with a smile and moving on to the next customer. She was attracted to Rowan but did not know why. He was the polar opposite to her usual male companions. She was unsure if he would fit into her world full time. Or, if she would be either welcome or comfortable in his.

# # # #

The cold garage air cut through the wool sweater Claire had gathered from her mom's along with some L.L. Bean duck boots she expected would be need to quad with her dad. She also had a small duffle filled with a change of clothes in case their quadding went sideways.

Rowan followed his daughter to the car dressed in flannel, jeans, and hiking boots. Claire first rolled her eyes when she saw her dad appear for coffee in his condo. But when he explained his *when in Rome* reasoning. Claire agreed that it was always best to dress for your audience.

The drive out of the city and up the interstate to Legend was an easy two and a half hours. It reminded Rowan of the trips he would take with both of his girls to soccer tournaments. The windshield time was high value for conversation and to catch up. He had a *no ear pods* rule that was often debated, accepted, then appreciated by each of his daughters. Rowan could keep the conversations going through questions, observations, and life history.

The drive through Amish country was always intriguing for his girls. The thought that anyone could live such simple and fulfilling lives without electricity and technology confounded both of them. *It's all in what you're used to* did not make any sense to them. Having grown up without computers and cell phones, that lifestyle seemed attractive to . He often called technology *life spoilers*.

The Sombrero parking lot, it was already two-thirds full, with the usual mix of pickups, jeeps, and cars when they pulled in. Rowan noticed on his drive-through that there were some higher-end vehicles, indicating that tourists had found the winery.

Rowan used some of the drive time to give Claire a high-level synopsis of how he found the Red Sombrero and some of its characters. He left out details about his feelings for Marnie, Janis's feelings for him, and some of the issues related to fights that could have happened over the business. He did mention Cousin Dave, including the details of his Whirling Dervish outfit, with the long flowing robe and canvas-covered thimble hat. Claire was hopeful to get a look at him before heading back to Pittsburgh.

"This place is kinda dumpy, dad." Claire said, without thinking.

She looked at the surrounding properties that were developed in a haphazard manner. There was an old barn that seemed to be unused and left to rot from the ground up. A field down below the firepits was intriguing. She wondered why they left it unused.

"That's part of its charm, sweetie," he answered. "It's like a dive bar in Five Points. It doesn't have to be pretty to be fun."

"Is it clean?" Claire asked.

"Define clean," Rowan answered with a smile.

As Rowan opened the door and motioned for Claire to lead him in, he noticed Marnie's Razor parked in its usual spot near the trees. Rowan was anxious to hear Claire's continued impression of the drinking establishment Marnie had built.

Claire's eyes immediately circled the room to create her first impression. She noticed the oil paintings that hung on the wood-plank walls that were not in sync with the rest of the building. She then saw three murals painted on the exterior walls of the bathrooms. Collectively, they were of the Beatles, the Monkees, and the four gunmen from the movie *Tombstone*, whom Claire did not recognize.

"This is kinda cool," Claire commented as she moved deeper into the room.

Rowan looked to the bar for a familiar face as he followed his daughter. The bartender was someone he had not met. He was not sure if Marnie was on the property or not; they had arrived earlier than he had expected.

"This deck is *fire*," Claire added as she looked out the back windows onto the deck then down to the firepit areas. "We could use something like this in COLA."

COLA was a locals and student term for Columbia. Rowan had used it once in a conversation with Claire. He was quickly chastised, told that the term was only for locals and students to use as a reference. From that point on, he made sure to use it whenever he could.

"This artwork is insane," Claire said walking to look at each piece. "This could be sold in town."

Rowan had surveyed Marnie's work before. He liked it and knew it was good. But he was hesitant to speculate on its market value. Selling art was harder than selling wine.

"This place is cool." Claire finished, to sum up her first impression. "I can see why you come here."

"There's music at night," Rowan qualified, as if needing to.

"Even better."

Rowan turned to look back at the bar. As he did, the front door opened, and Tom appeared, dressed in his usual weekend jeans and flannel.

"Rowan!?" he called out from the door. "I need to talk to you."

Rowan's heart started to pound as he watched Tom walk toward him and Claire. He was uncertain as to why Tom needed to see him.

"Tom," Rowan said, to slow him down. "This is my daughter, Claire."

Tom stopped abruptly to reassess the situation. He only had questions about the juice. But the presence of Rowan's daughter seemed to make talking business inappropriate. He nodded a greeting to Claire as he repositioned his approach to what he wanted to ask.

"We got a bigger than usual order of juice on Monday," Tom stated, to make his point without asking how.

"Yes," Rowan answered. "I need an hour with you and Marnie to talk about that. This afternoon, if possible."

Being included put Tom at ease. He knew Rowan was a smart business planner. His only concern was who would benefit from his plan. Tom was always skeptical of outsiders with schemes.

"Marnie's running errands. Said she'll be here at one or so," Tom said. "She left the Razor for you outside."

"Awesome," Rowan replied as he looked to his daughter. "I'm going to take her out for a run."

Tom looked skeptical about Rowan's declaration. The trails could get confusing, he did know that Marnie had taken Rowan on a fairly fail-safe tour across the ridge and down through the creek. He checked Claire's boots to see if they were waterproof.

"Meet back here around three?" Rowan asked.

"I'll be here for the rest of the day." Tom answered. "I'm doing bottling now. Could use a hand this afternoon if you're interested."

Rowan nodded. He knew Claire would have no interest. And without cell service, he was not sure how she would fill her time. He was curious to see if she liked the Sombrero's wine.

"Deal."

Tom started to walk away as he nodded confirmation to the three o'clock meeting time and bottling.

"Who was that?" Claire asked, trying to put pieces together.

"That...was the owner's ex-husband."

"And he still works here?"

Rowan gave a puzzled look before replying. He never really thought about Tom's work arrangement at the Sombrero.

"Works, volunteers, maybe barters for wine…. I don't really know."

"Well, it's nice they still can be in the same room together."

Claire's closing comment was meant more as a jab to her dad than a positive observation about two separating mates being able to tolerate each other.

"Yes, sweetie. I agree. It is."

Rowan put his hand on Claire's back to direct her toward the door. After taking a step, she decided to first hit the restroom before facing the cold again. Rowan thought that was a good idea and hoped Marnie's staff had cleaned it after their Friday night crowd.

Chapter 11

The wood and fire pit were hidden behind a cluster of rocks by the stream. Above the pit sat a copper coil elevated by a metal tripod that kept it above the coal bed.

Cousin Dave placed some dry grass on the ashes that were there then covered them with some dry, brittle sticks of various sizes he had collected from the surrounding pine trees. The firewood he had with him was split at his trailer and brought down on the back of his quad.

His design was simple and ingenious. It took advantage of a five-foot drop in elevation over twenty-five-foot run of creek. Cousin Dave trenched a hose under the moss bed that was below the pines from the high side pool in the creek to connect with the copper coil at the firepit. The fire would heat the coil and water that ran through it from below sixty degrees to above one hundred and thirty degrees as it circled its way through the copper. At the of the end of the copper tube, a second hose connected to tubing to deliver the hot water to a natural pooling area that was kept fresh by a hillside spring. A manual valve split the line to direct hot water either back to the creek or into the pool while he was bathing. The heated water and control valve allowed year-round al fresco bathing.

Cousin Dave blew on the grass as it started to accept the fire from his match. The smoke it emitted showed the grass was damp. As the smoke erupted into flames, the fire began to transfer from the grass to the sticks. Cousin Dave started the final stage of teepee-ing wood above the flames and under the coil to start heating the water. He then reached to turn the valve to direct the incoming stream water to the pool instead of back to the creek.

Claire's look toward her dad as she climbed into the passenger seat of the Razor showed a mix of excitement and concern. The fiberglass shell and hard plastic seats were not the comfort levels she was expecting for either safety or comfort. She looked at the scratched plexiglass windshield wondering if it was good for anything more than stopping bugs. As the engine started with its usual loud whine and vibration, Claire instinctively grabbed for her seat belt to ensure she would stay inside the small, plastic buggy should it decide to roll.

Claire was confused as she tried to latch the Razor's four-point belt seatbelt. She was used to reaching behind her door-side shoulder for the Mini's belt that would pull two straps across her to lock in by her hip. The part she found near the door only reached halfway across her chest. Rowan paused to enjoy her frustration before offering assistance.

"It confused me too," he said. "This is a harness. It has a left and right side that clicks in the middle.

Rowan handed Claire the driver-side half of the harness, showed her how to click it, then tightened the strap for security.

As Rowan shifted the Razor from park to drive, Claire noticed that he had not put his belt on.

"Dad. Really?" she asked, moving her eyes from his and to the unfastened belt, then back.

Rowan smiled at his daughter's concern.

"These are set for Marnie," he answered. "I don't want her to have to readjust them."

Claire rolled her eyes.

"Yes, because your life and health are so less valuable than her pulling the belts tight again," she answered.

Rowan knew his daughter was right, and that he was setting a bad example. He was trying to show some moxie to his daughter beyond his familiar anal-retentive, seatbelt-wearing dad in the super-safe Audi.

"Good point," he replied.

"Jesus, what's gotten into you up here?"

Rowan smiled as he clicked his belt. *Freedom*, he thought as he moved his foot to stomp on the accelerator.

Marnie always drove the Razor in two-wheel drive that delivered the power to the back wheels. As Rowan stepped on the gas, the buggy lunged forward and fish-tailed in the grass. Rowan calmly counter-steered toward the direction of the slide as Claire grabbed the handle and roll bar to keep herself steady. As they headed for the chute into the trees, an undulation in the grass tossed the Razor upward, giving her the impression they caught air. After a few moments of panic, Claire settled into the fast ride through the trees knowing her dad was going to make it fun without creating too much danger.

"How do you know where you're going?" she shouted over the noise of the engine.

"It's a circle," he answered. "If I don't miss a turn, it'll bring us right back."

Claire's eyes expanded at his *miss a turn* caveat. She knew from the ride into Legend that the forests seemed to grow thicker as the cell service disappeared. She wondered if her dad was just adding to the excitement, or if there was a real risk that he could actually get them lost. A quick check of the gas gauge showed half-full. She wondered how far they could wander, if lost, before running out of gas.

As they emerged from the trees into the meadow, Rowan slowed to a stop. He positioned the Razor toward the valley overlook to show Claire some of the unseen beauty of her home state.

"This is tailing off now," he said, as he pointed across the panoramic view. "Over the past few weeks, it was like a painting. Looked almost fake."

Claire studied the terrain and trees, noting gaps where selective forestry had been through to harvest some of the hardwoods that grew in the area.

"It's beautiful," she said. "You don't get this type of look at home, even from your apartment."

"Condo," Rowan qualified.

Claire gave him a questioning look.

"I own it," he replied. "Apartments are rentals."

Claire's return look sent the usual *whatever* message. The qualification was not important. The fact that he and her mom were apart was. That he had bought the place sent the message that their separation was gaining permanency. That reality stung. But she decided not to bring it up there and ruin the fun they were having.

"Do I get to drive?" she asked, touching the shifter knob that was sitting in between them.

Rowan thought about the trails ahead that landed in the stream. The aggressive driving that was required to plow into and through the water would probably be more than Claire was up to. But he also knew that Marnie had no idea of Rowan's courage to fly down a blind chute of trees and forge through the creek. There had to be a rescue option if he failed that test. Looking around the cockpit of the vehicle, the winch control answered his question.

"The part coming up requires some driving skills and courage," he answered. "Do you have what it takes?"

Claire had her harness unbuckled and was half out of the buggy by the time he had finished the question. The Razor was not much smaller than her Mini Cooper. The controls were limited to gas, brakes, steering wheel, shifter, and a two-wheel-drive/four-wheel-drive switch. The winch was something she did not recognize, and thought was likely something she would not need.

"I've got this," she answered confidently. "How hard can it be?"

Rowan smiled as he climbed out of the Razor to surrender control.

"I'll give you some driving commands," he answered. "Just don't question them, and we'll be fine."

Claire settled into the driver's seat and quickly locked and adjusted her belts.

"Got it," she answered, in an almost defiant tone. "She had just been given permission to drive through the trees the way she drove on the roads when she wasn't with him or her mom.

The noise from the engine's restart startled Claire. She pressed on the gas, noting the strong resistance of the gas pedal to her push. Rowan knew what she was thinking as she revved the motor a few times.

"You have to step on it," he said, as her comfort with it became apparent.

Claire shifted the Razor into drive then looked to her dad as if waiting for directions and permission. Rowan pointed to the clearing in the trees that began the run down the mountainside. Before he could turn, his body was pressed against the plastic seat as he grabbed the handle and roll bar.

"Be careful," he shouted without thinking.

Claire's focus on the opening as they finished crossing the meadow gave him confidence. When a small whoopee bump in the field did not cause her to decrease speed, he began to wonder if giving her the wheel was a good idea. Claire obviously got some aggressive driving genes from her mother.

As the chute narrowed, Rowan noticed the canopy that was above them when he first drove through with Marnie was about half gone. He knew it would not be long before all the leaves were down, eliminating the tunnel effect that was exhilarating. But that loss also added leaves to the trails that would adversely affect traction.

"Be careful with the leaves," he said loudly, to give Claire understanding that their footing was not good.

Claire kept looking forward without replying. There was exhilaration in her eyes that he remembered seeing after successful ski runs, amusement park rides, and soccer games. She was having fun doing something new.

As they rounded the last blind turn that headed down the steep drop to the creek, Rowan tuned back into the need to get Claire to go faster. Their speed had to put them far enough into the sitting pool of water to stay above it and get close to the shallower side of the confluence.

The unexpected drop startled Claire. She pulled her foot off the accelerator just like Rowan did when he first hit the decline.

"Faster, Claire," he commanded.

Claire looked at her dad showing complete disbelief that he wanted her to go fast down the steep drop into a black hole.

"Faster!?" she yelled back.

"Trust me," he answered.

Claire reluctantly stomped on the gas. Their increasing speed made her nervous as the landing zone of water began to appear.

Claire's reaction to stomp on the brakes was instinctive. It sent the buggy into a slide that was contained by the U-shape of the trail.

"Gas! Claire," Rowan barked, trying to sound confident instead of panicked.

Claire stomped on the gas, deciding to listen to her dad rather than question him.

When the Razor hit the creek, it sent a wall of water in all directions that blocked their view of the surroundings. Claire pulled her foot off the gas as the Razor came to a floating stop. As the buggy drifted, she looked at her feet to notice the water starting to fill through the floorboards as her dad switched from two to four-wheel-drive.

"Punch it!" he instructed, pointing to the far side embankment. "We need to get there before we sink."

"SINK!?" Claire replied as she stepped on the gas with a panicked look.

As the spinning wheels started to rooster tail the creek water, she felt the cold water surround her duck boots. Once they were moving and she felt more confident, she looked to her dad with a smile, noting his feet were on the dash, staying dry.

"Keep it floored," he said, as she turned her eyes back to the shoreline. "We want to get out over there."

The creek water was soaking her jeans and nearing the top of her boots just as the Razor grabbed traction to exit the creek. Once on solid ground, Claire stopped the vehicle to collect herself.

"That was AMAZING!" she declared as the water started to empty from the cockpit.

Rowan smiled, keeping his feet high and dry. He could see Claire staring at his feet with the same sucker's disbelief he showed Marnie.

"Feet dry?" she asked, with a look to throw guilt.

Rowan looked down to the floorboard for an all-clear before moving his feet back down to where they should be.

"All good," he answered. "You handled that like a pro."

Claire's back straightened at the compliment. Usually both her mom and dad were critical of her driving. To be able to do something so insane in a vehicle and then get complimented for it was beyond belief.

"Wait until I tell Mom," she said without thinking.

Rowan's smile shifted to a look of concern. He knew Mindy would find some reason to make the ride irresponsible and dangerous. And, in some ways, he would have to agree.

"I'd prefer that you NOT...TELL...MOM," he replied, knowing the odds of that happening were not in his favor.

As Claire reoriented in her seat, Rowan began to smell smoke from a fire. His recall of the area did not include any camps or cabins. But looking around, he noticed that the creek landing was near the uphill climb they just drove to reach the mountain top. The trail loop was not a circle, as he first thought.

He pointed off to the mud bog that he knew Claire would enjoy as much as the creek. His only concern was getting stuck and having to climb out into the stink to use the winch. But that was part of the adventure.

As Claire started their drive toward the mud bog, the smell of wood burning become more intense. Growing concerned, Rowan asked Claire to turn at the upcoming fork in the trail to investigate.

The pine forest they entered was familiar, with its moss carpet. A smoldering white cloud was coming from behind the rhododendrons. With the wet from recent rain, Rowan knew the fire had to be man-made. As they neared the location, the source of the fire, with the spiraling line of copper tubing above it, made Rowan first think of moonshiners.

"Claire, stop," he instructed, now growing concerned about what they had come across.

As he peered through the sparse vegetation, Claire pointed to a pool with a man in it.

"Over there," she declared.

Rowan's first thought seeing Cousin Dave in a steaming pool was relief, followed by concern. Cousin Dave's wave to Marnie's Razor was instinctive, as would be his getting out to greet her.

Rowan's fear was what Cousin Dave would *not* be wearing that would embarrass both him and Claire.

"Let's go," he instructed Claire as he noticed Cousin Dave start to stand.

"Claire! Step on it," he demanded.

"MARNIE!?" Cousin Dave shouted as he climbed out and threw a robe around him. "ROWAN!?"

"Hold on," Rowan told Claire, knowing he was caught.

Claire watched Cousin Dave tiptoe across the moss bed in bare feet.

"Who is this guy?" Claire asked.

"Something else you are not to tell Mom about," he answered.

As Cousin Dave trotted toward the Razor, Claire became more intrigued. He slowed to a walk as he finished his last few steps.

"Well," he said, taking hold of the Razor's roof to get a good look, "I was half right."

Cousin Dave looked to Claire then back to Rowan for an introduction.

"Cousin Dave," Rowan said in an amused tone. "This is my daughter, Claire."

Rowan looked at Claire to find a look of complete disbelief that her dad would be on a familial, first-name basis with the skinny-dipping country man.

"Nice to meet ya," Cousin Dave said. "Hot tub's fresh and perfect. You two up to join me?"

Rowan gasped in disbelief, wondering if Cousin Dave had just asked them to strip down to jump in his heated stream water.

"Not this time," he answered.

Cousin Dave's eyes bounced back and forth from Rowan's to Claire's.

"Well, it goes year-round," he answered. "Just turned on the heat. You and Marnie should come out when it's snowing."

Claire's face changed to concern with the comment and vision of her dad soaking naked in a fire-heated pool of creek water out in the middle of nowhere with a woman named Marnie.

"Another time," Rowan answered.

He gave Cousin Dave a wink to confirm it would be a go on a later date. With a single tap on the roof with his hand, Cousin Dave pulled away from the Razor.

"It was nice to meet you...Claire," he said. "Enjoy the rest of your ride."

Not waiting for a reply, Cousin Dave turned to jog back to the hot tub he had created. Rowan shook his head as he turned from the bouncing image to his daughter.

"These are your new friends?" Claire asked.

Rowan paused to answer as he turned to watch Cousin Dave drop his robe before jumping back into the pool. His naked, old man's backside confirmed Claire's vision of her dad and some *Marnie* woman joining him in like attire.

"That's a good question," Rowan answered. "Acquaintances...clients for now."

"You're not going to buy anything up here? Like a trailer or something?"

The condescension in Claire's voice was obvious. Rowan smiled at the brief thought of spending more time in a place where decorum was a choice instead of a mandate.

"No, not a trailer."

Rowan knew the answer, as he worded it, would both make Claire comfortable and wonder. As she shifted the Razor back into drive, he pointed toward the mud bog for their last fun-run before heading back to the Sombrero.

# # # #

When the Razor came into view, Marnie had just finished a discussion with Tom in the production bay. His report was that their inventory was full, with excess juice to produce more. His only concern was that the shelf life of the wine was limited because they did not pasteurize the final product. The juice they had could hold in the containers for weeks. They both decided that it was best not to risk losing inventory to spoilage. Marnie wanted to talk to Rowan about the excess he had ordered and why.

The silhouette of the two bodies in the Razor as it approached showed that Rowan was the passenger and the driver was female. A slight twinge of nervousness pitted in Marnie's stomach as her exposure to Rowan's person was about to drill deeper into his family.

As they climbed the final hill Rowan smiled and waved to Marnie before pointing to her reserved parking spot for Claire to park in. The Razor came to a stop with the driver's side positioned in between Claire's dad and his new...country...whatever.

"Welcome back," Marnie said as she walked toward the machine.

Claire nervously unbuckled her harness before starting to climb out.

"Always smart to lock in," Marnie added, shifting her eyes to see Rowan rolling his.

Rowan hustled around to be in position for introductions once Claire was out and standing. Marnie's first impression of Claire was as expected. She could model for J. Crew or L.L. Bean with the attire she had on. Her duck boots leaned more to L.L. Bean. Her look and figure were definitely Anglo. Marnie could see a lot of Rowan in Claire's face. It made her wonder how pretty his ex-wife was to create such a beautiful girl.

"Marnie, meet Claire..." Rowan started. "Claire, meet Marnie."

Their handshake was soft and brief. Claire could feel some roughness in Marnie's palm that she had not felt before. Even her dad's hands were soft. But she also noticed a natural beauty in Marnie look and skin tone. Her aura was intriguing. She wore no makeup and had let her hair go gray. And it worked extraordinarily well.

"It's nice to meet you," Claire replied. "I have to say, this is all a surprise to me."

Claire flopped her arms and took a step back to emphasize her point. She had no expectations coming home from school that the day she'd just had was even possible.

"Well, I hope in a good way." Marnie answered.

Her puzzled look to Rowan made him laugh lightly.

"Come in," she added, extending her hand to guide them into the production area.

Claire looked around the small fermentation area. Her initial impression was that it was simpler and smaller than she had expected. Like her father, she thought she would find big, wooden kegs full of aging wine neatly piled against a wall. Instead, she saw Tom draining purple liquid into a blue bottle from a plastic hose that connected to a stainless-steel vat. Her immediate thought was to ask a lot of questions. But she decided that it was likely best to keep them to herself to ask her dad on the ride home.

"This is neat," Claire said as she looked toward Tom and smiled.

"Not quite what you expected," Rowan replied, knowing what she was thinking.

"No, but what is these days?"

Claire's smile showed her pleasure at getting one in on her dad and his interests in the Sombrero. He gave her a small push forward to acknowledge her success. Marnie enjoyed the interaction between the two. It showed a side of Rowan she did not know was there. He was obviously a good dad.

# # # #

Rowan's face turned happy as he looked around the Sombrero bar to find the two people he wanted Marnie to meet. Maria's face looked different from the confidence she had shown at the brewhouse the night he'd had dinner there. There was a nervousness in her expression that forewarned that her brother was wondering why she would bring him to a winery in the sticks.

Maria and her brother, Tyson, stood as Rowan approached, Claire a step behind him. Marnie stopped to deal with something at the bar while Tom waited for her before moving over. Marnie's stop was more to buy time to think about where she had seen the two faces she was about to meet. Both looked familiar. She just could not place where and why.

Maria introduced Rowan to Tyson. Like his sister, Tyson had arms speckled with tattoos. He stood about six feet tall with a lean frame. His baggy jeans and black hooded sweatshirt with sleeves pushed up finished the stereotypical image of the hip, college-town entrepreneur.

Claire noticed the two as they stood. As she looked at them both, questions continued to grow. Why was her corporate banker dad dealing with a country winery owner and two tattooed twenty-somethings?

"Claire," Rowan said, "you're welcome to sit in, or to find a place to kill an hour or so."

Claire looked at her dad, then shifted her eyes to the two people she had just met. Marnie and Tom arrived at the table just as she was about to speak.

"If you're looking for internet," Tom said. "The best service is outside, over by that apple tree."

Claire smirked at the suggestion. She remembered losing service on the way up. As she looked to Marnie for confirmation, Marnie nodded to show her agreement.

"I think I'll stay here," she answered. "If you don't mind."

Rowan made the final introductions of Marnie and Tom to Maria and Tyson. Rowan had sent some framework for Maria to use to research and build upon for her brother's brewhouse. Her initial excitement was quickly extinguished by concern that her brother would continue to fail to see the bigger picture. Rowan told her that was going to be a common thread between Tyson and Marnie. Something that they were going to have to figure out on the fly.

Rowan opened by talking about the quality and local demand for both company's products. Although they were different, they both carried the same appeal of social atmosphere, great taste, and alcohol. Both were products used to celebrate successes and to drown sorrow. So both were recession proof.

Knowing in advance that both Marnie and Tyson saw growth as losing control of product and quality, Rowan began to build his case to have them share inventory. Marnie could sell Tyson's beer to get more parties of mixed drinkers to her winery. Tyson could sell Marnie's wine to get her crowd to his restaurant. The back-and-forth would build market for both of them as more and more people found their establishments and told others.

Tyson's initial resistance to the idea was to protect his brand. His meticulous approach to brewing, storing, and serving his beers made him suspicious that anyone would give them their needed level of attention. Looking around the Sombrero did not add to his confidence that Marnie would do either.

"How do I know my beer will be kept to the right temperature and served properly?" he asked.

Marnie moved to respond to what she felt was a stupid question as Rowan's hand squeezed her knee to keep quiet. His eyes reinforced his message not to stir the pot and ruin the opportunity.

Maria added her thoughts about joint marketing for tourists— that would share the cost and push business to either entity to produce revenue for both. Tyson's eyes closed a number of times as he thought about the proposal. Marnie continued to sit silent, with her arms clenched across her chest.

"That explains the extra juice," Tom said, excited about the potential to make more wine.

Rowan scanned the faces of Maria, Tyson, and Marnie to take a temperature on the room. A quick look to Claire showed that she was intrigued by what her father found and was trying to put it together.

"I guess we could set you up with growlers and cans to see what happens," Tyson said slowly.

A smile appeared on Maria's face as she listened to her brother give an inch.

Rowan turned to look at Marnie to see if she was going to respond. Tom nudged her to comment. His expression encouraged her to give the idea serious consideration.

"We have some extra inventory we can send over. It just needs to be room temperature. Served in a glass," she answered sarcastically. "How do we work the billing?"

Rowan's anxiety level began to drop when Marnie agreed to use the brewhouse and accept their beer.

"Straight inventory, each pays the other a week after receiving it." Rowan answered, knowing he had to add one more comment to build trust. "Let's be clear: no payment, no additional inventory is to be exchanged."

"Cash or check?" Marnie asked.

Rowan knew her thinking was that cash was relatively untraceable. Checks were a paper trail for the tax man.

"If you two want to build legit businesses, you need to operate like one," Rowan answered. "But I'll leave that to you to decide."

"Checks work," the two said simultaneously.

Rowan smiled as he saw the deal come together. He figured that both entities would see an immediate boost to sales as a result. From his own experience, he knew that most patrons were a blend of wine and beer drinkers. For both operations to offer the other's products made them more attractive to groups looking for somewhere that offered both beer and wine.

The next step was to get them to cooperate on some shared regional marketing and advertising. Rowan asked for them to let Maria prepare a plan for their review. He added that he would be available and involved in its development, but that Maria would be responsible for the legwork to build a plan that, once accepted, would be implemented quickly to build holiday traffic.

The meeting ended with unenthusiastic handshakes. Marnie and Tyson agreed to sell the other their product at sixty percent of their retail price to insure a profit for the reseller and an acceptable wholesale profit on manufacturing costs to the producer. They would review their sales and need for inventory from week to week, knowing they had the ability to make runs for more supply any time they needed it. Rowan asked Maria to have a marketing plan framed for discussion for their next meeting in seven days.

As the meeting separated, Tom clenched his hands, eager to return to make more wine. He saw dollar signs in Rowan's mating of the Sombrero to the brewery. The only downside was Marnie's smile and touch to Rowan's shoulder to thank him for the opportunity he created.

"That's a pretty cool thing you did there," Claire mentioned to her dad as he watched Marnie return to the bar.

"Teamwork," Rowan answered. "I added what I do best to what they do best."

Rowan thought about the statement that had just flowed from his mouth without thinking. Marnie still had challenges. The increase in revenue from the deal was her path to salvation. But she desperately needed to tighten her business practices to make sure that income was always greater than expenses. He sensed that Tyson counted every penny, which made him both comfortable and worried at the same time.

"Is there any way I can help with the marketing?" Claire inquired. "I am a marketing major and could maybe get credit."

Rowan responded with an inquisitive look. His daughter was shifting from child to capable adult in front of him. Her college perspective from South Carolina would be helpful to Maria to build a plan that would appeal to younger clientele.

"I think that's a great idea," he answered. "We can stay overnight. Go to dinner at the brewhouse. You can witness the Sombrero in full swing later. I have a cabin rented for the season nearby. It's kind of a hunting dump, but it's clean."

Claire began to regret her offer as Rowan presented that staying in a rustic, hunting cabin was her only option. She started looking for reasons not to stay.

"We don't have our things," she replied, hoping he would agree to go back to comfort in Pittsburgh. "I don't have my toothbrush, underwear, anything!"

Rowan smiled, recalling similar challenges a few weeks earlier.

"Walmart," he replied. "They've got everything."

Rowan would have mentioned Larson's. But he knew Claire's choices at that store would run close to a thousand dollars.

"Walmart," Claire repeated in a tone that said she would likely wait in the car.

Rowan put his arm around Claire to give her a loving hug. Although initially resistant to his suggestion of where to outfit for the weekend, she gave in knowing he would not let her go until he got a return squeeze.

Rowan and Claire separated as Claire went to visit the restroom, and he went to find Marnie to tell her that they were staying the night after leaving for a few hours.

"I'm taking Claire into Clarion to get some supplies for tonight," he said, when he found her.

Marnie's back was to him as she heard his words.

"I've also got another thing brewing for you to consider, but I'll talk to you about that later."

Marnie stood still and he waited for a reply.

"Marnie?"

Rowan walked to her. He placed his hands on her shoulders to spin her to face him. Her face was expressionless.

"What's wrong?"

"Why are you doing this, Rowan?" she said softly. "Why do you think you can just come in here and start deal making with my wine, without me?"

Rowan's hands dropped from her shoulders as he stepped back.

"I thought you'd be happy with the opportunity... opportunities," he answered, puzzled as to why she would object.

Marnie paused before speaking. She knew his intentions were good. His approach of just moving forward without discussion was what bothered her. She had to be careful.

"You know," she started, "I may be a shitty businesswoman. But I did build this business."

Rowan laughed at the self-deprecation. Her eyes were welling with tears that he knew he had to quell. Fact was, Marnie was no different from most entrepreneurs. Entrepreneurs were almost always more focused on product than business. And most companies run by entrepreneurs failed because their founders' mission-passion always took attention away from their business responsibilities. Tyson showed the same tendencies. And by the time most returned to deal with business issues that festered into real problems, their efforts were often hindered by a lack of expertise to fix them in time.

Rowan walked toward Marnie, who immediately took a step back. She knew he intended to hug her to provide comfort she did not want. But when she backed into the counter, she had nowhere to go to avoid his embrace. Reluctantly, she let him hug her.

"The Red Sombrero will always be your business. I'm just a banker trying to win the confidence of an owner of a business with awesome potential."

"That better be the truth."

Marnie's body remained stiff with her arms at her side as he squeezed her body to his. After a few seconds of resistance, she lifted her arms to hug him back.

"You're such an asshole," she mumbled, laughing.

Rowan continued to hold her tight as he enjoyed the fragrance of her perfume.

"I'd give you a business book to read that would show you that you're no different from most entrepreneurs. But I know you wouldn't read it."

"You got that right," she answered, as she let go of him.

"Do you trust me?" he asked.

"Do I have a choice?"

Rowan scowled at her question. It was not what he was expecting.

"Yes," he answered. "You do.... I can leave."

Rowan stepped back to move to the door. As he intentionally moved slowly, waiting for her answer, he felt her hand grab his. Marnie pulled him to her for another hug.

"You can stay...for now," she replied, laughing slightly again.

Rowan returned her hug before pushing her away gently. He cupped her face in his hands to give her a light kiss. As their lips parted, the sweet sensation of his affection ended when her eyes reopened to find Claire in the doorway watching.

Chapter 12

The drive from Legend to the Clarion Walmart was quiet. Claire walked away as soon Marnie's eyes met hers. Rowan followed her out to the car, looking for an opportunity to explain what his daughter had just seen. But during the chase, he realized that he really did not understand the situation himself. He decided to stay quiet until Claire was ready to talk.

To fill the twenty-minute drive, Rowan carried on a one-sided conversation, remembering trips he took with Claire to regional soccer tournaments up and down the East Coast. She buried her nose in her phone as soon as bars of service returned. He wondered who she was texting so feverishly.

"Who are you texting?" he asked, concerned it could be her mother.

"Mom," she answered.

"Claire..."

"Don't worry, Dad. I'm not mentioning Marnie. I'm just telling her we went go-karting, and that we're staying here." she replied. "You do know she dates, don't you?"

Rowan thought about Claire's comment. He wanted to correct go-karting to Razoring. But he knew Mindy would not understand Razoring. He also knew his soon-to-be ex-wife was dating. It seemed like a community of men lined up as soon as Rowan was out of the picture. Initially that upset him and made him jealous. But he also knew it was time for them to part in order to each find happiness on their own.

"Yes, sweetie. I do," he answered with a pained look on his face.

"Then you can too," Claire added. "You deserve to be happy... and loved. But up here? With someone so different than....us?"

Claire's segmentation of Marnie and the people in Legend as different from them and their community in Pittsburgh both disappointed and qualified things for Rowan. It was a different world with a different, and refreshing, approach and attitude toward life.

"I don't know what to say about that. I'm actually not sure what's going on."

Claire felt sympathy for her dad, who was desperately trying to frame something for her that he could not figure out himself.

"I guess just roll with it," she answered. "She's cool.... I like her."

"She is cool," Rowan agreed as the Walmart sign appeared above the tree line at the interstate exit. "Went to art school and lived in California."

"That's cool too," Claire added with a smile that showed approval. "This, however..."

Rowan got her insinuation that she was not excited to be visiting Walmart for supplies. But he also knew it was not her first time in one. He quickly checked for a Target as they exited the interstate to find nothing. He also gave Larson's another quick thought. But their needs were beyond just overpriced outerwear.

Having no other options, Rowan turned his one hundred-thousand-dollar Audi into the Walmart parking lot to find a spot that was close to the entrance but not in the mix of cars that would think nothing about dinging his door with theirs.

# # # #

Maria was excited to see Rowan and Claire walk into the brewhouse. She had already started compiling notes she had created over the past several months to build her brother's brewery and restaurant business. Walking through the rustic building, Claire was reminded of the microbreweries back at school in Five Points.

"It's amazing," she commented as she looked around. "You think your area is unique. Then you drive into somewhere else you think is completely behind the times to find that they're pretty much the same. Their cool...is our cool."

Rowan looked at his daughter as he thought about the days when the diversity between country and city was broader. He credited television, cable, and the internet for closing the gap. The offerings at Larson's showed that Clarion had most of the same sophistication as Pittsburgh. Both communities also had access to all internet retailers to get whatever they wanted as soon as the next day.

"There's definitely a difference between life here and life at home," Rowan answered. "But you're right—there is a lot of overlap that you wouldn't expect."

Rowan reintroduced Maria to Claire with an added offer to Maria for Claire to help her with insights from both Pittsburgh and Columbia. Reluctant at first, Maria saw Claire as a thunder-stealer. She was not only the big-city college girl who was going to get credit for all of Maria's ideas. She was Rowan's daughter. But as discussions pieced together through Maria's table visits, she realized that Claire's ideas and insights supported her initial concepts for marketing the brewery. She was particularly interested to learn more about Five Points and that maybe a trip to Columbia, South Carolina during the cold of winter could be a business trip.

When dinner ended, Rowan suggested the two women set a time to meet Sunday morning at the brewery to discuss their ideas. He charged Maria as the lead. He encouraged them both to work together, be honest with thoughts, and to not take any counter ideas personally. Both girls agreed and were anxious to get started. The mention of budget was framed as modest, to ensure that their focus was on bang-for-the-buck economy instead of just splash.

As Rowan and Claire were leaving, he took a moment to peer in the kitchen for Tyson. He found the young brewmaster standing next to his chef giving instructions on food preparation. A smile came to his face as the sight confirmed his impression that Tyson was a quality-passionate entrepreneur. A quick whistle and wave got a return smile and nod before Tyler turned back to attend to the food preparation. From that Rowan knew Tyson was in to build his business. He became more anxious to see what ideas Maria and Claire could build together.

# # # #

Darkness fell on the Sombrero just after 6:00 p.m. With daylight savings time approaching, Rowan knew the clocks would push back to bring sunset an hour earlier.

"I hate wintertime," Claire said as the Audi pulled into the cabin's driveway.

The Xenon headlights cut a clean window of vision down the path that extended from side to side but held a defined line at the top. Rowan slowed to keep the car from hitting bottom on the roadway as it began to undulate.

"Kinda spooky, isn't it?" Rowan asked, watching Claire lean toward the windshield for a better look.

"*Chainsaw* spooky," she replied. "I hope this place has running water."

Rowan did not respond to Claire's comment, waiting for her to look to him first. When her eyes shifted from the outside to his, he smiled to confirm that her fear might be true.

"OH MY GOD, Dad!" Claire shrieked. "Does it have an outhouse!?"

Toying with Claire was a fun pleasure he'd enjoyed since she was a child. On their way to vacations, he would look for a dilapidated cottage or house, pull into the driveway, and announce they had arrived. Claire's response, along with her sister's, would set Rowan laughing hysterically, while Mindy would frown and say *it was not funny*.

"No outhouse," he replied. "But it is a hunter's cabin. Meaning it is rustic and has animal heads on the walls."

Claire exhaled to show her discontent. The thought of dead animal heads looming over her while she slept was frightening. She knew driving back to Pittsburgh was not an option. But there were hotels near the university that seemed nice.

"Can't we stay at the hotels near the university?" she asked.

Rowan thought briefly about her request. It was a fair one. Claire had never been exposed to the level of rustic the cabin offered. Even at summer camp, with its metal bunks and screened walls, the accommodations were not as frightening as she was about to see.

"I'll tell you what," Rowan answered. "If you feel uncomfortable with the cabin, we can drive the twenty minutes back to town to get a hotel room."

The driveway ended in the parking area in front of the cabin. A single yellow light by the door gave Claire her first impression of what was to come. The cabin's simple design was cute and inviting. Her anxiety eased as Rowan put the Audi into park and opened his door.

When the cabin door opened, the yellow light from the porch leaked into the room to show hints of its simple accommodations. Rowan turned on the overhead light. Claire's first sight when the room illuminated was a twelve-point buck head mounted over the stone fireplace. At first, she gasped, then she settled to accept it as decoration before looking at what else was there.

"Dad, this place is a dump," she commented.

She pressed down on the old mattress covered by a faded, but clean, cover. The squeak that followed made her pull her hand back quickly. Her eyes bulged at the sight of the ancient facilities and rusted tub in the bathroom.

"The Sombrero bathroom is nicer than this one."

Rowan smiled as he listened to his child's disdain. He knew they were not staying. That meant he had to be careful with his wine consumption. Being twenty-one and a fan of all things alcoholic and sweet, he knew he could not count on Claire to drive him anywhere after seeing the Sombrero in action in a few hours.

"Okay," he agreed. "We'll get a hotel room in Clarion. But without internet service, we'll have to take what we can find later."

Claire nodded. A quick look into the refrigerator resulted in a gag reflex because of some food Rowan had left the week before that had gone bad.

"Do you really stay here?" Claire asked, surprised her dad would stoop to such levels.

"Only once," he lied. "A few weeks back. It's not that bad if you don't really do anything but sleep."

"I don't think I ever could here." Claire replied as she headed for the door.

Rowan opened the door to leave, and Claire took one last look around.

"I'm surprised you didn't wake to something sitting on your chest," she mumbled as they walked back outside.

Rowan's immediate thought as he shut the cabin door was that he should not have shown Claire the cabin. He knew, at some point, she would mention it to Mindy, which would result in two levels of response. One of disappointment in him for staying there. Two with outrage that he would expose their daughter to that level of living.

"Claire," he said, as they walked back to the car, "this is one…"

"…of those things we don't tell Mom. I get it."

The fact that she finished his thought made him smile. They were in sync. He hoped she would stay true to that promise and not disclose the cabin in some future outburst.

#####

The Sombrero's parking lot was fuller than usual for 7:00 p.m. The usual pickups and jeeps were there along with an array of quads and Razors parked in their designated area to the side. Marnie had the white Christmas lights lit to illuminate the path from the parking area to the front door.

"Looks like you don't have the nicest car in the lot tonight," Claire mentioned, pointing to two Range Rovers parked side-by-side.

The two black beauties both had Pennsylvania license plates with Pittsburgh dealer insignias. The Pittsburgh Steelers and Penguins logos showed they were from the city. Rowan was happy to see the high-end tourist crowd find the Sombrero, which was a goal he had for Maria and Claire to achieve.

"They should not be too hard to spot in the crowd," Rowan commented as he studied the cars further. "I stood out like a sore thumb when I first arrived."

Claire smiled to think about her dad as the fish out of water. What he was wearing now was different from the wide-wale cords and Polo flannel shirt he would typically wear on weekends at home. But even with his dialed-down fashion to fit in at the Sombrero, he was still a preppy who would be easy to find in this crowd.

Rowan parked the Audi in a spot near the door that Marnie had marked as reserved for EMS services. She had offered it to Rowan, saying that it was just something to keep a spot open for favored guests—not that he had achieved that status.

"Dad, this is the EMS spot," Claire declared as he pulled to a stop.

"It's a fake," Rowan replied. "Marnie said I could park here because my car looks like it belongs to a doctor. She actually thought I was one when we first met...a brain surgeon."

Rowan chuckled to the memory; Claire rolled her eyes.

"What if someone gets hurt or sick?"

"My guess is that the ambulance will pull close to the front door," he replied. "Easier access, in and out."

Claire remained puzzled as they climbed out of the car. She studied the area where she thought an EMS van would park to bring aid, then looked back at where Marnie had marked the parking spot.

"Why not just mark it reserved?"

"Because no one would respect that," Rowan replied. "Tow trucks don't circle around here for illegally parked cars the way they do in the city."

Claire nodded understanding. But she was still uncomfortable with parking in an EMS zone. As Rowan opened the door to enter the Sombrero, the crowd that was waiting was bigger and rowdier than she expected. It reminded her of her favorite bars in Columbia. Looking back at her dad, she noticed energy appear in his face as he looked around the room and then waved to Marnie.

"Our seats are reserved," Rowan said, pointing to his usual and the one next to it at the bar.

# # # #

"Welcome back, you two," Marnie said, happily.

"You're happy tonight," Rowan replied.

"Lots of people, lots of inventory. What's not to be happy about?"

Claire settled on to her stool as she watched Marnie reach for two glasses and one of the blue bottles that was sitting behind the bar.

"I need to see your ID," Marnie joked.

Claire, thinking she was serious, pulled her ID from her phone pocket for Marnie to study. Her exaggerated examination of the plastic card and photograph brought a smile to Claire's face.

"You're good!" she said, handing the license back to Claire and pushing a glass toward her.

Rowan was already pouring the red wine into a glass he was holding.

"This is different than what you're used to," he said. "It's sweet. So I think you'll like it."

"Oh, that's nice," Claire replied in an exaggerated, whiney voice. "Sweet for the sweet?"

The reaction on her face as the Dervish Red hit her taste buds showed it was not what she expected. Continued movement of her lips and mouth revealed that she was intrigued with the taste while deciding if she liked it.

"This is good," Claire declared, taking a second sip to run it again. "I like it."

Rowan nodded as he looked to Marnie to declare the young adult market as fertile.

"This would sell in Columbia," Claire added as she finished the first tastes Rowan had poured into her glass.

Marnie smiled more in admiration of the father-daughter interaction that was playing out in front of her than about the approval of her wine. It was a relationship she wished she had with her dad. Claire seemed to be a lot like Rowan while Marnie, as an artist, was a polar opposite to her dad, who worked a farm.

"I'll be back," Marnie said as Rowan and Claire disappeared into their own discussion.

They started talking about marketing to the twenties market in Pittsburgh. Rowan shared his experience with Vinnie and Sal. He laughed when he talked about the relabeling of Dervish Red to what Vinnie called Dago Red. Claire's face lit with objection as she heard her dad use the derogatory ethnic term.

"Dad," Claire stated, adamantly. "You can't use that term. It's not P.C."

Rowan smiled at his daughter's sensitivity. He knew she would object to it before he said it.

"I didn't," he replied. "Vinnie, my very Italian friend, and client, did."

Claire responded with a puzzled look.

"I still don't think you should call it that," she replied.

"We won't," he chuckled. "It will be called something else."

As Rowan took another drink of wine, a familiar face appeared behind him. Creeping slowly toward the bar, she put her finger to her lips for Claire to not react or say anything. A hand touching his shoulder then continuing down his chest made Claire smile as her dad jerked upright. The final clasp to hold him, along with a kiss on his cheek from behind, told Rowan who it was.

"Janis," he declared as he spun in his seat.

"Who's Janis?!" Nicki replied, stepping back in surprise.

Nicki's outfit was stunning. She was wearing leggings that disappeared into her knee-high patent leather riding boots. To keep warm, she had a turtleneck under her hip-length, black, puffy, down parka. Her Pittsburgh Steelers tassel cap finished her polished look for the flannel crowd. Rowan noticed the men behind her glancing repeatedly as their women looked away.

"Nicki," Rowan clarified, visibly surprised to see her. "I thought you were someone else."

"Hi Ms. Schmitt," Claire added.

Nicki touched Claire's arm to return her greeting.

"Surprised to see me?" she asked, knowing his reply from the look on his face.

"What are you doing up here?" Rowan answered as he looked around the bar for any others.

"We came up for the leaves. Dorsey said you found this fun winery. We thought we'd check it out before heading back."

Rowan ran his thoughts back to the parking lot. The two side-by-side Range Rovers were theirs. Dorsey was likely somewhere in the crowd with his wife, Charlotte, and others. Two Range Rovers meant they'd brought a party.

"Come on outside. We have a firepit to ourselves."

Rowan gave a quick look to Claire, who was eager to move away from the crowd. The thought of a warm fire in the open air with the smell of burning wood was inviting. As they both stood to walk with Nicki, neither noticed Marnie behind the bar near them. Her vantage point gave a head-to-toe look at Nicki. She saw her affectionate approach and kiss that Rowan seemed to enjoy. Nicki was a stunning woman, polished and obviously wealthy. Marnie began to feel angry that Rowan could be pulled so easily from his usual perch to disappear into the crowd with her.

"Marnie," Tom said as he walked through the kitchen area, "we...."

"Tom! Whatever it is, just fix it," she snapped.

"Jeez-sus," he answered. "Where'd happy Marnie go?"

The glare in her eyes answered his question. He had seen her upset many times. When it reached that look, he knew something had happened. He looked at the end of the bar, noticing that Rowan was not on his stool.

"Where's Ro..."

"TOM! Just shut it! Please."

Marnie turned away from him to wipe a clean counter cleaner. The hard, downward push on the rag was Tom's cue to just make whatever decision he was seeking from her happen. He turned away as Marnie stopped her wiping motion to drop her shoulders and head in despair.

# # # #

"Ro-wan. Ro-wan. Ro-wan"

Dorsey started the chant that erupted further through their friends as they saw him arrive with Nicki and Claire. Dorsey had the fire blazing high. Several Adirondack chairs were pulled close to the two-foot stone surround that many were using as seating.

"This place is awesome," Dorsey stated, holding up a blue bottle to offer both Rowan and Claire some wine.

Rowan smiled to the comment, disappointed that his friends had found his piece of heaven in the north country. But it was true, and nice to see them. They were always fun to be with. But the Red Sombrero was his escape from the city, and from them. Now that they had found it, he was not sure they would forget about it. That was good for Marnie's business. But not so good for his need to escape.

"Welcome to the Red Sombrero...and to north country."

Rowan pressed a fake smile onto his face to make his greeting seem sincere. He looked at his friends, who all appeared worn from a day outside touring, now settled with glasses of Dervish Red. He fully expected that they would be joining him and Claire in the search for a hotel room later. No one was going to be able to make the two-and-a-half-hour drive back to Pittsburgh after some *après-leaves* at the Sombrero.

"I see a bunch of tired eyes enjoying some craft wine outside by the fire." Rowan said as he looked around at his eight friends. "Where are you sleeping tonight?"

His eyes shifted to Nicki, thinking about her having to spend the night in the cabin Claire rejected. He also knew it was the end of leaf season, and that decent hotel rooms could be hard to find. At least hotel rooms suited to the comfort level his friends demanded.

"We're definitely heading back," Nicki said. "We'll stop for some dinner somewhere, then drive home."

Rowan smiled at her declaration. None of them had had dinner. Their situation was reminiscent of his first night, when he found the Sombrero and woke up with Janis's dog. The memory of Travis's foul breath made him gag and cough slightly.

"There's food here. But not dinner. There's also a fun microbrewery in Clarion," he offered, to both get them fed and on their way.

Dorsey put his arm around Rowan as he finished his suggestions.

"You can't get rid of us that easily," he declared. "We'll hang until we get cold."

Yeah, well keep drinking the antifreeze, and you'll be here all night was Rowan's thought that he was able to hold to himself.

Rowan settled next to Claire on the stone wall that separated the fire pit from the chairs. As he pulled her close, the warmth on their backs felt good. They breathed in the cold, fresh air. Claire stayed quiet through a number of conversations Rowan had with friends who rolled by to chat then moved on. He squeezed his arm around her shoulder to give her comfort and show his appreciation that she was there.

Marnie waited patiently, then finally agreed to surrender the stools at the bar after ninety minutes passed the return of Rowan or Claire. She wondered where he had strolled off to with the beautiful woman who accosted him at the bar. Although she felt no right to claim him, that did not deter the jealousy that was building as time passed and he was nowhere to be seen.

"Can I get two more bottles of red?" Rowan asked, as he finally returned to the bar with two empties.

Marnie looked at him, then away.

"Check with your server," she replied. "I'm busy."

Rowan frowned at Marnie's reply and looked to his stools, which were now occupied by other people. It was the first time she had ever given them away. But it was also the first time he had ever vacated his spot for any length of time. A quick look at the clock showed he had been gone for almost two hours.

Rowan followed Marnie down the bar to find an open spot to talk to her.

"Are you mad at me?" he asked.

Marnie wiped some glasses dry as she decided whether to answer his question.

"Why would I be mad at you?" she answered. "You're superman. You save the day."

Her response answered his question along with how mad she was.

"What's wrong?"

"Nothing, Rowan. Just go back with Miss Little Equestrian in her thousand-dollar boots and puffy coat."

Rowan smiled at the accusation. Marnie was jealous.

"Nicki?" he asked. "She's a childhood friend from Pittsburgh."

Marnie continued to dry glasses as she looked at Rowan.

"Why is she here?"

"There's a group outside from home," he answered. "They came to see leaves then remembered this place from a conversation I had with her brother at the Steelers game."

"Group? I did not see a group come through."

Jesus, Rowan thought. *How could you miss them?*

"They're...we're out at one of the fire pits. Come out, and I'll introduce you."

Marnie saw that Rowan's offer was sincere. But she also knew the tables would turn to make her the fish out of water in her own bar.

"I'll catch up with you," she replied as she gave him two bottles. "I need to get coverage."

"Don't you dare blow me off," he replied, smiling to show he knew what she was doing.

"Just go, Rowan."

Rowan disappeared into the crowd with the bottles as Janis settled onto the stool where he had just left.

"Seems like Clark's friends are more interesting than you are," she said in a snide tone.

"Fuck you, Janis."

"Marnie, you have to..."

Janis stopped talking as Marnie abruptly lifted her hand toward her. The hurt in her eyes told her best friend that it was not the time to take jabs at each other. Before Janis could apologize, Marnie turned to escape into the supply room to regather her thoughts and composure.

# # # #

Dorsey piled three logs onto the fire as it started to fade from the roar he wanted. The Sombrero firepit was similar to what he had in his back yard minus his formal landscaping.

As he surveyed the darkness, Dorsey noticed a white image cascading about, across the grass, in a random, twirling motion.

"What the hell is that?"

Rowan looked out to recognize the white, flowing shirt with its arms extended gliding effortlessly in circles across the grass. As it neared, the brown, canvas-covered thimble shaped hat became visible along with the face of Cousin Dave, who was in his own world while coming into land at the Sombrero.

"That's the guy from the creek," Claire observed.

"A little country color," Rowan said, patting Dorsey on the back. "He's an interesting character."

Cousin Dave twirled through the crowd as if seeking to greet anyone with a bottle. As he approached Rowan, Dorsey stepped back out of concern while Rowan lifted his blue bottle to pay homage to the Dervish. Cousin Dave extended his chalice shaped from tin. Rowan surrendered a generous pour into his cup before Cousin Dave toasted him and his friends, then continued off into the crowd.

"Friend of yours?" Dorsey asked.

"Acquaintance."

"Loony."

"Insightful," Rowan closed, to bring clarity to Cousin Dave's aura.

Nicki approached Dorsey, noting that it was after 9:00 p.m. She was cold, hungry, and wanted to leave. The rest of the group was fading as well, as the alcohol added to their exhaustion from a day of touring. They all knew there was no driving home. Claire remembered Tom's recommendation to get internet access by the apple tree. She was able to help everyone book suitable rooms in Clarion. Checking the brewhouse website, they were excited to find its kitchen was open until ten. They had time to get dinner. Claire would call Maria to let them know a table of eight was coming.

Rowan gave Claire his credit card for check-in to their room. She wanted to go back to the hotel to get warm, find strong internet service, and frame some thoughts for her meeting with Maria in the morning. Nicki urged Rowan to join them for dinner then more *après-leaves* at the hotel. Rowan declined, knowing that Marnie was still stewing. She never appeared to meet his friends as promised.

Dorsey settled the entire bill on his corporate American Express. Because Rowan was present, he declared the adventure a business scouting expedition to Clarion, Pennsylvania with his banker, investors, and fellow board member, Nicki. Rowan walked back through the main bar area to escort them, with Claire, to the Range Rovers. He made sure to tell them to be on the lookout for horse-drawn carriages.

Nicki took the opportunity to say goodnight to Rowan with a hug and unexpected kiss on the lips. She said he looked particularly sexy in his mountain attire. As she finished with a smile and touch to his cheek, he just shook his head in bewilderment. Rowan was anxious to see their taillights disappear into the darkness so that he could go fix whatever issues he had with Marnie. Marnie was thinking otherwise as she witnessed the goodbyes from the production bay service door to the kitchen.

As he returned to the bar, Rowan saw an empty stool near its center. Its position kept his back to the crowd but also put the front door and kitchen area in his peripheral vision. Marnie was nowhere to be seen. He wondered if she had finally given in and was outside looking for them. As he stood again to go search, he felt his arm grabbed from behind the bar.

"I'm here," she said.

Rowan stopped without turning back to look. A smirk appeared on his face that he knew he had to wipe clean before turning toward her.

"What makes you think I'm going to look for you?"

Marnie paused to avoid saying what first came to mind. He was there and not on his way off to be with his friends.

"Because you stayed behind instead of heading off with Miss High-Maintenance."

Rowan smiled as he reached to take hold of her hand. It was wet and clammy from the bar rag. But he held it anyway as its warmth returned.

"I'm not going to chase you," she added.

Rowan could see the hurt in her eyes.

"You don't have to. But I'm sure, at some point, you'll be looking to ditch me."

Marnie smiled, wondering if there would ever be any truth to that. Rowan's boyish grin was too captivating to let go of now.

"Jeez-sus!" Dorsey declared, as he sat next to Rowan at the bar. "No adventure in those people.... I'll need a ride to the hotel."

Rowan froze at Dorsey's presence and declaration. With Claire situated and safe in a hotel room with his friends, he was not sure if he was heading to Clarion for the night. And if Dorsey was going to drink more wine, he was not going to give his friend the keys to his car.

Rowan patted his friend on the back with a smile as he helped himself to the bottle of wine on the counter. The acoustic band was starting its first set of the night. Dorsey spun in his chair to both listen and survey the crowd. As he nodded his head to the music, he noticed an attractive blonde staring back at him. A quick smile received one in return as she disappeared toward the back deck.

"I'll be right back," he declared, heading off into the sea of bodies.

 Marnie turned back to her work serving customers. Before getting away, though, she was stopped by Rowan's grip of her hand. His eyes asked the question.

"We're good, Clark," she replied with a smile before walking away.

# # # #

Rowan kept his perch on the center bar stool, splitting his time between short conversations and touches with Marnie while also looking for Dorsey. His quick departure after unexpectedly returning to the bar seemed to be for the bathroom. But as the clock ticked past midnight, the crowd continued to grow, and Rowan's good friend, and client, was nowhere to be seen.

As Rowan turned back to the bar to find Marnie, he felt a bump on his back followed by a giggle he had heard before.

"Janis," he said, hoping he was right as he turned.

"Yup," she answered. "Look who I met."

Rowan continued his turn to find Dorsey struggling to stand, with his arm slung around Janis. The smile on her face sent the message that she had caught a bigger fish than her friend Marnie.

"So, you two found each other," Rowan asked, while trying to capture eye contact with his drunk friend.

"Yup," Janis answered. "He said you're his banker, and that he has lots of money."

Rowan took a moment to study his friend. The look on his face showed he was about where Rowan was on his first night at the Sombrero before waking up with Travis.

"That's not a lie, Janis," Rowan answered, as he watched Dorsey wobble. "Did he also tell you he's married and has young children?"

Janis's face fell as she was reminded of what she assumed through the ring impression on his hand.

"He said he's separated, just like you."

"Janis, he's drunk." Marnie said, quietly from the bar. "If Rowan said he's married, don't set yourself up for hurt."

Marnie's warning struck a nerve in Janis. Her body straightened as she steadied herself to respond.

"And what do you really know about him?" she asked, nodding at Rowan. "It's not like he showed you any divorce papers. He even brought his kid with him."

"Janis, stop," Marnie implored.

"We're heading back to my place. I'll take care of him like I did you."

Rowan shared a glance with Marnie to confirm Janis was lying.

"Let me drive him back to the hotel to stay with his wife," Rowan replied, to restate the fire she was playing with.

"No, I'll take care of him," she answered as she started to walk Dorsey to the door.

"DORSEY!" Rowan called out in a loud voice.

Dorsey revived from his stupor with a smile to Rowan's call of his name. He touched Rowan's face with his hand before tuning out again.

"Just let them go," Marnie urged. "It's not like he's in any condition to do anything...or remember anything."

Janis continued to pull Dorsey to the door the way an animal would pull prey back to its lair.

"You can pick him up in the morning," Marnie added, showing disgust in her friend's behavior. "You know how to get there."

Marnie could not resist adding the little jab. It was interesting that the two friends would act and end up the same way on their first night at the Sombrero. In some ways, their behavior confirmed the need for rentable cabins on her nearby property. But her concern was that there would be higher demand for hourly rentals instead of weekends.

Rowan thought about the possible problems Dorsey would have if he was not at the hotel in the morning. That would be a surefire indicator that he had found a place to stay. His wife's imagination could fill in the blanks.

"I can't go back to the hotel without him," Rowan declared.

Marnie thought she knew what his statement was meant to infer. He was looking for an invitation to stay at her place. She knew he had the cabin for the fall. But she also knew the novelty and willingness to accept that level of comfort had passed long ago. And, that he would never show that shithole to his friend.

"You're welcome to stay in my guestroom," she offered. "But don't get any big ideas."

Rowan smiled in response to Marnie's grin and line in the sand.

"I promise, Mother."

His tone was sarcastic. Marnie replied with only a puzzled look as she walked away. Rowan was watching her rear pockets disappear to the kitchen when a tin chalice clanked on the bar next to his bottle of red. Cousin Dave's bloodshot eyes showed he had success pilfering glasses from the crowd and was circling back for seconds.

"You should have joined me at the creek today," he said, as his eyes shifted from the bottle to his cup, then back. "I got the heater working."

Rowan shook his head as he filled the chalice to the top.

"Not with you naked and my daughter there," Rowan replied, serious in tone but finding humor in it too.

"It's all natural man..." Cousin Dave replied. "You can't let all of that societal decorum keep your spirit bound up. You've got to live!"

Rowan smiled at the truth Cousin Dave was sharing.

"That's just it," Rowan said as his face went blank. "I'm not willing to go all-in up here like you have. I like most of my life in the city."

Rowan was hesitant to admit that. But there was a definite release from the stresses and boredom of that life when he was in Legend. He knew that relaxation was a big part of his attraction to Marnie. Although she was uptight with her solvable business worries, her spirit was free, adventurous, and not tied to any societal conventions.

"No reason why you can't have both," Cousin Dave replied. "Marnie was away for as long as she lived here."

Rowan waited for Cousin Dave to add more insight to where he was heading. But he just fell into silence.

"Come for a soak and we'll talk," he finally said as he stood to leave.

"Next time you heat the pool, I'll be there."

"Sunrise, tomorrow. It's a beautiful time to soak free and naked in the cold, fresh air."

Rowan nodded with a toast of his glass, not certain he would make the dawn skinny-dip. Cousin Dave departed as quickly as he arrived, with a clink of his now-full tin goblet of red to Rowan's glass.

"Last call," Marnie declared as Rowan continued to ponder Cousin Dave's offer.

"Okay, but I'll need you to help me with something," he answered, trying to mentally set his Sunday ducks in a row so they could not fail.

Chapter 13

Rowan's plan was simple. Marnie followed him to the hotel to leave the Audi for Claire so she could meet Maria in the morning. He texted her the address to the brewhouse. He also added the address of the Sombrero for her to drive to after her meeting ended. He lied and said that he and Dorsey were safe in the cabin, to throw her and Dorsey's wife off the scent of anything beyond sleeping off the wine. He intentionally did not leave the cabin address so that he could find Dorsey then find their friends, rather than the other way around.

Part of the deal to get Marnie to drive the forty-minute round trip after 2:00 a.m. was that Rowan would drive the leg back from the hotel to her house. She gave him the address to plug into this iPhone, then curled against the door of her Wrangler to reclaim sleep she was losing by agreeing to his favor.

The twenty-minute drive back to Marnie's was surreal. It was the first time they had traveled together. Yet she was comfortable enough to trust him with her car while sleeping. Rowan touched her arm to confirm that she was really there. But he decided that instead of disrupting her quiet slumber beside him, he would just enjoy her innocent beauty as she slept away her exhaustion from the night.

As he pulled into the circular driveway in front of her house, Rowan looked across the valley to see a single light in Cousin Dave's camp. A quick check of his watch showed that he had less than three hours until dawn.

"Maybe next time, Cousin Dave," he mumbled as he put Marnie's car into park.

The interior light that lit when the car door opened woke Marnie. She checked her mouth for drool, happy to find none.

As Rowan walked around the car to get her, she opened her door and started to exit.

"Hey," was all she could think to say in her groggy state.

"Hey, yourself," he answered.

It was clear to Rowan that Marnie was still somewhere between sleep and consciousness. Her face was illuminated by the moonlight, enhancing her natural skin tone and beauty. Her eyes were inviting a kiss. Rowan leaned for a brief kiss touch before sweeping her into his arms.

"No funny business," Marnie declared, still groggy.

Rowan exhaled a small laugh at her comment and state. She was on her way out for the night.

"That's a promise," he answered.

"Good," Marnie replied. "Because I want us both to be there when we get together."

Marnie's phrasing and message both puzzled and excited Rowan. It was her first disclosure of interest in something beyond the friendship they currently shared.

"Me too," he replied, kissing her forehead.

Rowan laid Marnie on her bed then covered her with a quilt she kept folded at the bottom. Her home was extraordinarily neat. It was different from how she kept the Sombrero and not in keeping with his expectations for an artist.

Rowan pinched and moved a rogue strand of hair back from Marnie's cheek to behind her ear. A smile appeared on her face as she settled deeper into the blanket.

"Sleep well," he whispered as he left to find his bed.

Rowan woke before the sun rose. The house was still silent, with only the whisper of the forced-air heating system blowing more comfort into the room. He chose the living room over the guest bedroom, too tired to step beyond the full-length couch with the fleece blanket Marnie used when relaxing. The smell of her perfume lingered in its fabric, which made falling asleep more comfortable.

From the couch, Rowan could look out over the valley to Cousin Dave's camp. He noticed movement around the single yellow light Cousin Dave used to illuminate his outdoors. When the low rumble of a quad started, and a streak of light from its headlights lit the trees in front of it, Rowan knew Cousin Dave was heading off for his sunrise soak in his wood-fire heated creek water.

"No one will ever believe this," Rowan mumbled as he stood.

Rowan continued to question his decision to start moving toward joining Cousin Dave in the creek as he made his way toward the garage. He expected that Marnie would roll her eyes when he told her. But he was also interested to find the spiritual cleansing Cousin Dave said would happen. He looked in Marnie's hall closet for a towel. He was happy to find two plush beach towels he could use to keep him warm when he got out of the water.

There was enough light in the house for Rowan to find his way to the garage and Marnie's Razor. He expected she would be fine with his borrowing the four-wheeler for a morning run down to the creek. The garage door made a quiet hum when it opened that he hoped would not wake her. He pushed the Razor out into the open air and away from the house to keep its engine noise from being amplified back through the house by the hard garage walls.

As Rowan navigated his way down the tree chute to the creek, he realized that he had to get through the splash zone of cold water to get to Cousin Dave's hot spring. The narrow headlight-lit view of his path made him nervous about stepping on the gas to launch into the waiting pool of water. When he hit the final straightaway he knew was the launching pad to the water, he decided to set all caution aside and build as much speed as possible.

The splash into the water was different from what he had experienced in full daylight. It was a softer, slow-motion wall of erupting blur that shot up on impact then settled as the Razor started to fill with water. Rowan calmly shifted the all-terrain vehicle into four-wheel-drive and stepped on the gas. He noted that, this time, the effort was smoother, easier, and faster than the previous two, and that the creek water that found its way into the cockpit of the Razor barely covered the floorboard before he exited the creek.

As he stopped to shift the buggy back into two-wheel-drive, Rowan could smell the burning firewood. A smile came to his face as he slowly accelerated toward where he knew Cousin Dave was warming his tub. As he made the turn back toward the pool area he and Claire had visited a day earlier, he could see the yellow glow from the flames flicker to throw shadows of Cousin Dave stacking wood nearby. Rowan turned off his lights as he approached, to enhance the ambiance of the area.

"I would've bet you weren't going to show," Cousin Dave said as Rowan emerged from the darkness.

"I saw you milling around, then leave, from Marnie's," Rowan replied. "I figured, how many opportunities would I get to experience this?"

"You stayed at Marnie's?"

It was a casual question, but he also had obvious concern in his voice.

"On the couch," Rowan answered. "That's how I saw you moving around…through her living room window."

Cousin Dave nodded. "It really doesn't matter to me," he added. "She needs a complementing spirit to make her whole and happy. You've got good karma."

Rowan smiled as he reached to test the temperature of the now-steaming pool of water.

"Feels good," he said.

Cousin Dave began to undress as he put a final log on the fire. The sky was still dark but was starting to show hints of sunrise off in the distance.

"Get in," Cousin Dave said, now completely naked and stepping down into the pool.

Rowan started to disrobe, feeling the cold air on his body as his shirt came off. He paused to consider leaving his boxer shorts on as he got to the final garment to remove before jumping in *au naturel*. As his skin started to scream to the cold air, he quickly cast off his boxers and stepped into the hot water of the pool.

The extreme change from the morning cold to the heat of the pool relaxed Rowan's body. Each muscle released its tension as he closed his eyes to enjoy the endorphin rush he was feeling.

"Are you feeling it?" Cousin Dave asked, watching his new friend's pleasure from the heated water.

"This reminds me of an outdoor spa at Vail. But that was a much larger, glorified swimming pool at a hotel. Very sterile. Feels the same, though."

"Likely full of toxic chemicals heated by gas in an artificially lit area," Cousin Dave replied. "THIS is as God intended it...if you're into any type of religion."

Rowan looked at Cousin Dave feeling the truth in his statement. The Vail experience was artificial and expensive. Cousin Dave had created something better with two hoses, a copper coil, and creek water.

"You've created heaven here," he agreed as he watched the fire's golden light flicker off the rhododendrons.

Rowan watched Cousin Dave nod at the comment then drop deeper into the water with his eyes closed. The sunlight was starting to streak the eastern sky with an orange hue he could not take his eyes off. The silhouette of tree limbs and their remaining leaves created an intricate foreground of lines connecting isolated clusters. Rowan found himself running the lines of the limbs from cluster to cluster, thinking about nothing but feeling like he had solved the world's problems.

"Do you love her?"

The words that took a few moments to sink in. A smile came to Rowan's face as Marnie's face appeared in his mind. It was from when he first saw her behind the bar after he first walked into the Red Sombrero.

"Because I believe that love is like a switch. It just happens. You just feel it."

Rowan remained silent as he thought through his feelings for Marnie. Cousin Dave was transforming from the neighborhood nut to her concerned guardian, which he found surprising and refreshing.

"That's an interesting question and comment," Rowan answered. "She is all I think about. She's just so interesting, a truly gifted artist, strangely alluring, hard-working, and SO DAMN STUBBORN. I've never met anyone like her."

Cousin Dave gave a quick nod of his head.

"It's a different life up here, man."

Rowan locked eyes with Cousin Dave to address the challenge he had just presented.

"I've lived in the city, playing its cultured, competitive game for fifty years...and I'm tired," Rowan replied. "This feels right. I'm glad I tripped over this place."

Cousin Dave smiled as he felt Rowan reach the level of consciousness to make Legend and Marnie work with his spirit.

"You didn't trip over it. You were called here. Just like I was."

Rowan smiled, thinking that correlating their two paths to Legend as the same was a stretch. But he also knew that Cousin Dave had made a point to ponder. A number of stars had aligned for him to find Legend, Marnie, and the Red Sombrero.

The sun rose without notice as the two soakers withdrew into their own thoughts. Cousin Dave let the fire wane which resulted in the pond cooling. The two men stepped from the water to towel off and get dressed. On the drive home, Rowan realized that the air did not feel as cold as when he left the water. And that he felt extraordinarily fresh while driving back to Marnie's. A quick look at his watch showed the time approaching 8:00 a.m. With only a few hours of sleep, he should be dragging. But instead, he was exhilarated and looking forward to the day, hoping that Marnie was up and waiting for him.

# # # #

Claire woke in the hotel room surprised that her dad was not in the other queen bed, snoring as he often did on soccer trips. She checked her phone as she lay in bed to see if he had left her a message. She knew that leaving him at the Sombrero with Dorsey was likely going to end with them back at the cabin. She was happy to not be there now, and to have a decent breakfast waiting for her in the lobby.

Claire read Rowan's texted instructions then looked out into the hotel's parking lot to find the Audi. She was surprised he had left the car for her to drive by herself. He had never offered before because of its cost and power. The time on her phone read 8:15 a.m. She had almost two hours to eat breakfast, shower, and get to the brewhouse for her 10 a.m. with Maria. Rowan finished his instructions with the comment to not rush. He did not expect to be at the Sombrero until noon.

Claire appeared in the hotel lobby expecting to find the usual mix of families milling around the free breakfast buffet. As she passed from the hallway through the lobby, she saw Nicki and Dorsey's wife, Charlotte. Both women presented well under the circumstances but were in the same clothes they had on the day before. Claire smiled as she thought about them in the Walmart she and her dad had visited earlier.

"I guess the boys didn't make it back," Charlotte said to Claire as she approached the table.

"No," Claire answered. "My dad dropped his car and headed back. My guess is that they stayed at the cabin he rented."

"That sounds interesting," Nicki interjected, thinking about the luxury cabins she rented in Aspen and Vail.

Claire nodded.

"Interesting, is a good description," she replied. "My dad said to meet him back at the Red Sombrero at noon. I'm sure Mr. Schmitt will be with him."

"I'm also sure he'll also be in great shape to drive home. He was pretty lit when he jumped out of the car to go back," Charlotte added. "I wonder why he didn't drop Dorsey with the car?"

"Boys will be boys," Nicki replied, not wanting to say that Rowan probably wanted to spare Dorsey Charlotte's wrath for getting too plastered.

"Probably a good thing," Charlotte giggled. "He gets gassy when he's drunk."

Nicki smiled at Charlotte's TMI on her husband as she turned toward Claire. Her face showed she was trying to configure a question she thought Claire could answer.

"Claire," Nicki said before pausing. "What is it about that winery that draws your dad up here? I mean...its neat... But I wouldn't say it's anything you'd want to do more than once."

"Well, that's easy," Claire started, then she stopped, remembering who she was talking to. "It's an escape...a project. The winery needs his financial help."

Claire's initial reply was going to include Marnie, but she knew it was better for her dad that he not become the center of the rumor mill back home, which tended to grossly distort the simplest of stories.

"Seems like small potatoes compared to what he does for Dorsey."

Claire smiled to acknowledge her comment.

"I think he just finds it fun."

Nicki shared a glance with Charlotte.

"I don't see it," she replied. "He could do something like that a lot bigger and better in the city."

Claire took Nicki's comment as her cue to exit. She smiled in agreement and started to head toward the food line as the two women started a new conversation. She could feel Nicki's inquiry looking for hope that her dad was not being pulled north because he was either changing or, worse, because he had found a new love interest in the area. For the first time, Claire began to see the appeal of the area. She started to laugh as she left their line of sight to pour herself some coffee.

Rowan parked Marnie's Razor in the driveway in case she was still sleeping. He knew pulling it into the garage would rattle the timbers throughout the house and wake her. Even with the time it took to drive up the hillside, he continued to feel renewed from his experience at the creek and was anxious to tell her about it.

The house was quiet when he entered through the garage. He stopped to listen after removing his shoes to keep from making noise as he walked into the living room. With no sign of Marnie, he returned to the kitchen to scout for coffee and something to make for breakfast. He wanted to make a good impression by having something ready when Marnie appeared. He was anxious to see how put-together she was going to be when she finally showed.

After searching the cabinets and refrigerator for coffee, Rowan found what he was hunting for in a capped, ceramic cylinder next to the coffee maker. The coffee filter in the Mr. Coffee was a reusable screen. He filled the ten-cup machine with water, knowing he was good for at least six. Despite his awakening at the creek, his energy was starting to decline as his body ached for its usual morning jump-start of caffeine.

As the coffee started to brew, Rowan wandered back into the living room. It seemed bigger in the daylight. On the wall were paintings that ranged from abstracts to landscapes. He recognized a few of her chosen scenes from the Legend area and from San Francisco. Marnie's talent for clarity and depth was immense. Rowan studied a few pieces of work from a distance, then up-close, for textures and brush strokes.

After strolling the far wall, he turned to look out the bay window toward Cousin Dave's. He saw the old quad parked next to the door to the trailer. The last thing Cousin Dave said before he rode off from the creek was that he had *chores to do*. Rowan smiled as he looked at the small, plush, and expensive Airstream trailer, thinking Cousin Dave just may have solved all of life's questions.

As the smell of the brewing coffee filled the room, Rowan passed a table littered with photographs from Marnie's past. In the middle were several family pictures of Marnie as a child with her parents, grandparents, and siblings. A close look at her mother disclosed their shared features. Like Marnie, she was as '70s cover-girl beautiful as her daughter. She wore no makeup because she did not need it. Her skin tones were perfect. Marnie got her alluring good looks from her mom.

At the end of the table, a wedding picture of Marnie and Tom sat in a silver frame. They both looked much younger and leaner. Marnie's hair was a chestnut brown, remarkably different from the gray she had today. If Rowan had to choose, he thought the gray hair suited her face and coloring better. But the picture showed two young, happy people who were in love, excited to be together, and looking forward to life's adventure. How and when that all changed was a story Rowan was interested in hearing. But it was not one he was going ask about.

"Snooping?" she asked, as he was trying to quietly put the picture back onto the table.

The unexpected voice made his hand fly upward as he gasped.

"Jesus," he cried. "You scared me."

Marnie walked toward him to take the picture as he regained his normal breathing rhythm. Her hair was tousled from hours on the pillow. But it worked to create an even more natural, more beautiful image of the woman.

"You're a fantastic painter," Rowan said as he watched Marnie carefully resituate the picture on the table.

"Yes," she replied. "And there are thousands of really good painters. I'm just not good enough to make a living at it... particularly here.

Rowan hugged Marnie, knowing her statement was true. Her work was as good as what sold in the galleries back in

Pittsburgh. But she would have to step out of Legend to market it. He did not know if she would be up to it. Selling wine to those who came looking for it seemed to be a better fit for her personality.

"Well, I'd like one for my..."

"Oh my God! You smell like the creek!" Marnie cried out, pushing him away.

Rowan sniffed around and toward his shoulders, detecting nothing.

"Oh!" he said quickly, realizing what he wanted to tell her. "I was with Cousin Dave this morning. In his..."

"Hot tub," Marnie finished for him. "He's been doing that since he moved here. Everyone goes once, then the novelty wears off.... Did you make coffee?"

Marnie walked into the kitchen as the coffee maker chimed completion of the brewing process. She grabbed two oversized mugs from the counter and poured coffee into both.

"I only have almond milk and cane sugar," she mumbled as she opened the refrigerator. "Is that okay?"

"Perfect," he replied, knowing that his longtime interest in tasting almond milk was coming to fruition.

Rowan typically put half-and-half and pink Sweet'N Low into his coffee. He called it his hyphenated kickstart to his morning. As he stirred Marnie's milk and sugar into his coffee, the resulting color was darker than he was used to seeing. The taste lacked sweetness. But the flavor had a richness he was not expecting.

"This is really good," he commented.

"Folgers...Columbian," Marnie answered, expecting a snarky comment back for her choice in beans.

Rowan looked into his mug thinking his purchase of specialty beans that cost three times as much was probably a bad decision.

"I like it."

"Don't patronize me, Clark." Marnie replied as she started to dig into her refrigerator. "I have eggs, some sausage, and orange juice. I'm sure I have some bread for toast too."

Rowan walked to stand next to her as she piled items into her arms. When Marnie turned toward him, they bumped, causing some of the items to shift in her arms before settling again.

"It's very good."

Marnie shuffled to get by him as Rowan shifted to stay in her way.

"Kiss me," he said, smiling at her struggle.

"No," she answered. "I haven't brushed my teeth, and maybe I just don't want to."

"Me neither," he replied. "Except that I want to."

Rowan's smile sent a cold chill down Marnie's back. She shivered as he stood there waiting.

Marnie exhaled and closed her eyes, knowing he was not going to move until she gave in to his request. When she reopened them to look at him, his eyes were still locked on hers; and his grin was bigger. She took his preoccupation as her opportunity to quickly toe-up to kiss him before he had a chance to react.

"There," she said, as she swept by him to put her breakfast items on the island for preparation.

"So, you and Cousin Dave did your first naked hot creek ritual this morning?"

The mental image of the two soaking made her pause and smile.

"It was a religious experience," he answered.

"Yeah, well, that's his property. He can do with it what he wants."

Rowan looked through the kitchen door to the living room. The line of sight extended through the bay window over to Cousin Dave's. As he mentally tracked the trails to the creek where the hot tub was, it was over a quarter of a mile between the two. But maybe his campsite was separate from the Creekside bath he created.

"He owns that entire hilltop and valley," she added, knowing Rowan was piecing things together in his head.

"That has to be worth a few million dollars," he replied, thinking through the size of the property at a few thousand dollars an acre.

"He'll tell you he's poor when he talks to you. But he's land rich. Bought it all when he first arrived. Looked sort of like you then. Well, not quite as preppy...or pompous."

Marnie lowered her voice and smiled as she finished her thought. She meant to only say that to herself.

"That's amazing." Rowan began to think. "He's from Pittsburgh? There is a ton of family wealth there. What's his last name?"

Marnie stopped cracking the eggs into her mixing bowl to think.

"I don't know that answer," she replied. "He's just Cousin Dave."

Rowan set the breakfast table in the kitchen as Marnie put finishing touches on their brunch. He used some of the time to observe her home and to watch her move. At times she would catch him watching. She knew she was blushing when she could feel the heat run through her cheeks. It felt good that he was there with her.

"Breakfast...is served," she declared.

It was apparent from the taste of her simple offering that Marnie was an artist. The plate she presented was beautifully constructed with some added garnishments. The flavors of each item he tasted exploded in his mouth. He thought for a moment about Claire being stuck at the hotel with its lame, free breakfast she would pick over. A quick look at the clock showed she should soon be on her way to meet Maria at the brewery.

Rowan pulled his phone out to check with Claire to insure everything was fine.

"What are you doing?" Marnie asked. "No phones at the table."

"Just a quickie," Rowan answered, smiling at his choice of terms. "I need to check with Claire about her meeting with Maria."

Rowan's screen lit. He was surprised to have service and to see two messages. Claire was on her way to Maria's after having breakfast with Nicki and Charlotte. He stopped to think about how that conversation went. The second text was from Vinnie. He wanted to meet Marnie in Pittsburgh on Tuesday with Sal. They had ideas and concerns to discuss about the wine adventure.

"Rowan," Marnie declared.

When Rowan's eyes shifted from his phone to hers, he found her eyes shifting from his to his plate, then back.

"It'll get cold," she added.

Rowan put his phone facedown onto the table and picked up his fork. He smiled, happy that Claire was in good spirits, that Vinnie was ready to move forward, and that he was sitting across the breakfast table from the most remarkable women he had met in decades.

"Eat up. We have to be at the Sombrero for setup by eleven."

Rowan wanted to talk business with Marnie. But he knew they would have time on the ride over and during the final staging of the winery for Sunday to talk about Vinnie's need to see Marnie in Pittsburgh. He knew the early days of the week would be easy for her to manage. Claire was leaving Tuesday morning to return to South Carolina, so their last night of quality time together would be on Monday.

"What?" she asked when she looked up to find him smiling at her.

"Nothing," he replied.

# # # #

Rowan started the car then waited as Marnie ran back into the house. He was piecing together his thoughts to discuss how to deal with the ideas Claire was going to bring back from the brewery. He was thinking through even more how to get Marnie excited about Vinnie's interest in relabeling her wine to sell to the older Italian market. His concern was that after the thrill of the possible dollars wore off, the realities and stress related to the time and costs of production would set in. Those thoughts added to his anxiety as Marnie returned smiling to sit next to him in the Wrangler's passenger seat.

"Shouldn't you be driving?" he asked. "This is your car."

"I don't mind," she answered. "It's nice to be driven every once in a while."

She then went silent and looked out the window.

"Before we get to the Sombrero, I have two things to talk about."

Marnie turned, showing a look of concern. Her immediate thought went to *What have you done now?*

"Okay," she answered.

"First, Claire is going to come back wanting to discuss the ideas she and Maria have for the combined marketing effort. Please just listen and don't object or criticize. They're just ideas. You and Tyson will have final say on what you do together."

"But…"

Marnie stopped to Rowan's lifted hand. As she thought about his statement, she agreed that it would be rude to criticize free ideas. She also knew she did not want to sour anything with Claire.

"What's the other thing?"

"My client Vincent Giollota and his business associate Sal would like to meet you on Tuesday evening for dinner at his club in Pittsburgh to talk about Red Sombrero wine, particularly Dervish Red, being marketed at retail."

Marnie's eyes lit to the suggestion. She knew Rowan was working an idea that she did not know about.

"My wine in real wine and liquor stores?" she asked, starting to see dollar signs in her head.

"Your wine," he answered. "Just under a different label...for now."

Rowan added *for now* to ease any concern that would erupt within Marnie that her wine was not going to be sold under the Red Sombrero brand.

"Vinnie thinks your wine is really close to the old Italian table reds his dad used to make. He and Sal, who is in the liquor business, think there's an old Italian market for Dervish Red under a different name and brand."

Marnie shook her head.

"We can't do that," she answered. "Who would do that!?"

Rowan smiled at Marnie's naivete.

"Marnie, it's done all the time. All of those store brands you buy are made by the big manufacturers of the higher-priced brands."

"I still don't think it's a good idea," she replied, now feeling her stomach pit that Rowan would sell out her wine.

A question quickly began to build in her head as to whether he was just courting her for access to her wine.

"Just think about it," he said softly, to bring calm to the car. "Listen and then decide. No pressure."

"I have to drive to Pittsburgh?" she asked. "What kind of club is it? Where will I stay?"

Rowan smiled hearing Marnie sweat the details that he considered unimportant.

"Yes," he answered. "It's an old Italian club with the most amazing food you'll ever taste. And you can stay with me at my condo."

Marnie's stomach continued to tighten, seeing a lure Rowan was setting to get her to his home. Their relationship was beginning to smell funny, which concerned her.

"I—" she started, then stopped.

"You," he replied, "will have a wonderful time with fascinating company, and will stay in one of my two guest rooms, which have their own bathrooms."

Rowan added the details knowing Marnie was becoming cautious toward any possible alternative reasons she was being invited to the city.

"What do I wear? I mean, to the dinner?" she asked.

"Be yourself, Marnie," he answered. "Wear what YOU would wear to a nice dinner. They want to meet you for who you are."

Marnie reluctantly smiled at Rowan's attempt to comfort her into driving to Pittsburgh for an overnight. The premise for the invitation both upset her and made her nervous. Rowan's expectations, once back at his condo, also added to her anxiety. She was not ready to move that far with him, although she had been thinking about it more and more each week.

Rowan turned into the Sombrero parking lot and Marnie's usual slot. He spotted Janis' Razor parked on the grass knoll next to the deck. For the first time he thought about Dorsey being carried out by the black widow back to her nest. He was anxious to see if, and how, his friend survived his overnight with Travis.

# # # #

Dorsey was sitting on Rowan's stool, slumped over the bar, holding his face in his hands. The stool's location in the corner was helpful for balance, being where the wall and bar came together. He did not move when Rowan put a hand on his shoulder to see if he was still breathing.

"How's it going Dorse?" he asked, waiting for either some movement or a moan.

"I feel like shit," he answered. "I'm also hungry. She didn't feed me."

Rowan smiled as he looked to Marnie. Janis was nowhere to be seen, but she had to be somewhere in the building. Dorsey could not have driven the Razor anywhere in his current condition.

The women's room door flew open as he heard the sound of a flushing toilet. Janis was wiping her hands dry with a paper towel as she looked up to find both Marnie and Rowan staring at her.

"I'm returning your friend unviolated," she said in a snarky, sour tone. "Virginity still intact."

Janis did not stop to add to her thought or to chat. She continued to the door and disappeared without looking back.

"Well, that's good news," Rowan observed as Dorsey continued to suffer in the corner.

"I told you not to worry. Just make sure he doesn't throw up anywhere."

Marnie walked behind the bar then disappeared into the storage room. Rowan looked to the kitchen, then at the menu, to see if there was anything he could serve his friend other than some hair-of-the-dog he deserved. A quick look at the clock on the wall told him that Claire was still in Clarion. She could stop and pick up an assortment of McDonald's breakfasts on her way back. He unlocked the back door to the deck to find the apple tree that had internet service.

Rowan felt good that all of the things that he thought were highly questionable going into the weekend, along with everything that appeared unexpectedly, were all coming together. He was anxious to hear Claire's ideas. Dorsey's condition, although not healthy, was perfect for the handoff to Charlotte for their ride home. She would certainly give him hell for his condition, but she would not suspect that he did anything other than stay at the cabin. The unexpected infidelity aspect of his behavior would have to be discussed later between Rowan and his number one client.

Rowan was most excited that Marnie was coming to Pittsburgh for the meeting with Vinnie and Sal. He was looking forward to that discussion. But, more so, he was anxious to see her in his world. He was excited to show her his view of the city from Mount Washington, and to see if she either could or would fit into his lifestyle as comfortably as he was fitting into hers.

# # # #

Mondays were always Rowan's least favorite day of the week. But this one was different. His early evening drive up McArdle Road from the Liberty Bridge that crossed the Monongahela River in Pittsburgh was the final stretch of road to his condominium, where he would finally be able to relax. He confirmed dinner with Vinnie, which stuck in his head for most of the day. He was looking forward to having Marnie come to town. He knew it was going to test their relationship beyond the business dealings she was going to have to consider.

Claire's choice for her last *supper* before heading back to school was one of the new restaurants *up on the mount* near his condo. The building was a landmark with a glass wall that overlooked the city. Rowan reserved a special table for two, by the glass, to ensure the view was as good as the company and the food.

The restaurant was an easy walk along the ridge that offered the best sightseeing view of Pittsburgh's Golden Triangle. Pedestrians were protected from the severe drop-off by a heavy, ornate metal railing system that opened to several overlook platforms erected out over the hillside. With the sun gone for the day, the walk would be rich with the colors of the skyline that defined the buildings and companies that occupied them.

"Hi, Dad," he heard, as he walked through the front door. "I've got a surprise for you."

The muffled laugh in her voice gave Rowan the information he needed to guess what the surprise was.

"Hi Mindy," he called out before entering the room.

He knew his soon-to-be ex-wife had to be the surprise for Claire to get such joy out of it.

"Rowan," Mindy replied, as she stayed seated on his leather couch that overlooked the skyline.

Mindy was dressed in her usual fall attire of pants, turtleneck, and blazer that her tall, lean body wore well. Her hair was a shiny chestnut brown that she kept intact through regular visits to her stylist for color and touchups. Her skin tone complemented her hair with the added help of well-placed makeup. Rowan was always drawn to Mindy's physical allure. But their differences in personality and personal desires created a rub that overwhelmed their physical attraction as time moved on.

"Mom's going to join us for dinner," Claire announced.

Rowan's face lit with fake excitement. He thought about the trouble he went through to reserve a special table for two by the glass wall overlooking the city and its three rivers. He nodded his head as he pondered his options.

"I'll have to call the restaurant," he said quietly. "We'll need a table for three."

Mindy smiled, reveling in her husband's frustration. The fact that he would pick up the bill was an added bonus.

"I took care of it," Claire replied. "We're still on the glass. They had a cancellation."

Rowan took a moment to look at Claire. He smiled at her proactive effort to solve the problem she knew Mindy created. He knew it was good for Claire to see her mom over her fall break, even though Mindy chose a pleasure weekend at the beach instead of being home.

"Perfect!" Rowan declared. "Who needs a dresser?"

Dresser was Rowan's term for alcohol needed to warm up events. College football games had dressers, back in the day. He had a few dressers before his wedding ceremony. He also had a few dressers during many events throughout his married life with Mindy's family and others he knew he needed help to get through.

"Got any interesting reds?" Mindy asked with a smirk that showed she knew.

Rowan stopped his step toward his bar to study his wife's face, then to look at his daughter.

"How long have you been here?" he asked Mindy to assess how much Claire had shared.

"We spent the afternoon together," Mindy answered.

Rowan first nodded his head then started shaking it as he finished his trek to the bar.

"I have something I think you'll like," he answered. "It's from Napa."

Rowan knew his choice would disappoint Mindy. Her request was for a taste of Dervish Red that she had likely heard about from Claire, Nicki, and probably Charlotte. None of them could keep a secret. He imagined Mindy's phone lit up the moment each of the girls got home to share their news and observations of Rowan's find in the north country.

# # # #

The walk to the restaurant was quiet. The view was familiar to each of them as they worked their way toward the row of restaurants. Rowan insisted on stopping at an empty overlook to take a picture of Claire and Mindy. He made a soft jab that it would create a memory for them, since Mindy was at the beach for most of Claire's fall break.

The inside of the restaurant was elegant. From the door, the view immediately presented out through the glass wall toward the city. Rowan remembered attending a wedding reception in the same room when a powerful thunderstorm rumbled down the valley toward them. There was a slight hysteria as the clouds approached then encased the building in a dense, gray mist with flashing lightning and immediate thunder. At that time, the venue had a different name and purpose. The new management had done a wonderful job redesigning the space in tiers, so each table had a view to enjoy while dining.

When Claire and Mindy excused themselves from the table to visit the ladies' room, Rowan ordered a bottle of California red table wine. He knew he was going to drink at least three of its five glasses just to stay calm. He was sure Claire and Mindy would be in for at least two. He told the waitress to have a second bottle waiting.

The initial conversation at the table was pleasant, focused on Claire's fall and enjoyment of her classes and housing at South Carolina. As a senior, she was living in a duplex with a sorority sister. Both of them were Yankees. Below them was an overfilled three-room apartment that was initially filled by six boys. Claire shared that two were evicted due to police calls for noise. She added that the remaining four were mellow and more enjoyable to have as both friends and protection. The parking at the house also became easier with two cars removed.

Claire regretted mentioning the parking situation the moment she said it. She wanted to push through to another topic. But she knew an abrupt change would remind Mindy of her car's damage. That created a problem for her because she drove it to Five Points when she was supposed to Uber. It also created a problem for her dad because it was yet to be fixed a few weeks later.

"I saw the damage on the Mini," Mindy said, as she looked directly at Rowan. "That's your lane."

The use of the word *lane* was a term Mindy picked up and used regularly to define areas of responsibility. His lanes were well defined. Hers were as she decided they should be when she wanted control of them. The reality was that she could drift into his lane whenever she wanted. But he was to not cross the solid yellow line into hers. He smiled as he began to formulate his response.

"Claire's going to take it to Mini in Columbia to get fixed," he replied. "They'll get her a rental. It is taken care of."

Mindy shook her head as she listened to him.

"That could've been taken care of the week after it happened."

Rowan gave his wife a deadpan look as he held back on what he wanted to say.

"There is a benefit to waiting," he replied. "Maybe it will encourage her not to do it again."

As he finished his explanation, Mindy's eyes rolled to her wine as his turned to Claire, who was smiling.

"It's unsafe," Mindy mumbled as she brought the glass to her mouth.

The waitress appeared for their order, interrupting the Mini discussion. Claire and Rowan immediately lifted their menus to close the conversation and hide the smiles that they knew would frustrate Mindy. Each then ordered their meal as Rowan topped off their three glasses and added a second bottle to their order.

"Planning on getting lit?" Mindy asked as she looked at the three glasses.

"I'm walking home," he replied, knowing that would poke her. "You're welcome to stay in the guest room if you don't want to drive."

Rowan knew that was unlikely. Mindy did not have the toiletries with her that he knew were absolutes for both going to bed and for starting her day. Her ride back out to the suburbs was an easy eight mile run up the Allegheny River. But it was also a drive that ended with about three miles of winding country road back to the house where they raised their family.

Mindy did not reply to Rowan's offer. Although not saying it, they both were thinking about Mindy's probability of staying at Rowan's for the night. What he did not consider was that she thought staying at his place would be a good idea to avoid drinking and driving in front of Claire, as well as being able to send Claire off to school in the morning. Making the night longer and more awkward for him was an added bonus. Mindy took a large drink of wine as she continued to think about her options.

The conversation through dinner returned to Claire's classes and experiences through the fall. One of her classes was a senior year marketing workshop that worked case studies in groups to solve hypothetical problems in industry. Claire explained a project they completed that was similar to the opportunities and challenges she and Maria were working on for the Red Sombrero and the brewery. The moment Claire said *Red Sombrero*, Rowan's eyes closed as his stomach tightened.

As he looked to see what was waiting when he reopened his eyes, he saw Mindy sitting taller and drifting from side-to-side in her chair. He knew she had a slew of questions to ask him about the Sombrero that were meant to gather information as well as embarrass him in front his daughter. He knew she had a general idea of the Sombrero from peers' perspectives from Nicki and Charlotte. He was unsure what Claire had told her through the afternoon. He knew he would have to batten down his emotions and be selective in his words as he answered her questions.

"I've heard about this Red Sombrero winery," Mindy started. "How on earth did you find that place?"

Rowan smiled as he remembered walking into Marnie's immediate call-out that embarrassed him. He could see her face as clearly as if she were sitting in Mindy's chair. A warmth filled his chest that disappeared as the image faded back to his wife waiting for her answer.

"I was looking for a place to pee," he answered.

"DAD! TMI," Claire interjected.

"Sorry," Rowan clarified. "I was looking to find a rest room...to rest."

"Out in the sticks?" Mindy qualified. "Nicki told me it's more than two hours north of here."

Nicki, Rowan thought. *Of course, it was Nicki.*

"I was leaf touring. It was dark. My GPS took me there."

Mindy's face showed she did not believe his explanation.

"You looked for places to pee on your GPS?"

"Mother," Claire objected again, in a suppressed voice.

Rowan found his daughter's objection to the word funny. It was the term she used all the time when traveling.

"No," he answered. "I was looking for a restaurant, bar— anything that had a bathroom."

Mindy started to shake her head in disbelief.

"Why not just run off into the trees?" Mindy asked.

Claire flipped her hands up in desperation. Their nice dinner at an elegant restaurant was being taken over by an obsession about where her dad had to go to find relief.

Rowan started to laugh as he remembered the Sombrero waitress offering either the trees or the single-stall bathroom as his immediate options when he asked her for help.

"Never mind," Mindy finally added to appease her daughter. "I think the bigger question is why you keep going back there."

Rowan responded with a puzzled look. He was not aware that anyone knew of his weekly runs north to the Sombrero. He thought back through conversations with Dorsey and Nicki. He was certain he did not tell Claire too much. Then he thought about the cabin. He told her that he had rented it for the season. He was caught.

"Pressure release," he answered. "I find it peaceful."

Mindy did not like his answer. She shook her head as she wiped her mouth with the linen napkin.

"Jesus, Rowan," she replied. "Go play some golf or something. Hanging with hillbillies, and drinking cheap wine, is embarrassing."

"Marnie..." Rowan stated without thinking, then stopped. "I mean, Mindy, they aren't hill...billies. They're good people. Genuine."

Rowan checked both faces to measure the impact of his name error. That he called Mindy, Marnie, surprised him. They were polar opposite personalities.

"Who's Marnie?" Mindy asked.

"Marnie owns the Red Sombrero," Claire replied. "She's coming down."

Rowan stepped on Claire's foot to stop her comment. Claire's reaction told Mindy that Rowan did something to interrupt their daughter's news.

"Coming down...where? When?" Mindy asked. "*Why* also comes to mind."

Claire kept quiet until Rowan nodded permission for her to fill in the story gaps.

Mindy listened to Claire's detailed explanation of the Red Sombrero's wine, *Dervish Red*, that Rowan thought his client Vinnie would like. Mindy's head turned from Claire to Rowan seeking confirmation as Claire drilled deeper to explain a relationship he had created between a local brewer and the winery to cross-sell their products. Rowan nodded in agreement, impressed with Claire's ability to put together the opportunity as he watched Mindy's head start to fill with questions. Claire finished her story saying that the big meeting with Vinnie was tomorrow night to discuss final details with Marnie.

"So, this Marnie is coming here?" Mindy asked. "Where is she staying?"

Rowan gave a puzzled look to her question.

"After all of that, your question is where is she staying?"

Mindy leaned back in her seat trying to think of an adequate response. Her question showed a hint of jealousy that she knew Rowan would enjoy and would give Claire false hope.

"I guess that's none of my business," she replied.

"To answer your question," Rowan started. "She's arriving sometime tomorrow afternoon. And she is staying at my condo, in one of the guest rooms."

Mindy looked across the table at him in disbelief. She suspected there was more to their relationship than just a banker working to help a struggling business. Rowan worked deals worth high seven to nine figures. His clients were Dorsey Schmitt level. They were never entry-level lending to local businesses. She wondered why her husband was slumming.

"Well, again," Mindy said to end the conversation, "it's none of my business."

At the end of dinner, Rowan counted two-and-one-half bottles of wine consumed. The final bill for dinner was over four hundred dollars. Rowan added one hundred dollars as a tip for the exceptional service. The remainder of the bottle of wine was corked to take home. He offered it to Mindy as a party favor on their walk back to the condo.

"Thank you for dinner," Mindy said, as she kissed him good night on the cheek.

"You're staying over." Rowan insisted.

"I don't think that's a good idea," she answered. "I'm okay to drive home."

Rowan knew why Mindy did not want to stay. They both harbored feelings for the other that were undeniable. But the reality for both was that they were better apart than together. Thinking about the other with someone else was never pleasant.

Rowan insisted that Mindy Uber home. Claire was also in no condition to drive her home, having had two glasses of wine. It was not worth the risk to let either of them drive. The Uber arrived quickly. Rowan promised that Claire would drive out to her house early to return her car. That would give them an opportunity to have breakfast before she hit the road back to school.

Mindy liked the idea of additional time with Claire. She accepted the Uber Rowan offered, ordered, and paid for. She promised to text when she arrived home safely.

Chapter 14

Rowan knew Claire would still be sleeping when he had to leave for work in the morning. He took some time before going to bed to visit with her on the couch overlooking the glow of the city. Claire was happy with the outcome of the dinner she had set up to enjoy her final night at home until Thanksgiving. She snuggled next to her dad for reassurance he was still there for her despite anything that happened to keep her parents apart.

Claire did not mention Marnie by name. But she did say he seemed happier with his work and friends up north. They shared a laugh about the crazy guy named Cousin Dave in his white flowy shirt and brown thimble-shaped hat. Claire's recall reminded him to do some research on who Cousin Dave could be. Pittsburgh was loaded with old money, typically made from coal, steel, and timber in the region that was large enough to last generations.

The sky was still dark when Rowan left his bedroom dressed for work. He looked in Claire's bedroom for one last check on his oldest daughter. The sound of the door creaking woke her. She smiled as she saw her dad looking in.

"Just wanted to take one last look before leaving," he said, sitting next to her.

He reached to move some hair from her face as she sat up.

"Thanks for the fun weekend," Claire said, still half asleep. "I think the Red Sombrero is a cool project...and that Marnie is a cool lady."

Rowan hugged Claire in appreciation for her comments and permission. He pulled her close so that she would not see his eyes tear.

"It is a cool project," he replied as he kissed her forehead. "Keep working with Maria. Your ideas are great. And both of those companies need your help."

Claire smiled at her dad's encouragement. To work a real-world marketing project was exciting. She enjoyed Maria's perspective, which had overlap with hers, despite some differences.

"Enjoy breakfast with your mother," he added. "She never did text that she got home."

Claire smiled at his comment as she lay back down to sleep. Rowan waved as he left her room, emotional to be saying goodbye for a few weeks.

# # # #

The drive to Pittsburgh was familiar for Marnie. For many months up until her father's death, she would drive him into the city for care that extended his life and discomfort. After he died, she wondered if the added time was worth it. It was hard on her and her mother to see him suffer just for another day in agony.

The drive into the city from Interstate 79 was the least impressive approach to the city. It meandered down an ancillary Route 279 that ended on the North Shore, by the stadiums. Marnie used her phone's GPS to navigate the spaghetti of exits and bridges to get from that side of the rivers to Rowan's condominium building that sat above Pittsburgh's southside. She gave herself extra time to be sure she arrived on time. Rowan's text gave a gate code and said he left a key with the guard for her to access his condo when she arrived, knowing she would be nervous and leave early.

Marnie's drive up P.J. McArdle Road had her looking out over the vista as much as she looked ahead to where she was driving. As she reached the top of the climb, the road made a quick turn to the left onto a plateau before she had to turn right onto Rowan's street. Her GPS marked the end of her drive on the screen. That designation began to make her nervous about where he lived and who he actually was.

The building the GPS declared as his address towered high into the sky. Its secure parking area was gated. After Marnie entered the guest code Rowan provided, the gate slid open. Waiting for it to open completely seemed like an eternity. Her anxiety continued to grow as she pulled in to park at the ominous structure that housed Rowan's three-bedroom, three-bath home.

Marnie rolled her weekend suitcase into the front lobby, looking for a desk and guard for the key. She was immediately greeted by a well-dressed man in a sports coat and slacks interested in helping her find her way.

"I'm looking for the guard," Marnie said apologetically.

"That would be me," he replied. "You must be Ms. Gardner. Mr. Delaney said you would be arriving in the afternoon."

Marnie smiled, impressed with his recall of her name.

"I can help you with your things, if you need," he added as he handed her keys.

Marnie accepted the keys, which were on a leather key ring with the building's logo.

"That won't be necessary," she answered. "This is all I have with me."

The security guard walked Marnie to the elevator and pressed the button. He gave her the floor and door number as a reminder. Marnie thanked the man for his help, wondering if she should tip him. As the door closed, she felt embarrassed to not have offered him a gratuity.

When the elevator opened, Marnie walked out into a narrower-than-expected hallway that extended left and right. She noted some well-spaced doors that had to be entrances to each unit. Some had numbers and formal knockers while others were unmarked. She would realize later that the unmarked doors were service doors to the kitchens.

Marnie took a deep breath before turning the key to his condominium. Her heart was pounding in anticipation of what was waiting on the other side. She fully expected that it was going to be impressive, male-heavy in decoration, and overwhelming. When the door started to open, she whispered to herself to *calm down.*

The view of the city was immediate as the door opened to the small entrance hall that led to the living room. It was far more than she expected, and exponentially grander than the drive up the hill. As she walked into the living room, she looked around at the space that was larger than hers in a condominium that had more beds and baths than her house. She studied the decorations noting the original art on the walls. She now knew why Rowan appreciated her paintings. He was a connoisseur of fine oil landscapes, with several originals hanging on his walls. His art was similar to hers in subject matter and composition.

As she walked deeper into the room, the city view became larger. It was less impressive during the day, presenting as a dull, gray wash of buildings and rivers in the dingy fall sunlight. She wondered what made that view so special compared to the color-filled overlook her home and area offered. A quick look on a side table presented his family profile of parents, children, and the woman who had to be his wife. She was as pretty and polished as Marnie expected. Insecurity began to seep into her consciousness as she studied the face of the woman who preceded her.

"You're home early," called out a voice from one of the bedrooms in the back of the condominium.

Marnie was startled by the unexpected woman's voice, wondering if she was in the wrong condominium. She quickly laid the family picture back on its spot on the table as she spun to greet the person who called out.

The woman that appeared was familiar from the photograph and face Marnie had just studied. The feeling was surreal, making her wonder if she was hallucinating. She knew the woman standing less than fifteen feet from her was Rowan's ex-wife. Her face showed no surprise to see Marnie instead of her ex-husband as she studied Marnie from head to toe.

"You must be Marnie," Mindy said, as she walked toward the kitchen. "Can I offer you a drink?"

Mindy intentionally made it sound like alcohol to see if Marnie would bite. Her initial impression of the country bar owner was underwhelming. The woman wore no makeup and dressed simply.

"I'm guessing you're Rowan's ex-wife," Marnie struggled to say. "I'm also wondering why you're here."

Mindy waved off her question as if nothing.

"I just came over to get Claire on her way. She stayed here last night."

Marnie knew Mindy's reply was a lie. Claire had a nine-hour drive back to Columbia, South Carolina. That goodbye was hours ago.

"I'm sorry," she replied. "But I don't believe you."

Mindy laughed at Marnie's accusation. She knew she was caught lying about why she was there. But in her mind, she was doing this for her family's integrity and to keep Rowan from making a mistake, sowing his wild oats with a north country woman.

"I wouldn't either," Mindy confessed.

Mindy exhaled as she thought about how she wanted to say what she needed to say. Although she had been practicing all afternoon, her mental script had evaporated the moment she heard the door open.

"Look, Marnie," she started slowly. "Can I call you Marnie?"

Marnie nodded.

"I'm his wife," Mindy added.

"Ex-wife."

"Not yet," Mindy immediately qualified. "Not...yet. Our divorce is far from final. And I am reconsidering."

Marnie exhaled softly as she listened to Mindy try to stake her claim on their shared interest.

"Well," Marnie replied. "From what I understand, THAT takes TWO."

Marnie's reply was what Mindy feared. She did not deny interest in Rowan beyond a banker helping a client. The person who appeared to be a pushover at first glance began to grow into a formidable opponent. She was obviously tough and confident.

"It does," Mindy answered, trying a soft-sell approach. "Look around you. This is his life...what he's used to. How does it fit yours?"

"All this! Doesn't matter," Marnie replied, losing confidence in her remark. "We want the same things."

Mindy laughed at her comment.

"Do you now? You need to really think about that," she replied, "You're just a distraction. He is who he is. He won't take country simple for too long before coming back to this."

Mindy's message and sarcastic tone was piercing. Marnie looked around his condominium another time. She wondered if Mindy's comments were true. If her initial fear of being just an exotic tryst for him was right.

"I don't believe you," she replied, trying to appear strong.

"That's up to you," Mindy answered quickly, as she picked up her clutch to leave. "Personally, I would."

Mindy knew the dagger had been set. She quickly left through the kitchen's service door to the hallway to give Marnie time to think and no opportunity to reply. As the door opened and shut behind Rowan's *wife*, Marnie's anxiety, originally driven by excitement when she arrived, had just been squashed and replaced by nerves over whether Rowan Delaney's interest in her was just for money or a romp in bed.

As she continued to think about Mindy's words, she decided it would be best for her to leave Rowan's condo and return to Legend. Marnie returned the keys to the guard. He looked puzzled as he took of the keys from her. Rowan had taken more time to set up her arrival and to explain her appearance than she spent in the building. From his enthusiasm, it was apparent Rowan was excited to be hosting the woman.

"Is there anything I can do to help you?" he asked. "Should I tell him you were here?"

Marnie's pained look told him something went incredibly wrong during her short stay upstairs.

"Yes," she replied. "Please tell him I was here…and decided to return home."

The guard shook his head at her words.

"He'll be disappointed," he replied. "Mr. Delaney is one of the good guys."

Marnie smiled as her eyes teared. She did not want to get into a discussion about either Rowan as a person or why she had to go with this man she had just met. As she pushed the door out into the cold afternoon air, the emotions she was desperately holding inside released and she walked to her car sobbing.

Chapter 15

Rowan arrived at the condominium excited to greet Marnie. He was anxious to see her response to his home and view after having a few hours to absorb it after sunset. Seeing the transition from day to the night lights was what he hoped she would find most impressive. He was devastated to not find her waiting for him when he walked in from the hallway.

A quick call to the front desk confirmed that Marnie had arrived and left quickly. The guard had no additional information except to say she seemed happy when she arrived then visibly upset by something when she left. Rowan dialed Marnie's cell to see if he could reach her before she reached the no-service zone around the Red Sombrero. The immediate rejection of his call to voicemail said she was avoiding him instead of just unavailable.

"Damn it, Marnie," he exhaled as he thought about her emotionally driving home for over two hours.

He knew he would have to attend the dinner with Vinnie and Sal. He could give a health excuse for Marnie's absence then fill her in on the details of their offer. Her unexpected departure continued to bother him as he looked around to see what she could have seen to upset her.

"Dad?" Claire's voice answered, concerned about the unusual timing on his call.

"Hey sweetie. Where are you now?"

"Just south of Charlotte," she answered.

Rowan did some quick math in his head. Claire was gone for at least eight hours. She would not have overlapped with Marnie.

"What's wrong?" Claire asked. "Is Marnie there?"

Rowan paused, wondering if he should answer. He looked around his living room looking for anything out of place. He noticed the family picture Marnie had been holding lying flat on the table.

"Mindy," he said, not thinking Claire was listening.

"Mom?" Claire asked. "She came back to the condo with me to pack after breakfast. She had to go to the bathroom. So, we said goodbye in the parking lot. Then she went back upstairs for her purse."

"Okay, sweetie. Drive carefully."

"Is everything okay, Dad?"

Rowan smiled to stage his response in the positive.

"All good here," he answered. "Don't be like your mother, and ping me with a text when you get back to school. Love you."

Rowan's comment was a dig on Mindy while also reminding Claire to text him when she arrived. He knew he had a fifty-fifty chance of that happening. Claire, in many ways, was her mother.

Rowan tried one more time to reach Marnie before readjusting his night for damage control. Marnie rejected his call immediately with a *sorry, unable to talk* text message. Mindy did something to frighten Marnie. He knew he had to fix it quickly. He also knew Mindy would never admit anything.

# # # #

Vinnie and Sal were courteous about Marnie's no-show, understanding her need to stay in Legend to attend to her mother's urgent medical needs. They conveyed the opportunity they saw for Dago Red. It continued to be a name that made them both laugh nostalgically when they said it. At the end of the evening, they both admitted that they had to create a more politically correct name to brand the wine they wanted to buy from the Red Sombrero.

Rowan knew that one of Marnie's concerns was that her wine would only be used to confirm the Italian market for her wine. After that, Vinnie and Sal could find another source to manufacture the product. Rowan felt his relationship with Vinnie was strong enough to seek his word that their intention was to use the Red Sombrero as their primary source for wine.

"It'd be good for the winery," Rowan explained. "It'd be good for the region for some additional jobs up there."

Vinnie and Sal exchanged looks and nodded in agreement.

"Rowan, I'm a builder. I don't know shit about making wine," Vinnie replied candidly. "Sal here, he just sells it. Making it is too much trouble. We'll take the margin."

Rowan smiled, feeling embarrassed to have asked.

"But I will say," Vinnie added, "I'd be interested in being a very silent investor in a facility wherever you thought it would work best, if that's needed."

Sal nodded in agreement. That offer told Rowan that the two men had a big vision for their brand of *Dervish Red*.

The meeting ended with the details Rowan needed to take to Marnie and Tom to discuss production. The initial outlook was promising. He knew it would be enough to enable Marnie to start digging out of her financial troubles and get the Red Sombrero back on its feet. It would also offer some desperately needed new employment to the region. His concern was whether Marnie would either accept the opportunity or even give him the opportunity to present it.

# # # #

Two days and six unanswered voice messages cemented Rowan's impression that Marnie was shutting him out. He considered a drive to Legend to find her for a clear-the-air discussion about what happened and what she was thinking. He knew where he could find her. He was concerned about her reaction and Tom's response should she give him the green light to pound on him.

Thursday ended without either any answers or callbacks. Rowan had the cabin for the weekend and could take a half day Friday to drive up to Legend to find Marnie before the Friday crowd, and Tom, appeared. He decided to make the trip to see if the opportunity for the wine still existed, as well as to see if any hope remained for them to be together.

# # # #

Rowan pulled into the Red Sombrero parking lot, anxious to see who would be there at 2:00 p.m. He was surprised to see a number of pickups and quads parked in the customer areas.

As he got out of his car, the cool air chilled his body. He reached into the back of his car for his suit jacket. Having left straight from the office, he was still in his work uniform. As he finished settling into his jacket, he began to look for Marnie in production bay.

"Go home, Rowan!" she shouted from the darkness of the supply room. "Go back to your big-city life!"

Rowan kept walking toward her voice, trying to find her in the darkness.

"Marnie," he called back. "At a minimum, you owe me an explanation about why you're acting this way."

"Just go away. I'm not interested in you anymore."

Rowan stopped to think about her push off. The hurt in her voice was deep. He wondered if he could resolve the damage that was inflicted during her time at his condo.

"Go off and have fun with your buddy, Dorsey. There are lots of small towns out there with gullible women."

Rowan began to see the clearer picture take shape. He knew trying to use reason to break through her emotional wall was not going to work. She had to first come down from her fear to see the potential they had as a couple.

"Marnie. If anything, let me give you the business details to consider. Then I'll go. If that's what you want."

Marnie did not reply. She waited to see if he would turn and go. His stubborn resistance to leaving started to irritate her. She was tucked in a corner where there was nowhere for her to go without him seeing her. She decided to step out to face him.

"I'm not interested," she declared, appearing from the shadows. "I'm not interested in any deals, any money, and most of all, I'm not interested in you!"

"Marnie," he replied as he took a few steps toward her.

"Rowan, go away," she said again, holding her hand up for him to stop.

Rowan stopped to respect her wish. He reached into his satchel to pull out a bound document of the business proposal between the Red Sombrero, Vinnie, and Sal. It included Vinnie's offer to invest in more production equipment and projections for the Red Sombrero winery and any other company created to host the larger, private-label production.

"I don't know what happened at my condo. Larry, the guard, told me you were happy going in and emotionally distraught when you left. I know my ex-wife, Mindy..."

"Wife," Marnie corrected.

Rowan's chin lifted at the confirmation that Mindy was the catalyst for Marnie's retreat.

"Soon-to-be EX-wife was involved."

Marnie's emotions started to show in her eyes and face. She began to tremble as she looked at him.

"We're just too different, Rowan. You need a Mindy, not a Marnie."

Rowan took a step toward her to offer comfort.

"Stop, and please go," she commanded.

Rowan realized that her position was absolute by how she was standing firm to his advance. He dropped the proposal onto the ground.

"Read this," he replied. "Let me know. I'll work to make it happen whether there is an us or not."

His head began to shake from side-to-side as he wondered if he was saying goodbye for good. He knew in some ways it would be challenging to blend their lives. But he also knew that she was the freshest breath of air he had tasted in decades. His body began to ache as he thought about leaving. But he also knew he had to go to give her time to think to be able to complete her deal to save her business.

Rowan gave one last forced smile before turning back to his car. Marnie did not move as she watched the back of his perfectly tailored suit flow with each stride. She took time to admire his butt one last time as he reached to open the door to his Audi. As he took off his jacket, his white shirt with cufflinks highlighted his trim body and the accent colors of his silk tie. What was standing before her was perfect for her. But she had to let him go.

The Audi left the parking lot, and Marnie watched until it disappeared into the pines. She then turned to head into the storage room, leaving Rowan's proposal on the ground where he had dropped it.

# # # #

There were few times in his adult life that Rowan cried. The deaths of his parents and sadness that surrounded those were two. He tended to get emotional when his daughters were performing in sports, on stage in school productions, or when he dropped them at school for the semester. Pride was one of his triggers to get emotional. It took great sadness to make him cry. As he pulled the Audi onto the main road from Legend, he resisted the urge to cry, but finally broke down in tears and struggled to keep a clear view of the road ahead.

As he traveled down the road, he noticed a cloud of dust approaching from the berm ahead of him. His initial concern was that it was an Amish horse-drawn carriage. He slowed to ensure that he would be able to pass without startling the horse or putting his car unsafely in the opposing lane. As he approached the cloud, no carriage appeared. It was a quad running at full speed with a familiar figure driving.

Rowan matched the speed of the quad as he pulled next to Cousin Dave. He was wearing World War II aviator goggles along with a leather skullcap and a long scarf. The look fit his personality and offered a needed laugh to change Rowan's disposition.

A quick honk of his horn got Cousin Dave to look over. He was used to cars slowing for second looks and often ignored them. When he saw Rowan waving to him, he pointed ahead to his upcoming driveway for Rowan to follow him back to his trailer.

Rowan lost sight of Cousin Dave as he slowly worked his Audi up the rutted driveway. He knew there was no way to get lost and nowhere for Cousin Dave to disappear. He did not know why he was being called to talk to him, or why Cousin Dave happened to be riding on the road on his way out. He just needed to talk to someone before leaving.

"The loyal soldier," Cousin Dave exclaimed as Rowan stepped out of his car and put his suit jacket on. "You've got the uniform perfectly outfitted and the shoes polished."

Rowan smiled, knowing Cousin Dave's disdain for the establishment.

"Got a minute?" Rowan asked.

Cousin Dave finished setting out two chairs for them to sit.

"I've got as much time as you need," he answered.

Rowan studied Cousin Dave's stance as he walked toward him. He ignored the painful reminder that sat across the valley as an overwhelming urge pushed him to clear up one thing.

"Who are you?"

"People here call me Cousin Dave," he answered. "You know that."

"I do," Rowan replied. "But what's your real name? I've never been formally introduced to you."

Cousin Dave pointed to the chair he wanted Rowan to use.

"What difference does it make?" he answered. "It's all bullshit. A moniker to differentiate you from the others...to designate your clan, your...rank, in society, whether you earned it or not."

"I don't know," Rowan replied. "I just like to know who I'm talking to."

Cousin Dave chuckled at his comment.

"Why are you here, Rowan?" he asked.

The directness of the question startled him. Cousin Dave's ambiguous aura had just reached clarity.

"No bullshit?" Rowan replied.

Cousin Dave stayed quiet; his eyes locked on Rowan's.

"Marnie's done a complete about-face on me, and I can't figure out why."

"What'd you do?"

Rowan thought about his question. Everything he tried to do was positive. Every approach he'd made toward her was respectful. He knew Mindy had done something to spook her.

But he could not figure out what it was without Marnie telling him.

"I developed a plan to save her business without giving her money."

"Money's evil."

"She needs it for her business to survive," he replied. "And she, as well as her employees, need that business to survive."

Cousin Dave pondered Rowan's declaration. His expression changed to show he agreed.

"I don't know what she's thinking. But I do see you two as two intersecting universes that will have a lot of sparks and friction before you align. If that's important to you, you'll have to push through it. That said, if Marnie is really over you, you'll never be able to pull her into your orbit. You will lose on every effort you make. And, you just may have a painful run-in with Tom as the result."

Rowan's face shifted to show agreement, and concern, at Cousin Dave's last thought. Tom was a hair-trigger waiting to fire on someone. And Marnie was his powder keg.

"Suggestions?" he asked.

"Time. Little expressions of interest. Maybe some hope," Cousin Dave replied. "You can't force it. But you can't neglect it either. The universe will allow a properly tended garden to grow and flourish if it's intended to be."

Rowan smiled and stood to end the conversation that he saw going nowhere. Cousin Dave was evaporating from clarity back into his own sphere of consciousness.

"That's a lot to think about. It's been a pleasure knowing you...really."

"It's like the wine," Cousin Dave added unexpectedly, "Everyone likes their own blend. Sweet, dry. Red, white, or in between. You like what you like. Marnie never will complete herself here. Her balance will be through someone like you...not...anyone here."

Rowan looked across the valley one last time as he smiled. He extended his hand to Cousin Dave to say goodbye. He was surprised when Cousin Dave quickly returned the customary handshake to end their time together.

"I do have to ask you," Rowan added, as he stopped from turning away. "What's with the Whirling Dervish thing you have going on?"

Cousin Dave thought for a moment and smiled before he answered.

"The Dervish take a vow of poverty," he replied, waving his arm toward his simple homestead. "And it gets me free wine...and easy conversations with the girls."

Rowan smiled and shook his head as he turned toward his car.

"Walker," Cousin Dave blurted as Rowan looked back to wave. "David Walker."

Rowan smiled and nodded to confirm the information.

"Nice to finally meet you. But I like Cousin Dave better. It works for you."

Rowan drove out Cousin Dave's driveway as gingerly as he drove in. As he accelerated on the two-lane road back toward Pittsburgh, his mind started running *Walker* through his mental industrial registry.

"Walker Steel," he mumbled.

Walker Steel was a metals fabricating company that was sold in the early 2000s. Rowan's recall on the valuation was over three hundred million dollars. He did not know Cousin Dave's rank in either the family or the company. But it was only forty years old, making only three generations of inherited dilution possible. It was clear that Cousin Dave's share could have been north of ten million dollars before taxes.

"That explains owning the mountain and the Airstream," he said to himself, solving an interesting piece of the Legend puzzle that had been bugging him.

# # # #

Marnie continued to watch the door as she worked the light crowd at the bar. The customers that knew her could sense through her tone that something was wrong. Her usual friendly, chatty nature was reduced down to the order and the transaction. No one had the courage to ask her what was wrong.

When the door opened with an unusual vigor, Marnie turned to see who was coming in with such urgency. When she saw Tom absorbed in a bound booklet with a fancy cover, her adrenaline spike quickly nose-dived to depression.

"Marnie!?" he called out, without looking.

When she did not reply, he looked up to find her. As he scanned the bar, he found her staring back at him, surprised that he was reading something.

"I found this in the parking lot," he said. "It's some sort of business proposal for our wine."

Tom put Rowan's document on the bar. He then reached to his back pocket to pull out a sealed letter on Rowan's personal stationery. Ignoring the proposal, Marnie picked up the envelope and studied its exterior.

"This was inside the book," Tom said.

"See this?" she asked Tom. "This is the signature of an arrogant asshole from the city."

"Seems kinda girly to me for a guy to have his own stationery."

"That's what society does to you," she replied, spinning it in front of them to show the thickness of the paper the envelope was made of.

Marnie placed the unopened note on top of the proposal then turned away.

"Aren't you going to read it?" he asked.

"No," she answered. "It's all bullshit. Full of empty promises. His interest in me was to sell out our company."

Tom gave her a puzzled look. He leafed through the proposal again looking for anything, other than wine, to be sold, and anything Rowan would be paid for doing.

"Marn, I'm not educated like he is. There are a lot of numbers here. But I don't see any that go to him."

Marnie picked up the report and thumbed through the logically presented summary proposal and financials. Tom was correct. Unless Rowan was being paid outside of the deal by his investors, he was not being paid anything for his work to put the deal together.

"Where is he?" Tom asked, excited to ask a lot of questions.

"He left. I told him to go."

Tom's eyes grew large as he pondered the opportunity dying with Rowan not part of it.

"Call him back!" he demanded. "Shit, Marnie. No bank's ever been interested in helping us."

Marnie smiled at the truth in Tom's statement. For the most part, the Red Sombrero was self-financed through a family land grant, sweat equity, and reinvestment of earnings that were not reported to the government.

"Just let him go," she replied. "There's too much other stuff I just can't handle. Besides, we have the plan. We can go to another bank."

"What's the note for?"

"Jesus, Tom! Don't be so nosey. It's just schmoozing to get me to close his deal."

"Why's it on his personal stationery?" Tom asked. "Wouldn't he write that on bank stationery?"

"Letterhead," Marnie corrected, as she picked the envelope up again. "Company letters are on letterhead, not...expensive, personal, asshole stationery. I'm going to put this in the office to review later."

"Marnie," Tom implored.

"I have customers," Marnie answered, in a tone to say the discussion was over.

She turned to walk the proposal and envelope into her office. As she put the two items on her desk, she thought about Tom's comments. She had to at least read what he had written. But then an image of Mindy appeared from their meeting in Rowan's condominium, reminding her of their two different worlds and the friction and boredom that could occur as one tried to fit into the life of the other.

Marnie put her hand on top of Rowan's note to secure it in place and to touch the most personal thing he left for her. The weight of the envelope presented an energy she could not resist. Marnie sat in her chair, opened the envelope, and sat back to read what Rowan had to say.

Marnie,

If you are reading this note, it means you have sent me packing. Please review this proposal and contact Vincent Giollota directly. He will know who you are and will take your call. Use the numbers inside for your negotiations. You can make all of this work to secure your business and future as well as everyone that works for you now and will work with you through the new jobs you will be creating.

I don't know how Mindy got to you. But her fingerprints are all over your sudden change of attitude. She will do anything and say anything to ensure I am never happy again. But know I would walk anywhere with you and give up everything, short of my children, to be with you, because only that will make me happy again. You have to believe that to believe in us.

All my love,

Rowan

Marnie lowered the note to her lap as she thought about his words. She struggled to filter out the truth from his letter as Mindy's words ran through her head. In her heart, she wanted to believe him. But she also knew joining their two worlds would be difficult, if not impossible. That it would be easier if he just disappeared as quickly as he arrived as the right person, in the right place, at the right time.

# # # #

"This has good karma!" Cousin Dave commented as he pushed his tin cup toward Tom's bottle of Dervish Red.

Tom frowned as he began to pour more red into the metal container he knew was just a prop to get free wine. But Tom knew he needed an ally to convince Marnie that Rowan's plan was not only a good opportunity, but also one that required Rowan to help make happen.

"That's what I told her," Tom added. "If it makes sense to me. It should to her. Right?"

Cousin Dave smiled as he took a pull of wine.

"It's much deeper than that for her," he replied.

Tom looked off from their table over toward the bar to check on his ex-wife. He always got a warm wash through his soul when he saw her. Marnie appeared preoccupied with a small cleanup until she felt Tom's eyes on her. She gave him a warm smile when she looked to see him admiring her.

"She's so hard to let go of," he mumbled. "But we'd kill each other…. And she deserves to be happy."

Cousin Dave nodded agreement, knowing that Tom had come to a number of life conclusions.

"I didn't like him at first either," Cousin Dave said while looking into his cup. "I knew too many Rowans in my earlier days to think he was anything other than an all-about-himself person."

"Well," Tom conceded, as he slouched back into his chair, "how can you not be suspicious of someone that's so different and shows up out of nowhere with all the answers?"

"You have to make them prove themselves."

Cousin Dave tapped his index finger on the proposal that was sitting between them on the table.

Tom gave in to his reluctance to agree with Cousin Dave. Rowan showed his mettle by leaving the proposal he could have taken with him. The business plan he offered seemed sound. It also carried Rowan's credibility, as a senior corporate banker and business financier as its author.

"Where'd you get that!?" Marnie asked to disrupt the two's personal gratification at solving her problems. "Damn it, Tom! I told you to leave it alone."

Tom sat silent, looking guilty. He wanted to explain his reasoning for showing Cousin Dave Rowan's work. He needed confirmation that he was correct in his assessment that the plan was solid from the only other educated city person he knew.

Marnie's eyes shifted back and forth between the two faces that would not look back at her. Her anger with Tom began to grow as both stayed quiet.

"Fine," she declared, grabbing the proposal. "You two just stay out of my business."

"Our...business," Tom replied. "Marnie, we may not be married, but I am still your partner here."

"We will be fine, Tom."

Tom paused, wondering if he should state publicly what they both knew.

"No, Marn. We won't. Without this, the Sombrero won't make it."

Marnie gasped as she took a quick look around to see who might have heard that declaration. Cousin Dave's eyes were still hanging low, although it was clear he was still listening. Everyone else seemed absorbed in their own conversations about other things.

"He's a good person," Cousin Dave said, as his eyes moved up to meet hers.

The clarity in his thought added a sincerity that Marnie could not ignore. She knew Cousin Dave was talking about Rowan. The fact that it came from a disgruntled, rich, privileged city person who found his way to the northern territory to live a rustic life added validation.

"Is the universe telling you that Dave?" she replied in a snarky tone. "Some drunken, whirling inspiration!?"

Marnie raised her hand to stop Tom from speaking as his face lit to interject into their conversation.

"I think it's telling YOU that," Cousin Dave answered. "You're just refusing to look and listen."

Marnie stepped back as she thought about the comment. She was used to Cousin Dave talking in confused circles. His directness now was suspect.

"Yeah, well it's got a funny way of communicating as it continues to crap all over me," she finally replied.

"That's all in how you want to see it," Cousin Dave answered softly.

He avoided eye contact with her to let his thought sink in.

Tom and Cousin Dave kept their focus on their goblets of Dervish Red as they waited for her to give up and return to the bar. Neither looked toward the other until she disappeared from their peripheral vision. A quick glare at them when they finally dared look showed she was still angry about their intervention. It was clear that would be their last discussion on the matter.

# # # #

Marnie quietly maintained a watchful eye on the door through last call. She kept the end barstool empty with a reserved marker despite lots of interest. As the clock ticked toward the Sombrero's 2:00 a.m. closing time, Marnie had lost hope, concluding that Rowan was back in Pittsburgh looking for new opportunities with his own kind.

"Anything?" Janis asked as she took a seat at the bar.

She could sense her best friend's tension and disappointment.

Tom had told her earlier about Rowan's proposal, the unopened note, and Marnie's adamant desire to let him go.

"Marnie," she demanded. "Just call him. He'll come back."

"Janis, he's gone. And we're better off for it. He isn't like us. We were not a good fit."

Marnie's eyes were beginning to show the tears Janis knew she was trying to hold back.

"Just call him."

Janis's command was a sincere as she could manage as a smile appeared on her face.

"No!" Marnie exclaimed, not looking up to see her friend's face, which would have angered her more.

"Who's not a good fit?"

The voice that asked the question was familiar. And as happy as she was to hear it, she resisted showing a smile as she turned to look at him.

"What are you doing here, Rowan?" Marnie asked, walking out from the bar to confront him.

"I called him...from your office," Janis answered. "Went through his friend Dorsey. I took his business card from his wallet while he was passed out with Travis. That asshole had no idea who I was. He only answered because his caller ID said *Red Sombrero*."

Marnie remained still as she studied the man in front of her. It was the first time Janis was unable to read her best friend's mood to see if she had done a good thing or not. Marnie exhaled softly as her eyes first looked at Janis, then back to Rowan.

"Well...Clark Kent," she scowled, as she stared at him then started laugh and cry. "In or out?"

"In!" he replied, stepping toward her with a smile.

As the distance between them closed, Marnie's stern look softened and she let her resistance fall.

"Then close the damn door…it's cold outside," she uttered with an emotional stumble.

"Way ahead of ya, babe."

Marnie let him take her in his arms before returning his embrace for a long kiss. As their bodies touched, she felt all her tension release, and her body seemed to melt into his.

"Closing time?" she asked, as they separated slightly. "You waited until closing time?"

Rowan smirked as he looked at Marnie's face, which was lit with joy.

"I wanted it to be dramatic," he replied glibly. "And I wanted to be one hundred perfect sober to feel every…single…tingle through our first night of the rest of our lives together."

About the Author

Milo Hays is a retired fundraising consultant who spent his career helping nonprofits of all shapes and sizes tell their great stories to get funding. Today, he is splitting his time between Pennsylvania, which is home, and South Florida, where it is warm when Pennsylvania is cold.

Other Milo Hays Books can be found on amazon.

Two Once Removed   Stand-Alone Story/Book 1 of 3
Two Once There   Stand-Alone Continuation/Book 2 of 3
Two Once Settled   Final Story of the Series/Book 3 of 3

1200 Miles.

Made in the USA
Coppell, TX
03 November 2023

23791504R00187